John Ashton

The Adventures and Discoveriers of Captain John Smith

Sometime president of Virginia, and admiral of New England

John Ashton

The Adventures and Discoveriers of Captain John Smith
Sometime president of Virginia, and admiral of New England

ISBN/EAN: 9783337197292

Printed in Europe, USA, Canada, Australia, Japan

Cover: Foto ©Raphael Reischuk / pixelio.de

More available books at **www.hansebooks.com**

THE
ADVENTVRES AND DISCOVRSES
of
Captain IOHN SMITH.

THE PORTRAICTUER OF CAPTAYNE IOHN SMITH ADMIRALL OF NEW ENGLAND

These are the Lines that shew thy Face; but those
That shew thy Grace and Glory, brighter bee:
Thy Faire-Discoveries and Fowle-Overthrowes
Of Salvages, much Civilliz'd by thee
Best shew thy Spirit; and to it Glory Wyn;
So, thou art Brasse without, but Golde within.

If so; in Brasse, (too soft Smiths Acts to beare)
I fix thy Fame, to make Brasse Steele out weare.
Thine, as thou art Virtues,
Iohn Davies. Heref:

The
ADVENTVRES
and
DISCOVRSES
of
Captain IOHN SMITH,
fometime
Prefident of VIRGINIA,
and
Admiral of NEW ENGLAND.

Newly Ordered
by
IOHN ASHTON,
(Author of Chap Books of the Eighteenth Century,
Social Life in the Reign of Queen Anne, &c.)

With
Illvftrations taken by him
from
Original Sovrces.

LONDON, PARIS, AND NEW YORK:
Printed and Publifhed by Caffell & Company, Limited.
1883.

TABLE OF CONTENTS.

PREFACE.

AMERICANS are utterly aftonifhed at the apathy fhewn by the Englifh to the memory of a veritable "Worthy," Captain John Smith. On the other fide of the Atlantic they would fain claim him as their own, if they could, and they cannot comprehend the indifference to, and ignorance of, the details of his life, in this country. It cannot be from lack of interefting particulars, for his life was one peculiarly adventurous, bordering almoft on the romantic, and his adventures were related by him-felf, and others, with a terfe and rugged brevity that is very charming.

In all Biographies he is ftyled "an Adventurer," and in all probability would never have received a notice at all, had it not been for the peculiarly romantic connection between him and Pocahontas. Modern fcepticifm has, of courfe, endeavoured to throw doubts as to the reality of Smith's ftory, but a moment's reflection will fhow that it was put to the fevereft teft, and it was never once contemporaneoufly queftioned. When Pocahontas came over here, in 1616, Smith wrote a letter to Queen Anne (confort of James I.) commending her to Her Majefty's care, and detailing her various fervices to himfelf and the Colony at large. Of her faving his life he writes thus: "After fome fix weeks fatting among thofe Salvage Courtiers, at the minute of my execution, fhe hazarded the beating out of her own brains to fave mine, and not only that, but fo prevailed with her father, that I was fafely conducted to *James Towne.*" Can any one ferioufly think, that if it were a fabrication, he would fo write the Queen, well knowing that Pocahontas was here in the country, would be fure to be queftioned on the matter by every one that came in contact with her, and that either fhe, or her hufband, John Rolfe, could at once explicitly deny it, and thus caufe inftant difcovery, if it were a falfehood?

So alfo the truth of his fervices in Tranfylvania, his flaughter of the three Turks in fingle combat, and his captivity in Tartary, is plainly attefted in the grant of arms made to him by Sigismund Bathor, which grant was affirmed to him by Sir William Segar, Garter King of Arms.

Thus, then, when we have such irrefutable testimony of the truth of the most improbable events in his career, we can well give him the credit of verity in all the other portions of his narrative, which (except in some of the details of his very childhood) has been strictly adhered to.

The portrait of Smith is undeniable, as it appears in more than one edition of his works published in his lifetime, and that of Pocahontas is by the same artist, so that there is very little doubt as to its being genuine, the high cheek-bones and straight hair clearly evidencing her Indian descent.* It may

* These engravings are by *Simon Pass*, or *de Passe*, and were both executed in the same year. The supposed original painting from which the likeness of *Pocahontas* is taken, is in the possession of *Hastings Elwin*, Esq., J.P., of Gorleston, Yarmouth ; and many have been the speculations respecting it. In 1859 a writer in *Notes and Queries* (2nd Series, vol. vii. p. 307) says : "Her descendants, through the marriage of her grand-daughter *Anne Rolfe* with *Peter Elwyn*, Esq., are numerous in Norfolk. Her portrait remains in that family." This statement remained uncontradicted until 1875, when, in the same periodical (5th Series, vol. iv. p. 104), another writer says : "In 1859 a contributor of yours stated, erroneously, that *Anne* Rolfe, the grand-daughter of Pocahontas, had intermarried with Peter Elwyn, Esq., and that in her family

not be generally known that many families in America claim her for an anceftrefs, through her marriage with John Rolfe. The record of her burial is ftill preferved at Gravefend.

I know both thefe portraits, and all the other engravings (except the Colonial Seal of Virginia, which was taken from a document at Lambeth Palace, and kindly given me by F. C. Price, Efq.), to be thorough fac-fimiles, and they are, in my idea, far more interefting than they would be had the events depicted been drawn by a modern artift.

JOHN ASHTON.

the portrait of Pocahontas was preferved *at that day.* Poca-hontas only left one child, a boy ; he married, and died, leaving only one child, a daughter *Jane,* not *Anne,* who was married to Col. Robert Bolling, of Virginia, A.D. 1675. When John Rolfe, the hufband of Pocahontas, left England after her death, he gave his only fon Thomas to the keeping of a brother, and *the* Anne who married Mr. Elwyn may have been a defcendant of that brother ; and as the care of the child was committed to him, it is very probable that he, alfo, was the cuftodian of the portrait of the brother."

This theory is very pretty, only Smith, who knew all about her death, &c., exprefily ftates that the lad was left in charge of Sir Lewis Stukely, and Mr. Elwin, who moft courteoufly replied to my inquiries on the fubject, fays that the picture " was given to my grandfather by a Mrs. Zukelley, and nothing more is known of it beyond what is infcribed upon the picture, all of which is reproduced in the engraving."

PROLOGUE.

I WELL call to mind how we boys, that is to fay,
I and my brothers, did fomewhat chafe and fret
when our good father firft made us keep a Diurnal,
or daily record of fuch events as occurred ·in our
fmall lives worthy to be noted. At firft, until we
had grown accuftomed to it, and could not think
of fleeping unlefs it was duly written up, he would
make us fhow them to him every day; for, as he
truly faid, "I do this, not only to note your
different difpofitions—and growing powers of mind
—but for your own good, as you will thank me
hereafter, in order to implant in you habits of
obfervation, and of method, which will be of mighty
ufe to you in your way through the·world."

Thus it came to pafs that our Diurnals were
part of our daily life, and became a pleafing duty
which never was omitted; and they grew apace,
from noting things in brief, to writing long
defcriptions, and recording converfations of the
many notable perfons known to my father, who was
Alderman of his Ward, and had been both Sheriff

and Mayor. But of all our father's friends, the one we boys loved moſt was our near neighbour, Captain *John Smith*, for he liked us well, and would tell us tales of his life by the hour together; ſuch tales as made our blood leap through our veins, and held us with our mouths open, our eyes aſtare, and our hearts going pit-a-pat. Thoſe were the tales for our Diurnals; nor only ſo, we would act them over among us. Sometimes *Dick* would be the Captain, and *Harry* would be the Turbaſhaw, whilſt *I* and *Jack* were *Grualgo* and *Bonny Mulgro*, or one of us would be *Smith*, and the others Indians; and, indeed, we taught our little ſiſter *Mary* ſo well, that ſhe would play the part of *Pocahontas* to admiration.

Now that I am writing the Captain's ſtory from thoſe old leaves, with their faded ink and ſchoolboy writing, how vividly I call to mind how that ſtory was told, and methinks I now ſee our dear old friend in his big, high-backed arm-chair, with his tankard of ſpiced ale, a roaſted apple bobbing in it, and his pipe of *Virginia* (for he had uſed to drink Tobacco), and with his hand, perhaps, on *Dick's* curly pate; for we boys would ſit on footſtools round him, or lie on the floor with our elbows on the ground, and our chins reſting on our wriſts, drinking in every precious word with great eagerneſs.

His countenance was fomewhat rugged and weather-beaten, as whofe, indeed, would not be, after leading a life of fuch adventure? But though the crow's-feet were about the corners of his eyes, and the wrinkles in his forehead, his complection was ruddy, although funburnt, and he had a pleafant fmile and a loud cheery laugh. It is true that his hair was getting fomewhat thin atop of his head, but it was of a fine warm brown colour, though fomewhat ftreaked with grey, and it was curly and long enough to reach his ruff or ftanding collar. He wore on his face all the hair that nature had given him, but his thick, grifled beard was carefully trimmed, and his whifkers* were ftrong and briftly, and were trained fo as not to come over his mouth, and be in the way of his eating and drinking, but ftraight out on each fide, which made him look very fierce, and like the old lion that he was.

And yet he was not old, for he was but in the 53rd year of his age, when it pleafed the Lord to call him to Himfelf; but his many perils and privations had told upon him, and the pain of that terrible wound he had received, when he was treacheroufly blown up, would at times, in fpite of his ftout heart, bring a look of care and trouble

---

* Mouftaches.

upon his countenance. He was about the laſt of Queen *Elizabeth's* old adventurers—men, who like *Davis,* and *Frobiſher,* would ſtart on a voyage, the end of which none could foretell, with but ſcant means, either of men or of victual, and with ſhips all too ſmall; yet they recked little, but kept their eyes ſteadily fixed on the purport of their expedition, and *did it* if it was in the power of man to do. Perhaps you will ſay that the hope of gain was the power that urged them on. I think not. Undoubtedly it had ſomewhat to do with it, for the riches that *Cortes, Pizarro,* and *Hernandez de Soto* met with were enough to make men's mouths water. Who knew but what Captain *Smith,* too, in ſome Indian land, as yet unknown, but to be by him diſcovered, might not meet with a people who valued not gold nor pearls, ſave for their prettineſs, and would fain exchange them for beads, and knives, and looking-glaſſes. Everything that was unknown was, of courſe, magnificent. Yet I think it was more the love of adventure, than of gain, that led them on, for they muſt have ſeen that no Engliſhman ever made his fortune through his adventures, although he might be honoured, in his lifetime, and make for himſelf a name in the hiſtory of his country.

This was ſpecially the caſe with Captain *John Smith,* who, although he had, in his latter days, enough of this world's riches to fuffice for his fimple wants, had got but little pelf, and not even the barren honour of a knighthood, from his long life of toil and adventure. In his very own words now lying before me, and which, methinks, I can hear him fpeaking yet once more, let him tell his own ftory. "Having fpent fome five years, and more than five hundred pounds in procuring the Letters Patent and fetting forward, and near as much more about *New England*, &c. Thus thefe nineteen years I have here and there not fpared anything according to my ability, nor the beft advice I could, to perfuade how thofe ftrange miracles of mifery might have been prevented, which lamentable experience plainly taught me of neceffity muft enfue, but few would believe me till now too dearly they have paid for it. Wherefore, hitherto, I have rather left all, than undertake impoffibilities, or any more fuch coftly tafks at fuch chargeable rates; for in neither of thofe two countries have I one foot of land, nor the very houfe I builded, nor the ground I digged with my own hands, nor even any content or fatisfaction at all, and I fee ordinarily thofe two countries fhared before me by them that neither have them, nor know them, but by my defcription."

This was not faid in a fpirit of grumbling—for he was too large-hearted for that—but there is no doubt he did feel keenly, not his want of fortune or title, but the fact that in his mature years he was set aside for younger men, who had none of his experience, except that which they might learn from him. Better by far, for the Colony of *Virginia*, would it have been, had my old friend been sent out to settle their difficulties, for his good found sense, his active mind, his undaunted courage and his long-sighted sagacity, eminently fitted him for a position of command. But it was ordered otherwise, and our old friend was left at home in his last years in neglect—but not in idleness, for he could not be idle: indeed, he was hard at work writing a *History of the Sea* when he died.

So he perforce stayed at home, and in his leisure hours told his adventures to us boys, and, methinks, I cannot do better than to tell the story of his life to you, my reader, as near as possible as he told it to us; it will be better than if I put it in my own words, yet must it needs lack the thrilling interest of a narrative personally delivered.

DISCOVRSES

OF

Captain IOHN SMITH.

CHAPTER I.

WAS born in the year 1579;* that year when Jack Spaniard invaded *Ireland*, bringing with him a holy banner bleſſed by the *Pope*. Much blood and time it took before the rebellion was put down, and the Dons were all either killed, or put in ward. But the work was done thoroughly, and with a good heart, ſo that none, methinks, ever went back home to tell the tale. Ha! but we paid them out well, and made them dance a Coranto to a pretty tune when they tried the ſame ſport, on a larger ſcale, with their Invincible Armada. Invincible, quotha! my Lord *Howard* and his old ſea-dogs found joints enow in their harneſs, I trow; and *Ireland* proved even more unkind to them than before, for ſeventeen of their ſhips were taken or deſtroyed, and much over 5,000

---

* He was baptized on 6th Jan., 1579, and his baptiſmal regiſter is ſtill to be ſeen at Willoughby, Lincoln.

B

men were killed or taken prifoners on that coaft, which, I warrant me, they love not now.

I mind the time well, though I was but a young-fter of nine years old, for the whole land was drunk with joy, and of courfe my native village muft be a piece with the reft of the world. My Lord *Willoughby* did give two great oxen to be roafted, and alfo good ftrong October; both of which were given without ftint to all comers. Ay, and he provided alfo a bull to be baited, which was the firft I had ever feen of that rare fport. I remember it fo well, more by token that our dog *Tyke* muft needs be very valiant and join in the fray, but he limped on three legs ever after, and it had nigh coft him his life but for the great care, and good nurfing, he received.

There was dancing round the May-pole, too, and it would have been kept up till night, but old *Jack* the crowder* got overcome early in the after-noon with too much October, which he kept pouring down to make his arm liffome, for he faid it ached with conftant work ; fo many of us betook ourfelves to *Alford*, to fee the two Frenchmen with their bear and monkey.

And the year after, too, did Sir *Francis Drake* and Sir *John Norris* give the Dons and Portugos

---

* Fiddler.

a pretty fright, when they marched up to *Lifbon*, and laid the country wafte. With all this, can any man having a grain of fenfe wonder that there never can be peace beyond the Line? It is all very well at home here to be commonly civil, and a man may even go fo far as to fay, fhould he meet a Don, " Tengo el honor de faludar á ufted, Caballero," but once acrofs the Line I hold there fhould be no peace. *Neptune's* baptifm wafhes away all cuftoms and civilities due to them, and the motto of every good Englifhman fhould be, all over the *Spanifh Main*, " Guerra al cuchillo."

My birthplace was the village of *Willoughby* in *Lincolnfhire*, about three miles from *Alford*, and feven miles from *Spilfby*, and it has belonged for many hundreds of years to the family of the *Willoughbys*, although when my Lord was made a Baron, in the reign of that peerlefs virgin, Her Majefty the Queen *Elizabeth*, he took the ftyle of *Willoughby d'Erefby* from his manfion of that name near *Spilfby*. My father was a yeoman, and came of a good ftock, the ancient family of Smiths, of *Crudley* in *Lancafhire*; while my dear mother came from the family of the *Rickards*, who had ufed to live in *Great Heck* in *Yorkfhire*. She was called to her reft when I was but young, and my father forrowed greatly, but I myfelf mind little of her, fave that fhe was always kind and gentle with me, whilft

my father, as is the wont of many men, was somewhat hasty, and apt to be cholerick.

He, good man, would fain have me book-learned,
and in his heart he had, I believe, a great wish that,
when old enough, I should enter the Church ; but
books were not to my taste. I was sent to *Alford*,
to the Free School there, as being the best place
for learning, not too far from home. It had not
been long founded by a merchant of *Alford* named
*Spanning** for the godly and virtuous education of
the youth of *Alford* and the neighbourhood, and to
teach the A B C, and also to read both English and
Latin. But I was young and silly, and although
I mastered the A B C and my hornbook, yet I
made not much progress in my English and Latin,
so that my father, whose dearest wish it was that I
should be a scholar—in which, doubtless, he was
most right—removed me from *Alford*, and sent me
to the Grammar School at *Louth*, which was founded
by His Majesty *Edward* the Sixth, of pious
memory, who endowed it with the property of some
of the ancient guilds of the town, and the tolls of
some markets or fairs.

It has turned out many fair scholars, but I was
not among them. I learned more of the ferula
than the Latin grammar, for many beatings did I

---

* 1565.

receive, not only for my lack of induftry, but for ftraying out of bounds, birds'-nefting, orchard robbing, and other acts of mifchief and childifh roguery, until I fickened of being always chid, and made up my mind to run away and go to fea. I know not why boys who are impatient of reftraint always think of this. Perhaps they are like the young turtles, whofe parent, having laid her eggs in the fand, well in fhore, leaves them to be hatched by the warmth of the fun. What does my little turtle as foon as he is hatched? Why, he makes direct for the fea. You may turn him round, and try and force him inland, but you cannot conquer his inftinct and liking for the fea; and the moment he is let alone he will make ftraight for the water.

Matters had got to fuch a pitch with me, and I had fo fet my mind upon brave adventures, and to get fomehow to the fea, that I fearched about for the means—one of which was money—for I had fenfe enough to know that I muft have food on my journey. At laft I found a man who confented to purchafe my fatchell, books, and all that I had, for a trifle. He muft have been a fcurvy knave, to have taken advantage of the want of knowledge in a child, nor only fo, but to cozen him out of fome paltry coins into the bargain. However, at the time, I thought not of it; indeed, I thought it was very good and kind of him to help me.

With my little ftore of cafh in my pocket, I
turned back to fchool, meaning to take the firft
opportunity to efcape, when on my arrival, I was
told that the head mafter would fain fee me at once.
I liked not this, for my interviews with him were
never very pleafant ones, at leaft, not for me, and
befides, I knew I had done wrong, and was going
to run away. Methought, perhaps he has found it
out, and knows all about it, and my face was very
red, and my body very warm all over, when I
reached his room. But what furprifed me moft
was that he told me in a very foft and
gentle manner to be feated, and then he regarded me with a kind and compaffionate
look, and faid, as if to himfelf, " Poor boy!
poor boy!" At laft he afked me how my
father was. To which I made anfwer that when
laft I heard of him he was well. At this he feemed
much furprifed, and told me that for fome time
paft he had been ailing, then that he was ill ; after
a paufe, that he was very ill indeed, and when he
had thus led me on, he told me gravely and quietly,
that I had a great lofs, but that it was my father's
gain ; that God had taken him away, and I fhould
never fee him alive again. For fome time I could
hardly realife the blow, but it flowly came to my
mind, and then I fell to a fobbing as if my heart
would break. My good mafter left me to myfelf

awhile, and when he heard my fobs getting fainter
and quieter, he came back and told me that as foon
as arrangements could be made to fend me home,
he would do fo. On the morrow a fitting opportunity ferved, and I went home in time for the
funeral, which, I remember, was at night by torch-
light, and that everybody, for miles round, came
and ate and drank, till they could do fo no longer.

I was now but thirteen years of age, and quite
alone in the world, for although I lived with one of
my guardians, yet no heed was taken of me, and I
was left to do what I pleafed. I had liberty
enough, in all confcience, but never a penny in my
pocket, for my kind guardians liked my little ftore
of money fo well that they kept it to themfelves,
and gave me none of it, which had one effect, that
I could not get beyond fea, though I had not loft
the hankering for it. So things went on until I
was fifteen years of age, when they, for very fhame,
could not keep a great hulking fellow like me
idling about and doing nothing. So they therefore
bound me apprentice to one Mafter *Thomas
Sendall*, of *Lynn*, in *Norfolk*, who was the greateft
merchant of all thofe parts, with whom I was not
long, for I difliked the work about the warehoufes,
and the general difcipline, being as yet untamed.
Neither did I like the ftate of fervitude I was in.
I muft not fpeak to my mafter or miftrefs, even out

of doors, unlefs bareheaded; I muſt always call
them Sir, and Madam, and wait upon them at meals,
getting the half-cold fcraps afterwards, as my ſhare
of the feaſt. I hated wearing the flat cap, the
badge of the 'prentice; in ſhort, I could be content
with nothing. All I wanted, and the only thing
that would fatisfy me, was to go to fea; and at
length, weary of my fervice, I aſked Maſter *Sendall*
one day to fend me to fea, at which he only laughed,
faying, " No, *John*, I have needs of thee on land.
Thou art my apprentice, lad, and wouldeſt be of
no fervice to me at fea." "Thy flave, more likely,"
thought I. So after thinking it over all night as
I lay awake, immediately breakfaſt was over, I
managed to flip out, and fairly ran away, and I
faw not Maſter *Sendall* again for the fpace of eight
years.

    This was the beginning of my life of adventure.
I ſhould never have fettled down to the quiet life
of a merchant; my blood was too quick and mer-
curial, and my limbs were meant for other work
than to ſtand behind a counter, and ferve goods.
Every man to his taſte, and I never have regretted
that I ran away, although my life has been fomewhat of a rough one.

    I managed to get back to *Willoughby*, and there,
my guardians not caring to have me again on their
hands, thought to provide for me, by getting

leave for me to go with young Mr. *Peregrine Bertie*, who was going to *Orleans* to join his brother *Robert*, who afterwards became Earl of *Lindſey* and Lord Great Chamberlain of *England*. They were the ſons of that noble man, and famous ſoldier, the Right Honourable Peregrine *Lord Willoughby d'Ereſby*, who was chriſtened *Peregrine* becauſe he was born when his father and mother were voyaging in foreign parts. My guardians liberally gave me (out of mine own eſtate) ten ſhillings to get rid of me, and this was the modeſt fortune with which I ſtarted in life.

Now, indeed, this was the life I loved. Here was I, the runaway apprentice, transformed into the companion, albeit alſo the page, of a young nobleman, with brave clothes on my back, and a horſe to carry me. Ha! Maſter *Sendall*, would thou couldeſt have ſeen me then. I fear me thou wouldeſt not have known thy ſullen apprentice in this gay young ſpark that curvetted and caracoled along, ſinging gaily for pure joy.

'Tis true, I ſang another tune very ſhortly after we left *Dover*, for the ſea, of which I was ſo fond, did not ſeem to love me much, but treated me very roughly, and, being new to it, ofttimes I thought our little bark would have been ſwallowed up by the waves, and that we ſhould all be drowned. Yet this feeling ſoon diſappeared when

we fet foot on fhore at *Calais*, where every other
fenfation did give place to admiration; for all
things, the place, the people, and the language,
were new.

We ftayed no longer at *Calais* than to reft and
recover from the effects of our voyage, and to buy
frefh horfes, and then we ftarted on our journey.

When we came to *Orleans* we found my
young nobleman's brother, with his tutor, or
governor, who was to take them, and fhow them
the chief cities of *Europe*.

And here a mifhap befel me, for their governor
thought there were as many people attendant on
his charge as was neceffary, and that a new arrival
like myfelf, was one too many, fo he decided that
I fhould return to *England*. This was fomewhat
hard on a boy of fifteen years old, and my Mr.
Peregrine did loudly intercede for me to be allowed
to ftay, but the governor was obdurate, and read
him a long lecture on the virtue of obedience to
thofe fet over him: fo that he was filenced, if not
convinced. But, if I had to part from them, they
were determined I fhould not go empty-handed, fo
thefe two honourable brethren gave me money
more than fufficient to meet my charges, and we
faid good-bye to each other.

With money in my pocket, good clothes on my
back, and my own mafter, with perfect liberty to

come and go as I would, do you think I was going
to return to *England?* Indeed, no! that was the
fartheft from my thoughts. I went to *Paris*,
into which the King had lately entered, and where
an Englifhman was fure of a hearty welcome; for
was not our moft gracious Queen helping the
French King, with both men and money, to drive
the rafcal Don out of his dominions? And in
truth I did mightily enjoy myfelf, and fo did an
acquaintance that I made, one Mafter *David Hume*,
a Scotchman, who fhowed me all the fights of the
city, and, perhaps, thinking that this confiderate
behaviour ought to be rewarded, took to borrowing
my money, as long as I had any to lend. Mafter
Hume talked greatly of his friends in *Scotland*,
how powerful they were, and fo forth, and by way
of acknowledgment of my loans, which I think he
did never intend to repay, he gave me fome letters
to thefe mighty friends, to prefer me to the Scotch
King for employment, and he would have me
think that this was a certainty, for, after he had
given them to me, he would ofttimes fay, " There,
lad, now is thy fortune made." I never thought
at that time, but have done many a time fince, why,
if his friends were fo powerful, did he not ufe their
intereft in his own behalf, inftead of borrowing
my money?

However, with thefe letters in my bofom, I felt

mighty fine, and ftarted on my journey homewards.
I was fo young that I did not know the value of
money, and fo it fell out that by the time I had
got to *Rouen*, I found I had nothing like enough to
take me to *England*, fo I made my way as beft I
could to *Havre de Grace*, where were fome Englifh
troops, a portion of Sir *John Norris's* force, then
helping King *Henry*. Being a ftout and lufty
lad, without friends and with no two coins to
jingle againft each other in my pocket, needs muft
that I fhould turn foldier, and they never faid me
nay. I was ftrong enough to handle a pike, and,
although the morion, back and breaft plates, and
buff coat were fomewhat heavy, and hot, at ftarting,
yet every day I got more ufed to them, until I felt
them not; and, befides, I was then fo mighty
proud of being a foldier, that I would have borne
anything, no matter what hardfhip, without complaining, and with a fmile upon my face.

I faw no fervice, however, in France, and
indeed I was not forry, for I had much to learn;
I knew nought of martial exercifes, or even the
words of command, or of the different movements
by which bodies of difciplined men are made effec-
tive in warfare. I had to learn all the terms of
fortification, for I knew not a counterfcarp from a
traverfe, or a baftion. Nor was it poffible for me
to be actively employed, for, when our troops and

the French together had driven Jack Spaniard out of *Brittany*, our Queen recalled her forces under Sir *John Norris*, and sent them ftraitways to *Ireland* to put down the rebels there.

But ftill there was work to do, and I was in love with a foldier's life; my comrades had been kind in teaching me, and I had been willing to learn. So it came to pafs that when Sir *John Norris* left, fome of us adventurers, or volunteers, ftayed behind, for the Spaniard was far fuperior in number to the French, in the *Low Countries*, fo that the French, now they had no longer the Englifh to help them, were fain to afk the Hollander to come to their affiftance, which he did, both with men and money. Captain *Jofeph Duxbury* was making up a company, and I joined him, and ferved under his colours fome four years. We were fomewhat of a motley lot, for, as the French King could not truft his own troops by themfelves, he was very glad of help elfewhere, and no adventurer was ever turned away. There were Englifh pikemen, German lanfquenets, and the Switzer, who is always ready for a fight, provided that the pay is good, and reafonably certain. Among them all I learned how to take care of myfelf, and I well call to mind that there are worfe places than the *Low Countries* to live in, provided a man will look to himfelf, and is not fqueamifh.

Peace was concluded in May, 1598, and this threw me out of work, so that I felt the neceffity of doing fomewhat to further my fortunes. So I bethought me of the letters I had from Mafter *David Hume* to his kinfmen in *Scotland*, and I felt fure, now I could ride a horfe, could ufe my weapons with effect, and coming ftraight from the martial fchools of the *Low Countries*, that an appointment of no mean fort would be the fruits of their influence with the King of *Scotland*. So, finding a fhip that was about to fail to *Leith*, I took a paffage in her, but we had a ftormy and difaftrous voyage, being fhipwrecked by ftriking on fome rocks off *Holy Ifland*, near *Berwick*. Luckily it was daylight, and I managed to reach the fhore on fome floating wreckage, but was fore buffeted and bruifed by the waves and rocks before I got on hard ground. The poor folk here were very kind to us, after they had refcued all they could for themfelves from the wreck; but my bruifes, and my bath, were too much for me,. and I felt grievoufly fick of a fever. For a long time I lay there, not knowing whether I fhould live or die, but the fimples my nurfes gave me, and my natural good conftitution, got me through it, and although, when the fever left me, I was very weak, yet I foon felt hungry, and began to eat hugely, fo that my ftrength came back to me.

With some difficulty I made my kind friends accept of some slight payment for the trouble they had been at with me, and I left them, walking along the causeway which connects the Island with the main land, at ebb tide, having had enough, for a time, of the sea, and set out on foot to deliver my letters. But how shall I tell of my bitter disappointment? Master *Hume's* fine friends turned out to be very decent people, and grudged me nothing in their hospitality. As a friend of their *Davie*, all that they had was at my disposal, but they utterly lacked, as he must have well known, the power to help me. They had no sort of influence at Court, and indeed they told me that if they had, nothing could be done without money, which must be given away judiciously; so I had to put the best face upon it that I could, and make the best of a bad bargain.

Of course it was no use stopping there, so I bade them farewell, with many thanks on my part for their kind hospitality, (nor would they let me go unless I promised to return very shortly, and pay each of them a long visit in turn,) and set my face toward my native village.

It was worse at *Willoughby*, for I was there looked upon as a prodigy—one that had seen the world, had travelled in foreign parts, and could speak with foreign tongues, nay, had fought hand to hand with the hated Spaniard. Never had they feen or heard tell of the like, and I knew not a moment's reft; nothing but feafting and drinking, vifiting and being vifited, fo that in a fhort time I was glutted with too much company, wherein I took fmall delight, and being aweary of it all, I put a ftop to it by turning a kind of Eremite. That is to fay, I retired myfelf into a little woody pafture, a good way from any town, environed with many hundred acres of other woods, and there, by a fair brook, I built myfelf a little hut, or pavilion, of boughs, and there, on a bed of leaves, I did ufe to lie at night and fleep in my clothes.

It was a pleafant enough life while it lafted, for my wants were few, and were all fatisfied. The woods fupplied me with food, and even venifon was not lacking at my meals, and in hunting and cooking, a good portion of my day went. Befides which, I had my horfe to groom, water, and exercife, and, having my lance with me, I would practife tilting at the ring, and other martial fports. Was I ftudious? I had *Niccolo Macchiavelli's* Book of the Art of War, and *Marcus Aurelius* as well; and did I lack anything? a man paid me a vifit now and then, and brought me all I needed. This my life, however, was not deftined to be of long continuance, for it fet people's tongues a

wagging, as they marvelled hugely at my turning
Eremite; fo, by way of drawing me from my
retreat, they perfuaded a noble Italian gentleman,
Signor *Theodora Polaloga*, who was of the houfe-
hold of *Henry*, Earl of *Lincoln*, to pay me a vifit.
He was a man of totally different ftamp to my
country acquaintances. His companionfhip charmed
me. He had travelled and read much, and fpoke
feveral languages; moreover, he was a moft noble
and excellent horfeman, and, what with the charms
of his converfation, and the glowing accounts he
gave me of the many horfes I fhould have to ride,
if I would but pay him a vifit at my Lord of
Lincoln's place at *Tatterfhall*, I at laft confented,
and went with him. But I foon wearied of it;
this fort of life did not content me; I was ufed to
one of more action, and I could ftay no longer in
England, fo I took fhip, intending once more to
vifit the *Low Countries*, with which I was familiar,
and which, at that time, was the fchool of war for
all Europe—a fort of centre from whence forces
could be recruited for any purpofe, and where a
foldier of fortune was fure of employment.

On my arrival, I found that fighting was to be
done with the Emperor *Sigifmund* againft the Turk,
and, as I would much rather cut heathen, than
Chriftian throats, I made up my mind to proceed
thither, and put my fword at the Emperor's difpofal.

c

And now I muft tell of a moft notable villany which happened unto me. I fell in company with four French gallants, nice pleafant fellows, full of good comradefhip, but who were four of the greateft rogues unhung, as you fhall hear. If you pleafe, what fhould one of them feign himfelf to be but a great Lord, and the other three were his friends, and they were all well attended.

Mighty kind they all were to me, knowing all the time—the fcoundrel knaves!—the trick they were going to play me. Oh, yes! and was I really going to fight the Turk? that was exactly what *my Lord* would like to do, and he could have his will, but he had his duties to attend to in *France.* However, *my Lord* was glad it was in his power to be of fome affiftance to me, and that he would be only too happy to afford. He had taken a violent fancy to me, and if I would but accompany him to *France*, why, he would introduce me to no lefs a perfon than the Duchefs of *Mercury*, with whom he was fo intimate, that on his reprefentation, fhe would inftantly write me letters of favour to her Noble Lord, the Duke, who was then General to the Emperor *Rudolf*, in *Hungary*. What a poor, filly boy I then was! I believed them thoroughly, and furely thought I was now on the high road to fame and fortune—and how the villains muft have chuckled fecretly to themfelves, knowing all the time the fcurvy trick they did intend to play me.

I joined them, and took a paffage with them in the fame fhip, and, in the innocence of my heart, I delighted to fhow them that I had plenty of good apparel, and moreover, that my pouch was well lined. We had a fomewhat rough paffage, it being winter-tide, and when we came to the broad fhallow inlet of *St. Valerie fur Somme*, the arch Knave, *my Lord*, who had agreed the plot with the rafcal captain, did fo arrange that their, and my, trunks were with themfelves landed, and the boat was to return for me. After fome time methought the boat was fomewhat tardy in coming back, and, to fhorten my tale, I waited in good footh all the next day until towards the evening, when the boat returned, and the captain came aboard. Oh, he had his lie all ready and pat ; the fea had been fo high he could not put off before ; indeed, his coming then was at the peril of his life. " Well," faid I, " if fuch be the cafe, put me on fhore now, that I may join my Lord and his comrades." Then began he to ftammer fomewhat, and faid my Lord had gone to *Amiens*, and had fent word by him that he would there ftay my coming. But there were fome foldiers on board, one of whom, I found out afterwards, knew my knaves, and as they had feen more of the world than I had, they cried "fhame" upon the captain for being in league with fuch rogues. The paffengers alfo joined in the fame chorus, and there was fuch an outcry, that the captain was nigh being flain for his treacherous villany, and there was great talk of feizing the fhip, which affuredly would have been done, had they only known how to navigate her.

When the hubbub had fomewhat calmed down, I reflected that I could do no good by flopping on board the fhip, fo I was put on fhore, having but one coin in my pocket, and that about the value of an Englifh penny, fo that I was in great ftraits; fo much fo, that I had to fell my cloak to pay for my paffage. And, indeed, it had fared hard with me, had not one of the foldiers who had been on board, called *Curzianovere*, proved him- felf a true comrade to me. He, it feems, knew *my Lord*, and he told me that this great Seigneur, *my Lord Depreau*, was nought but the fon of a lawyer in *Lower Brittany*, and his companions, who were named *Curfell*, *La Nelie*, and *Monferrat*, were three young citizens, as arrant cheats as *my Lord*. He faid if I would go with him, he would bring me to their friends, and, in the mean time, I muft fhare his purfe. I thankfully accepted his offer as frankly as it was made, and we fet out upon our journey.

We travelled together till we came to *Mortain*

in *Normandy*, where we found *Depreau*, from whom, alas! I could get no fatisfaction, but the news of his cozenage made me kind friends everywhere.

Here I parted from my comrade, and wandered about from port to port, trying in vain to find fome man-of-war, until at laft all my money had been fpent, and I was reduced to fuch diftrefs, that one day, going through a foreft, I fank down by a fair fpring, nearly dead with cold and grief. Here, without doubt, I fhould have perifhed, had not a rich farmer pafled by that way, and he, like the good Samaritan, relieved me, to my great content, and kindly tended me until I was again able to go on my way.

Ah! but my journey was not all forrowful. I had my little bit of fun, and it was none the worfe in that I had it all to myfelf. One day, as I was pafling through a great grove of trees between *Pontorfon* and *Dinan*, who think you that I came fuddenly upon? It was one of my knaves called *Curfell*, and he was even in more evil cafe than I was. You may fancy I did not ftop long a bowing to him, my injuries were too late, and too keen; and he, too, knew what it muft come to; fo without even a word pafling between us, we both drew our fwords, and flew at each other. The fight lafted but a little time, for I fore wounded Mafter *Curfell*, and he fell to the ground, and, the village folks coming around, I made him confeſs his villany before them; and then he told us how, in the dividing of the ſpoil, the rogues fell out among themſelves, but that for his part he was quite innocent in the matter. The canting knave was not worthy of being kicked, and ſeeing that he was ſore hurt, I cared not to be further cumbered with him, ſo I left him among the villagers.

I bethought me of a nobleman with whom I was acquainted, and who lived not far from hence; the Earl of *Ployer*, who during the war in *France* had been brought up in *England*, together with his two brethren. I called on him, and was by him welcomed right heartily, ſo that I was better refurniſhed than ever. I ſtayed with him for ſome days, during which time I was ſhown all the places of note within the neighbourhood, and, when I took my leave, I was provided with plenty of money for my charges.

I will not weary you with the ſtory of my journey to the ſouth of *France*, whither I was bound; ſuffice it that in due time I came to *Marſeilles*. Here I found a ſhip ſailing for *Italy*, ſo I embarked in her, but the ſhip was driven by ſtreſs of weather into *Toulon*. When the ſtorm ſomewhat abated we ſet ſail once more, but it came on again to blow, and although it was not more than an Engliſh ſeaman would laugh at, yet the failors in thofe parts are very timorous, and too much given to calling upon faints to help them, and not reefing their fails themfelves. So we muft needs creep in fhore and anchor clofe to the little ifland of *St. Mary*, which is clofe by *Nice*, in the Duchy of *Savoy*.

I had noted that, for fome time paft, my fellow-voyagers, who were moftly a rabble of pilgrims going to *Rome*, had looked afkant at me, and formed in little knots muttering, whilft fome went from group to group whifpering, but always cafting a glance at me. I cared not for the rudenefs of their manners, for I had no knowledge of having done aught to offend them. At laft they began to curfe at me, which I repaid as beft I could ; and then they took to calling me a Huguenot, thereby intending to reproach me with being of the Proteftant religion —they could not fay enough to infult me. I was Englifh dog, Englifh thief, Englifh pirate— all Englifhmen were pirates ; and they wildly railed againft my dread foverain, Queen *Elizabeth*, and, what think you it came to laft of all ? *They never fhould have fair weather as long as I was aboard.* I was *Jonah*, and they were fuffering for my wickednefs. So it came to pafs, that from words, they began to huftle me about, againft which I defended myfelf as well as I could, but, owing to their numbers, I was but a child in their hands, and, when the cries

of *Jonah* got louder and louder, I was feized hold
of and thrown overboard.

The diftance between the fhip and the ifland was
not great, and I was a good fwimmer, fo that I was
not very long before I was on firm land, although
I was fomewhat bruifed and fore from being dafhed
againft the rocks, and fcrambling among them to
get a landing. Yet was I thankful, for I had
rather be alone by myfelf, in any land, than in the
midft of fuch a crew of howling devils as I had juft
been. There was light enough for me to fee what
fort of place I was caft on, and I found there were
no houfes, or inhabitants, and only a few kine and

goats. So I got the beft fhelter I could, and lay down in my wet things to fleep.

The next morning, when it was dawn, I perceived two fhips anchored clofe to the ifland, driven alfo there for fhelter from the fury of the weather. I hailed them, and very fhortly a boat was lowered, and I was fetched off; and when aboard of one of them, the *Bretagne,* I was well refrefhed, and fo kindly ufed, that I was fain to caft in my lot with them. More efpecially, when the captain of the veffel, Captain *La Roche,* of *Saint Malo,* knew that I was a friend of Earl *Ployer,* who was his near neighbour when he was on land, and at home, he was very kind to me, and entertained me with the beft he had, for the Earl's fake. Our fhip was oftenfibly for trading purpofes, but Captain *La Roche* had other ideas in his head, and failed to *Alexandria* in *Egypt.* Here we difcharged our cargo, and afterwards vifited feveral ports, merely to fee what manner of veffels were about; and then we cruifed about and lay to, between the ifland of *Corfu* and *Cape Otranto,* in the kingdom of *Naples,* that is, at the entrance of the *Adriatic Sea.*

We had not long been cruifing about, when we efpied a Venetian Argofy, which was fure to be richly laden. My captain bore down upon her, as if he were defirous to fpeak her, but the Venetian, not liking our looks, and having a moft rich cargo

aboard, fired a fhot at us to make us fheer off.
Although this fhot killed us a man, yet did our
captain rejoice, for it gave him the very opportunity he wanted, of attacking the Argofy, although
it was double our fize.   We had privily made
ready for action beforehand, and we at once gave
the enemy our broadfide, then our ftern guns, and
our other broadfide.   The Venetian would not wait
to fight us, but endeavoured to outfail us, fo we
had to purfue, ufing our chafe guns, and with them
we did fo maul her fails and tackling, that fhe was
at laft fain to lie to and defend herfelf, exchanging
fhot for fhot.

When fhe hove to we grappled her, and twice in
an hour and a half did we board her, but they
managed to get clear, and at the third time the
enemy fucceeded in fetting our fhip on fire.   This
was a fore trouble to us, as it divided our crew,
and, of courfe, thofe who were putting out the fire
could not fight; but at laft, and with fome difficulty, the flames were quenched.   This fire ferved
us a good purpofe, for it fo enflamed our men with
rage, that each man fought like three, and went
at their work luftily, and with a will.   Nay, the
gunners were more careful than ever over laying
their pieces, and fhot her fo oft between wind and
water, that the enemy was beginning to fink, which
perceiving, they yielded, and we ceafed firing.'

Our work was not yet done, indeed we had a bufy time of it to come—for, befides that we had loft fifteen of our crew in this action, part of us had to ftop the leaks, to prevent her finking; more had to guard the prifoners, whom we chained together; and part, of courfe, rifled the fhip. I worked with this party, and we kept hard at it for twenty-four hours. What can I fay of the exceeding riches of this veffel? Indeed it was no wonder they defended it fo ftubbornly and valiantly. It was worth having a fight for. Not only was fhe laden with rich filks, velvets, cloth of gold, and rare tiffues, but fhe had a goodly ftore of piaftres, fequins, and Turkifh gold coins. Ah! I like to think of that time; we worked with a will, not only becaufe we were coining money, but we were fain to haften our work, that we might not be interrupted by any other veffel, which we might have to fight; and that we wanted not, in our crippled condition. We felt no pain, nor fatigue, until we had loaded our fhip with all fhe could carry, and then, fore againft our will, we gave over, and fuddenly became thoroughly tired out with toil. When we caft her off there was not a man of us but whofe heart went with her, for fhe had enough rich ftuffs left in her yet to freight another *Bretagne*, for our burden was but two hundred tons, whilft hers was four or five hundred.

CHAPTER II.

ALTHOUGH we won the fight, yet were we fore damaged, and our captain would fain have put into fome port of the coaft of *Calabria*, to repair and refit; yet, hearing there were fix or feven galleys at Meffina, he turned for *Malta;* but the wind coming fair, he kept his courfe along the coaft of *Sicily*, by *Sardinia* and *Corfica*, until he came to the roads of *Antibes*, in *Piedmont*. Here I parted company with my friend Captain *La Roche*, with many kind fpeeches on both fides, bidding him to remember me, on his return, to Earl *Ployer*. I landed in far better cafe than when I fet out, for my fhare of the fpoil was valued at five hundred fequins, which the Captain gave me, and I had, befides, a little box *which God fent me*, and, of courfe, I did not refufe, with near as much more.

Bidding the *Bretagne* good-bye, I fhipped myfelf on board a veffel for *Leghorn*, as I wanted to fee *Italy*. After landing at *Leghorn*, I journeyed through *Tufcany* without meeting with any adventures, until I came to *Sienna*, where I found thofe two noble gentlemen, and honourable brethren, my Lord *Willoughby* and his brother. They were in a fad plight, both being cruelly wounded in a defperate fray, yet to their exceeding great honour.

They could hardly believe that the cavalier before them was the fame as the lad of fifteen, whom they fent back to his home ; and they marvelled greatly when I told them of all my adventures, and how their parting with me had been the means of making a man of me.

With them I abode fome days, but I was not one who could ftop long in one place, fo I ftarted once more on my travels, nor paufed until I had reached *Rome*, where I had the good fortune to fee Pope *Clement* the Eighth, with many Cardinals, creep up the holy ftairs, which were brought from *Jeru-falem*, and which they fay are thofe our Saviour *Chrift* went up to *Pontius Pilate*. On thefe ftairs, wherever the drops of blood, caufed by His being pricked by the crown of thorns, fell, a nail of fteel is driven in. And up thefe ftairs none dare go, fave on their knees, and they muft kifs every fteel nail. Clofe by, alfo, is a chapel, where hangs a filver lamp, which burneth continually, and yet they fay the oil neither increafeth nor diminifheth. I alfo faw the *Pope* fay mafs at the ancient church of Saint *John de Laterane*.

After leaving Rome, I travelled till I came to *Gratz*, in *Styria*, where I met with an Englifhman, and an Irifh Jefuit, and by their means I made the acquaintance of many brave gentlemen of good quality, efpecially Lord *Eberfhaught*, who was very good to me, and introduced me to Baron *Kiffell*, the General of the Artillery, who, in his turn, made me to know the Earl of *Meldritch*, who had the rank of Colonel in the Army. I joined his regiment, and went with him to *Vienna*.

But I ftayed not long there, juft time enough to furnifh myfelf with arms and munitions, and I joined the Army in *Hungary*, where things were going fomewhat in our disfavour, the Turk having juft taken *Caniza*, and was now befieging the ftrong town of *Olumpagh*, with twenty thoufand men. My friend, Lord *Eberfhaught*, was fhut up within the town, but it was invefted fo ftraitly that he was cut off from all intelligence, and hope of fuccour.

Now it happened that when I had met this nobleman at *Gratz*, he and I had talked over what fhould be done in a fimilar ftate of things, and we had arranged a plan by which we could communicate with each other, without the knowledge of any other perfon. Of this I told our General, Baron *Kiffell*, and, in truth, it was fimple enough to thofe who underftood it. It was but this: I climbed a mountain, feven miles from the city, and there I fhowed three torches, at equal diftances from each other. This fignal the Governor underftood, and replied to by fhowing one. Then we commenced operations by fignalling with the torches. We divided the alphabet into two parts, from A to L, and from M to Z. The firſt part, from A to L, was ſignified by ſhowing and hiding one link ſo often as there were letters from A. Thus B would be twice ſhown and C thrice, and ſo on ; and from M to Z two torches were employed in the ſame way, and when a word was thus ſpelt three lights were ſhown.

It was thus I ſignalled to him this meſſage : "On Thurſday night I will charge on the eaſt ; at the alarum, ſally you ;" and *Eberſhaught* replied .that he would.

This plan was carried out with ſuch ſucceſs, and with ſo much damage to the Turks, that, in diſguſt, they raiſed the ſiege, and retired to *Caniza*.

For this exploit *Kiſſell* received great honour, and he rewarded me by making me a captain of two hundred and fifty men in the regiment of Colonel *Voldo*, the Earl of *Meldritch*.

Indeed I now felt happy, for I had command of men, who moreover were cavalry, and I thought I ſaw my way into being a great general ; but there was a general rumour of peace, and this ſomewhat damped me, being ſo newly promoted. Yet the Turk intended no ſuch matter, but levied ſoldiers from all parts he could. Thus, I could not feel but over-joyed, when news came that the Emperor had raiſed three armies. One of theſe, led by the Archduke *Mathias*, the Emperor's brother, who had for his lieutenant Duke *Mercury*,* to whom I was attached, was to defend *Lower Hungary.*

Duke *Mercury* had an army of thirty thoufand men, and with thefe he laid fiege to *Stal Weiffenburg* (otherwife called *Alba Regalis*), in *Lower Pannonia*, which place was fo ftrong, both by nature and art, as to be confidered impregnable, and the Turks fallied forth, and did us great hurt, flaying many hundreds of our troops, both German and French; but by means of fire-balls, which I caufed to be thrown into the town, and by affaulting the town at an unexpected place, we gained poffeffion of it. Then, turning our own, and the captured, cannon upon the Citadel, we reduced it, and Earl *Meldritch* took the Bafhaw prifoner with his own hands.

During this time, the Great Turk *Mahomet*, the third of that name, had raifed an army of 60,000 men to relieve the town; but the Duke *Mercury*, knowing that this raw levy could not be worth much, left a ftrong garrifon in *Alba Regalis*, and started off with 20,000 men to meet the Turk in the plains of *Girke*. The armies met, and fought hand to hand, till the night parted them; by which time

---

* Mercœur.

we had well learned not to defpife the raw Turks under *Haffan*, for the regiment of Earl *Meldritch* was furrounded, and we had to cut our way through the enemy. This, at length, we fucceeded in doing; but, alas! with the lofs of near half our regiment. I myfelf was fore wounded, and had my horfe fhot under me; but I was not long unmounted, for there was choice enough of horfes that wanted mafters.

This reverfe was terrible for us, and we had hard work to hold our own againft the Turk, when, happily, at the approach of winter, he raifed the fiege, broke up his camp, and retired.

Duke *Mercury* now divided his army into three parts; he fent 7,000 to affift *Caniza*. The Earl of *Meldritch* with 6,000 men was to affift *George Bufca* againft the Tranfylvanians, and the reft he kept himfelf. The ftory of his life from this point is very brief. He returned to *Vienna* in great triumph, as if he had conquered all *Hungary*. The Archdukes, and all the nobility, received him with great honour, nay, his very picture was confidered fo fortunate, that thoufands kept it as a precious relic. But the day after a feaft at *Nuremburg* he was found dead, and two days after, his brother-in-law died fuddenly, and their hearts were fent into *France*. Much did people goffip over this, but not loudly, for it is not for the commons to call in queftion what happens among princes.

D

I accompanied Earl *Meldritch*, but he, fearing treachery from *Bufca*, formed the idea of joining his enemy, the Prince Sigifmund, inftead, and endeavoured to perfuade his troops to go with him.

Nor did it take much to perfuade them ; the promife of free liberty to make booty of all they could get poffeffion of from the Turks, was fweet, indeed, to men whofe pay had not been regular, and who were worn out by hard travel. For myfelf, I owed nothing to the German Emperor, but much to my noble Lord the Earl *Meldritch*, and as, when in *the Low Countries*, I had seen enough of fighting with Chriftians againft Chriftians, fo that I fomewhat loathed it, (faving againft a Spaniard,) yet never did I fee harm in fighting the Turk. So I joined with him heart and foul.

I need not to fay that the Prince was glad of fo brave a commander as the Earl of *Meldritch*, and the addition to his forces of fo many expert and ancient foldiers; fo that he gave us all neceffary relief in the way of provifions and other things, but alfo what freedom we defired to plunder the Turks.

The Earl was not a man to remain long idle, fo, after haraffing the enemy by all the means in his power, he, being joined by Prince *Moyses* with 9,000 men, lay fiege to the town of *Regall*.

It was not till we had well fettled down before

the town that we found out how hard was the nut
we had undertaken to crack ; for the plain on
which we were entrenched, was ſo commanded by
the ordnance of the town, that we ſpent near a
month in entrenching ourſelves, and in raiſing our
mounts to plant our batteries therein.

Ay, and it galled us much to be taunted and
derided by the Turks, for they would call out to
us at times, aſking us, " Were our ordnance at
pawn ? " and they would ſometimes tell us that they
could ſee we were growing fat for want of exerciſe.
And this, I ſay, nettled us, for we could not as yet
help ourſelves ; yet to me did it bring a mighty
honour, as you ſhall hear.

One day they had been reviling us as uſual,
when a trumpet ſounded, and a ſmall company
ſallied forth, bearing with them a white flag of
truce. They aſked to ſee one of our leading Commanders, and when he had come and demanded
their meſſage, they ſaid how it was commonly reported within the town that we ſhould never aſſault
their city, but would go as we came, and that,
therefore, rather than it ſhould be ſaid we had had
no fight with them, and to delight their ladies, who
were getting ſomewhat dull by reaſon of their ſeeing no ſport, their lord *Turbaſhaw* had ſent them
with a meſſage, and a challenge to any captain who
had command of a company, to fight with the one

who was willing, and durft do fo, each for the other's head.

Think you there was lacking one among us to take up this challenge? I trow not. On the contrary, everyone wanted to fight this proud Turk; and, the fubject being difcuffed, men waxed warm: fome claimed it as a right, but all wanted to fight. Seeing this, it was propofed, and in the end decided, that choice fhould be made by lot, and, to my great delight and pride, the lot fell upon me.

My fellows envied me, as in like cafe I fhould have envied them, but they cheered me up, and I was overwhelmed by the offer of horfes, arms, and armour. But I would none of them, preferring mine own harnefs, in which I had fought many a time, and which fhowed by its dints, that it had been well proven.

A truce for a time, until that the combat fhould be ended, was agreed upon; and, indeed, it was a pretty fight to fee—all our troops drawn up in array on three fides, leaving us a fair field in the centre for the combat, whilft the walls were crowded by the Turks and their fair dames, whofe bright-coloured dreffes lent a charm to the fcene, which, perhaps, would have been more brilliant had we been able to fee their faces, which were veiled after their manner. I felt no dread, but my blood ran hot and quick through my veins, as I faw this noble concourſe, which had met together to ſee either my victory, or my death, and I ſaid to my-ſelf, " *John Smith*, this day thou haſt need of all thy ſkill and cunning ; think of nought but victory, and fight as thou haſt never fought before, for the honour of the army."

The *Turbaſhaw* was the firſt to enter the field,

His three ſingle Combats
His Encounter with TVRBASHAW

and he came well mounted and armed—his horſe curvetting and caracoling to the ſound of the haut-boys by which he was accompanied. He was indeed mighty fine to behold, for on his ſhoulders were fixed a pair of great wings, moſt curiouſly made of eagles' feathers ſet within a border of ſilver, and his dreſs was richly garniſhed with gold and precious ftones—and he came with a Janizary before him, bearing his lance, and two others, one on each fide, leading his horfe.

I kept him not long waiting, but with a flourifh of trumpets, and with only a page bearing my lance, I rode into the fpace; and after having courteoufly faluted my adverfary, I took up my ftand. All things being arranged, at the found of a trumpet we charged, and I had fuch good fuccefs, that my lance ftruck the Turk through the fight of his helmet, and went through his face, head and all, fo that he fell to the ground dead: which feeing, I alighted, and unbracing his helmet, I cut off his head. As the challenge was only for each other's heads, I defpoiled not the body, which the Turks took; but, bearing the bleeding trophy, I returned, without having received the flighteft hurt at all. The head I prefented to the Prince *Moyfes*, our General, who kindly accepted it, and I was welcomed back again with joy by the whole army.

The Turks chafed exceedingly at the overthrow of their champion, more efpecially his bofom friend, who was called *Grualgo*; and he, for very madnefs, fent me a particular challenge, in order to regain his friend's head, and take mine, or lofe his own—together with his horfe and armour, which were but lawful fpoil. So next day

His Combat with GRVALGO. Cap.t of three hundred horsmen.

was the fame fpace cleared, and the fame fcene enacted, for I could not with honour have refufed his challenge, even had I been fo minded, which I was not.

At the found of the trumpet we made our

charge, and met with a great fhock, fo that our lances were completely fplintered, and the Turk was nigh unhorfed. It had been agreed that in this event our next weapons fhould be piftols, fo wheeling round and again charging, we each dif-charged a fhot. The Turk's bullet hit me upon the placard or breaftplate, and glanced off, but mine took effect in his left arm, fhattering the bone, fo that it hung helplefs, and hindered him of all control of his horfe. Whether it was the agony of the wound, or the reftivenefs of his horfe, I know not, but the Turk fell to the ground, where he lay bruifed and ftunned. Need I fay, I was foon off my horfe—and he loft his head, as his friend before him. I took, as was agreed, his horfe and armour, but his body, and his rich apparel, were fent back to the town.

The Turks made fome fallies every day, but to none effect, and the fiege went on but flowly, for we had not completed our works and approaches to the neceffary height. So that to fill up the time, I, being then young, and fomewhat fool-hardy, fent a meffage to the ladies of the Turks, that I was not fo enamoured of their lovers' heads but that I would give them to any one of their rank who would redeem them by combat; but that to win them, he muft alfo take mine, or I would have his.

This challenge failed not of its effect, and it was accepted by a Turk of rank called *Bonny Mulgro.* We fought next day on the same ground as before, but under somewhat different conditions, for the Turk would have no lances— perhaps becaufe he had feen how I could handle

How he flew BONNY·MVLGRO·

one—but had battle-axes in their ftead. After the trumpet had founded, we rode at each other and difcharged our piftols, by which no harm was done; and we then fell to with our battle-axes, and that fo ftrongly, that fometimes one, and fometimes the other, had hard work to keep the

faddle; and, indeed, it was near going hard with me, for I received fuch a blow that I loft my battle-axe, and was nearly unhorfed; fo that a great fhout went up from the ramparts, to encourage my adverfary. He profecuted his advantage to the uttermoſt of his power, and had it not been for the readineſs of my horſe, and my own judgment and dexterity in ſuch matters, I muſt have been ſlain. But by God's aſſiſtance I not only avoided the Turk's violence, but, having drawn my falchion, I pierced him through back and body, ſo that he was obliged to alight from his horſe, and he ſtood not long, ere he loſt his head, as the reſt had done.

The whole army was ſo pleaſed with me that they took me in triumph to the General's pavilion, with a guard of 6,000 men and three ſpare horſes, before each of which was borne a Turk's head upon a lance. Prince *Moyſes* received me with great honour, embracing me with his arms ; and gave me a fair horſe richly furniſhed, a ſcimitar and belt worth three hundred ducats; and Earl *Meldritch* made me Sergeant-Major of his regiment.

CHAPTER III.

SOON afterwards we completed our ſiege operations, having mounted ſix-and-twenty pieces of ordnance fifty or ſixty feet above the plain ; and theſe were worked with ſuch good effect, that

within fifteen days two breaches were made, which
the Turks defended as valiantly as men could do,
whilft their flothful Governor lay in a caftle atop of
a high mountain, afking feebly, what the matter
was? The general affault was made, but our
troops fuffered feverely by logs, &c., being rolled
down upon them, and bags of gunpowder thrown
in their midft, two regiments lofing half their men
in this manner : but at length we overmaftered
them, and gained poffeffion of the city ; the Turks
retiring into the caftle, from whence they fent a
flag of truce, defiring terms.

But the Turks had cruelly murdered the father
of Earl *Meldritch*, and he forgot it not ; fo that
he turned all the ordnance in the town upon the
caftle, and fo battered it, that next day we took it ;
and then he did avenge his father's murder ; for
all that could bear arms were put to the fword,
and their heads fet upon ftakes round about the
walls, in like manner as they had ferved the
Chriftians when they took it. Then Prince
Moyfes had the ramparts repaired, and our works
deftroyed. There was great plunder in the town,
for it had, for a long time, been an impregnable
den of thieves. Our loffes, however, had been
very great, and Prince *Moyfes*, not thinking the
Turks fufficiently punifhed, left a ftrong garrifon
in *Regall*, and took and facked the towns of

Veratio, Salmos, and *Kuprouka*. After which, with
two thoufand prifoners, moftly women and children,
we went and encamped at *Efenberg*, not far from
Prince *Sigifmund's* palace.

Here the Prince paid us a vifit, and was prefented with the prifoners, and fix-and-thirty enfigns;
and a *Te Deum* was fung, and thanks returned
to the Almighty for our victories. And here,
alfo, as if to puff up my pride to the full, Prince
Sigifmund was made acquainted with the fervices I
had done at *Olumpagh, Stal Weiſſenberg*, and
Regall, and the Prince, at an audience I had with
him, gave me great honour, and granted me, by
patent, under his hand and feal, a grant of arms:
namely, On a fhield vert, a chevron gules, between
three Turks' heads proper; and for the creft, an
Oftrich or, holding in its mouth a horfefhoe
argent. I had to take an oath ever to wear them
in my colours; and, befides this, my gracious
Prince gave me his portrait in gold, and three
hundred ducats yearly for a penfion. I confefs
that I am, in a great meafure, very proud of thefe
arms, and contemplate them frequently with huge
fatisfaction; for I hold it to be no fmall matter, that
a boy, friendlefs, and alone in the world, fhould
carve out for himfelf, entirely by his own deeds, a
title to fuch rewards from his Prince as this gift of
coat-armour. This is the original grant, given me

fome long time afterwards, but I will tranflate it
from the Latin tongue in which it is writ :—

"Sigismund Bathor, by the Grace of God,
Duke of *Tranfylvania, Wallachia,* and *Moldavia,*
Earl of *Anchard, Salford,* and *Growenda ;* to all
whom this Writing may come or appear.

Know that We have given leave and licence
to *John Smith,* an Englifh gentleman, Captain
of 250 foldiers, under the moft generous and
honourable *Henry Volda,* Earl of *Meldritch,*
Salmaria and *Peldoia,* Colonel of a thoufand
horfe, and fifteen hundred foot, in the Wars of
Hungary, and in the Provinces aforefaid under our

authority; whose service doth deserve all praise and perpetual memory towards Us, as a man that did for God and his country overcome his enemies. Wherefore out of Our love and favour, according to the law of Arms, We have ordained and given him in his shield of Arms, the figure and description of three Turks' heads, which with his sword before the town of *Regall*, he did overcome, kill, and cut off, in the Province of *Transylvania*. But Fortune, as she is very variable, so it chanced and happened to him in the Province of *Wallachia*, in the year of our Lord 1602, the 18th day of November, with many others, as well Noblemen, as also divers other soldiers, were taken prisoners by the Lord Bashaw of *Cambia*, a country of *Tartaria*; whose cruelty brought him such good fortune, by the help and power of Almighty God, that he delivered himself, and returned again to his company and fellow soldiers, of whom We do discharge him, and this he hath in witness thereof, being much more worthy of a better reward; and now intends to return to his own sweet country. We desire, therefore, all our loving and kind Kinsmen, Dukes, Princes, Earls, Barons, Governors of Towns, Cities or Ships, in this Kingdom, or any other Provinces he shall come in, that you freely let pass this the aforesaid Captain, without any hindrance or molestation, and this doing with all kindnefs, we are always ready to do the like for you.

"Sealed at *Lipfwick* in *Mifenland*, the ninth of December in the year of our Lord 1603.

SIGISMUNDUS BATHOR.

"With the proper privilege of His Majefty."

And more than twenty years afterwards, I had thefe arms regiftered in our own College of Heralds, as this writing of *Garter's* fheweth. This, too, is in Latin, which I tranflate thus :—

"To all and fingular, in what place, ftate, degree, order, or condition whatfoever, to whom this prefent writing fhall come ; I, *William Segar,*

Knight, otherwife Garter, and Principal King of Arms of England, wifh health. Know that I the aforefaid Garter, do witnefs and approve, that this aforefaid Patent, I have feen, figned and fealed, under the proper Hand and Seal Manual of the faid Duke of *Tranfylvania*, and a true Copy of the fame, as a thing for perpetual memory, I have fubfcribed and recorded in the Regifter and Office of the Heralds of Arms.

"Dated at London the nineteenth day of Auguft, in the year of our Lord 1625, and in the firft year of our Soverain Lord *Charles*, by the grace of God, King of Great Britain, France and Ireland; Defender of the Faith, &c.

WILLIAM SEGAR."

But, if I was fomewhat elated with my good fortune, it was deftined that my pride fhould have a fall, for the *Crim* Tartars came in fuch hordes, and did fo harry us, that we met with much lofs, and our ftrength was greatly reduced. Warring with favages, the war was carried on favagely. I mind me fpecially at *Rebrynk*, where the enemy was entrenched too ftrongly for us to harm him. Neverthelefs, whenever we could catch a few of their men, we cut off their heads, and rolled them up and down before their trenches: whilft they flayed alive feven of our porters, and hanged their fkins upon poles.

E

After a time, however, things came to fuch a pafs that we muft either fight or be cut in pieces, flying; fo, of courfe, we offered battle, although the odds of numbers were fearfully againft us, 11,000 of us againft 40,000 of the enemy. We did our beft, but when night came, only fome 1,300 or 1,400 horfe had managed to fave themfelves, cutting their way, under Earl *Meldritch*, through the enemy, and fwam the river; all the reft were flain, or taken prifoners. And on that bloody field that night, lay nearly 30,000 dead bodies, fome headlefs, fome armlefs or leglefs, but all cut and mangled, and the *Crim* Tartars admitted that they never paid dearer than they had done that day. Twelve Englifhmen went that day into the fray, well and hearty, and nine paid with their lives; they did all they could do, and when they could do no more, they left their bodies there in teftimony of their minds. Two efcaped, but I was fadly wounded, and lay among the flaughtered dead bodies.

That was a night I fhall never forget; how I lay there tortured by thirft, and groaning with the fierce agony of my wounds; fo that I was even glad to fee the pillagers coming, thinking they would moft probably cut my throat, and thus put me out of my mifery. But they, judging from my habit and armour that I fhould be more valuable to them for ranfom alive than dead, took me prifoner, with many others, and ufed me well until my wounds were healed.

When I was fairly found again, I was fent with a batch of Chriftians to *Axopolis*, where we were fold for flaves in the market place, as if we were beafts. None but thofe who have undergone this degradation, can have any conception of the feeling. Stripped naked in order to fhow the foundnefs of our limbs, with mufcles being handled and felt, as a butcher does an ox; a kick, a blow, or a lafh from a whip, and a curfe, were you not quick enough in obeying fuch orders as " Turn round," " Put out your arm," &c.; whilft now and then we were fet a-wreftling, one with another, in order to fhow our ftrength.

I was purchafed, at laft, by a Bafhaw named *Bogall*, and inafmuch as I was of better quality than moft of my fellow-flaves, he thought I fhould make a nice prefent for his fair miftrefs at *Conftantinople*. So we were fent to *Adrianople*, and from thence, chained together round the neck by twenties, we marched in long files to *Conftantinople*, where we were delivered to our feveral mafters, and I to my future miftrefs, the young and pretty lady *Charatza Tragabigzanda*.

This noble gentlewoman had great compaffion on my misfortunes, and my youth, (for I was but

twenty-four years of age,) and, knowing fomewhat of
the Italian tongue, fhe would oft converfe with me,
as well as fhe could; and at times, when fhe fhould
have gone to the bath, or to weep over the tombs,
as is their wont, fhe would feign ficknefs, and would
queftion me, how it was that *Bogall* had taken me
prifoner, and whether I was, as he had written her,
a Bohemian Lord, conquered by his hand, as he
had conquered many others, whom, ere long he
would prefent to her, and whofe ranfoms fhould
adorn her with the glory of his conquefts.

To this what could I reply but the truth? I
protefted I was nought of the kind, and that I had
never fet eyes on *Bogall* until that he had bought
me at *Axopolis*; that I was an Englifhman, who by
my own adventures had been raifed to be a captain
in thofe countries. I think fhe would fain have had
me a Bohemian Lord; but as I ftill fturdily avowed
that I was but a fimple Englifhman, fhe inquired
diligently of many French, Dutch, and Italians,
who could fpeak Englifh, and their report confirmed my ftory. This, if poffible, made her more
compaffionate to me than before; fhe would not
keep me herfelf as a flave, and, as fhe much feared
that her mother might fell me, fhe thought the
fafeft plan was to fend me to her brother, *Tymor*,
Bafhaw of *Nalbrits*, in the country of *Cambia*, a
province of *Tartaria*. She did it for the beft, but

my heart fank within me when I thought of my life about to be paffed in flavery, in thofe deferts; and miferable enough was my captivity there, as you fhall hear.

It took us many days to journey from *Conftanti-nople* to *Nalbrits*, where *Tymor* Bafhaw then lived, in a vaft ftone caftle, with many great courts about it; environed by high ftone walls.

Up to this time I had been well treated, but now was I to experience a thorough change, and that entirely owing to my ladv's well-meant kind-nefs; for in the letter fhe wrote to her brother, and which was delivered to him the fame time as I my-felf was, fhe had faid fo much in my favour, and pleaded fo for my good ufage, that he more than fufpected her liking for me. For fhe alfo wrote him that I was but to fojourn there to learn the language, and what it was to be a Turk, till time made her miftrefs of her own actions. This pro-voked all the bigotry of the proud and haughty Turk. What! fhould his fifter think kindly of, nay, even fo love a Chriftian dog, as to wifh him to be well treated, and in courfe of time be advanced (he turning renegado) to who could tell what pofi-tion by her favour? Never, with his confent and affiftance. The dog fhould be treated according to his deferts. So, after fpitting in my face, and reviling me with all the bitter words his tongue

could command, he called his tafkmafter, or drub-
man, to him, and gave him orders what to do with
me.

The man, feeing his mafter fo incenfed againft
me, took a devilifh delight in putting me to the
utmoft indignities. He ftripped me naked, and
fhaved my head and beard as bare as my hand ; he

rivetted a great ring of iron, which had a handle,
bowed like a fickle, for anyone to catch hold of,
around my neck, and clad me in a hair coat trimmed
with undreffed fkins. There were many more
Chriftian flaves, and nearly a hundred criminal
Turks or Moors, murderers, thieves, or worfe. Of

thefe, being the laft comer, I was the flave of flaves, kicked, cuffed, and fpat upon by all. The treatment was fuch that even a dog could not have lived to endure the very beft of it, and although we laboured hard for them, having the whip always before our eyes, or on our bodies, they regarded us no more than as beafts.

I like not to dwell upon that time. I was always thinking over my fad lot, and the only confolation I could find, the only ray of light in that deep, difmal, darknefs, was the hope that fooner or later *Tragabigzanda* would inquire after my welfare, and fhould fhe even get a glimmer of the truth, fhe would at once ufe her utmoft endeavours to releafe me. I often debated the profpect of efcape with fome Chriftians who had been flaves there for a long time, but they had long fince given up all hope of fuch a deed, becaufe they could fee no way of effecting it with fafety. But God helpeth his fervants when they leaft think of help, and fo it happened to me.

I was put to threfhing by myfelf, at a barn in a large field more than a league from the Bafhaw's houfe, and *Tymor* often would ride over, as he did to overlook the other portions of his land, and whenever he came, he took occafion to beat, fpurn, and revile me. On one occafion he carried this to fuch an extent, that I could no longer bear it, but

forgetting all reafon, I fell upon the tyrant with my
threfhing bat (for they ufe not flails) and beat his

Capt SMITH Killeth the BASHAW of Nalbrits and on his horfe efcapeth.

London Printed by James Reeue

brains out. Seeing that if I ftopped, I fhould moft
furely be killed, and that if I was caught trying to
efcape, I fhould but meet the fame fate, I determined
to try and get away.

I ftripped the Turk of his clothes, and dreffed
myfelf in them, after which, I hid his body under
the corn. Then, filling a bag with corn, I mounted
his horfe, and fled into the defert at all hazards.
For two or three days I wandered about I knew
not whither, and I met no man of whom I could
afk my way. Yet did God in His goodnefs direct

me to one of their great roads, which crofs thefe large territories. There are pofts with figns on them directing the way to the different countries, and I chofe that which had a crofs upon it, to fhow it led to a Chriftian country—in fact, to *Mufcovy.*

For fixteen days I travelled in fear and trembling, fearful of meeting at any moment fome one who fhould fee my collar of flavery around my neck, and who, by reading the writing on the fame, would difcover whence I came, and deliver me back to certain death, or make me a flave once more. I have fcarce any recollection of how I fared during this long time, how I fed, how I refted. I know I feared to approach any rock, or even any clump of bufhes, left behind them fhould be enemies. Judge of my joy then, when, on the fixteenth day, I came in fight of *Æcopolis,* a town on the river *Don,* and a garrifon of the Mufcovites. Here I was brought before the Governor, who examined me ftraitly as to my life and adventures, but at laft, being convinced that I was a true man and no rogue, he had my iron collar taken off, to my hearty joy and great relief.

Here, too, I found, as I have always done when in misfortune, kindly help from a woman ; the good and charitable Lady *Callamata,* whom God preferve, and whom I fhall always hold in reverence, largely fupplied all my wants, fo that indeed I felt as if I were in heaven after my fufferings in captivity, and the hardfhips and horrors of my efcape.

With them I ftayed until a convoy arrived, which was going to *Coragnaw*, where the governor of that place received me with wonderful kindnefs, owing to my letter of recommendation from the governor of *Æcopolis*, and, indeed, all through my journey to *Hermonftadt*, in *Tranfylvania*, I never met, in all my life, with more refpect, mirth, content, and entertainment. There was no governor, wherever I came, but what gave me fomewhat as a prefent, befides bearing all my charges, fo that I could fcarce contain myfelf for joy after my late hardfhips.

Once arrived in *Tranfylvania* I found fo many good friends, that had I my will, and had I not longed once more to fee my native country, I fhould hardly ever have left them, for indeed I was glutted with content, and near drowned with joy. But I minded me that I had to report myfelf to my Prince, inafmuch as I was ftill in his fervice, having been captured whilft fighting for him. As he was not in *Tranfylvania*, needs muft that I fhould go and feek him; fo I travelled to *Prague*, in *Bohemia*, and at length found him, together with my old .Colonel and companion in arms, the moft noble Earl *Meldritch*.

After hearing my cafe Prince *Sigismund* condoled with me mightily, and moreover ordered me to be given fifteen hundred ducats of gold to repair my loffes, and to fomewhat recompenfe me for the hardfhips I had undergone. It was then, alfo, that he gave me that writing I have already fhown you, in which he requefts all perfons under his jurifdiction to fhow me help, at the fame time giving me the boon I afked of him, my difcharge from his fervice.

I was now my own mafter, and at liberty to do as I chofe for myfelf, fo I travelled throughout *Germany*, *France*, and *Spain*.

CHAPTER IV.

THEN, hearing of the wars in *Barbary*, I went from *Gibraltar* to *Tangiers*, and thence to *Saffee*, where I made the acquaintance of a Captain of a French man-of-war, named *Merham*, and we became very good friends. Although the country was much difturbed by civil war, I went about and faw many curious things, as, being an Englifhman, I was unharmed; for *Muley Haffan*, a former

Emperor, had a great liking for Englifhmen, and, having no good artificers of his own, he welcomed handicraftfmen from *England*, fuch as goldfmiths, watchmakers, plumbers, carvers, and polifhers of ftone.   He allowed all thefe a ftanding fee of ten fhillings a day, a fufficient quantity of linen, woollen, filk, or what not, for their apparel, and ftinted them not in diet, befides which, they could tranfport, or import, what they would, cuftoms free.   One of them, Mr. *Henry Archer*, afterwards came over to *England*, and fet up in bufinefs as a watchmaker.

Concerning this *Archer*, there is one thing more worth noting.   Not far from *Mount Atlas*, a great lionefs, in the heat of the day, did ufe to bathe herfelf, and teach her puppies to fwim, in the river, *Canzeff.*   This was a good breadth, yet fhe would carry them over the river, one after the other; which fome Moors perceiving, watched their opportunity, and, when the river was between her and them, ftole four of her whelps; which perceiving, fhe paffed the river with all the fpeed fhe could, and coming near them, they let fall a whelp (and fled with the reft), which fhe took in her mouth and fwam the river back again.

They gave a male and female to Mr. *Archer*, who kept them in the King's garden, till the male killed the female, when he brought him up like a puppy-dog, having it to lie upon his bed, until he grew as great as a maſtiff, and no dog could be more tame and gentle to thoſe he knew, than he was. Being about to return to *England*, Mr. *Archer* gave him to a merchant of *Marſeilles*, who preſented it to the French King, who, in his turn, ſent it to King *James* as a gift.

It had been in the *Tower* ſeven years, when one *John Bull*, who had been ſervant to Mr. *Archer*, went with divers of his friends to ſee the lions, not knowing his old friend was there; yet this rare beaſt ſmelt him before he ſaw him, whining, groaning, and trembling with ſuch an expreſſion of acquaintance, that, being informed by the keepers how he came there, *Bull* ſo prevailed, that the keeper opened the grate, and *Bull* went in. But no dog could fawn more on his maſter than the lion on him, licking his feet, hands, and face, ſkipping and tumbling to and fro, to the wonder of all the beholders. *Bull* was quite ſatisfied with this recognition, and managed to get out of the grate; but when the lion ſaw his friend gone, no beaſt by bellowing, roaring, ſcratching, and howling, could expreſs more rage and ſorrow, nor would he either eat, or drink, for four whole days afterwards.

While I think of it, however, I muſt tell you another lion ſtory. In *Morocco*, the King's lions are all together in a court, environed with a great high wall. To thofe they put a young puppy-dog. The largeft lion had a fore upon his neck, which this dog fo licked that it was healed. From that time the lion took him under his protection, and defended him from the fury of all the reft, nor durft they eat till he and the dog had fed. This dog grew great, and lived amongft the lions many years after.

I foon gave up all hope of feeing any fervice in this country, for their ways would not fuit me, fo I could not ftay, but returned with Captain *Merham* and his companions to *Saffee.*

Now, after our arrival, *Merham* invited me and two or three more to go on board his fhip, and he gave us as good a welcome, and fpared not anything that he had to exprefs his kindnefs towards us, that the time ran on fo that it was too late to go on fhore, and we were of neceffity conftrained to ftay aboard. To this we had no objection, for we were in right good company, and a fairer evening could not be; yet, ere midnight, fuch a ftorm did arife that we were obliged to flip cable and anchor and put out to fea. The ftorm was fo great that we could carry no fail but juft one small one, which kept us spooning before the wind, till we were driven to the *Canaries.* There the weather got calmer,

and we put ourfelves to rights fomewhat, hoping
that fome good might come out of this evil
chance; nor was it long before we took a fmall
bark coming from *Teneriffe*, loaded with wine. Three
or four more we chafed, and took two, but found
little in them, fave a few paffengers, that told us
of five Dutch men-of-war, about the *Ifles*, fo that
we ftood for *Boyadora*, upon the African fhore,
betwixt which, and *Cape Noa*, we defcried two
fails.

Merham, wifhing to know who and what they
were, hailed them. According to the ufual courtefy
at fea, they very civilly danced their topfails, and
defired *Merham* to come on board of them, and
take what he would, for that they were but
two poor Buccaneers. *Merham*, however, was
too fhrewd an old fox to be fo caught, and feeing
himfelf in the lions' paws (for truth to tell, they
were two Spanifh men-of-war, and well appointed),
he fprung his luff. One of the Spaniards tacked
after him, and came clofe to his nether quarter,
when he delivered his broadfide and then luffed up
to windward. Her confort, the *Vice-Admiral*,
did the like, and in the courfe of an hour they
attacked us one on each fide, and tried to board us;
but we beat them off, and they left four or five
of their men dead, and fprawling on our gratings.
So they battered us for another hour, and then

boarded us once more. This time, however, they threw on board of us four kedgers, or grapnels, with iron chains, in order to have torn down our grating, but the *Admiral's* yard was fo entangled with our fhrouds that he could not fheer off, which gave Captain *Merham* time to difcharge two crofs-bar fhots, and divers iron bolts made for that purpofe, full againft the *Admiral's* bow, in which it caufed fuch a breach as made us fear we fhould both fink in company. The Spaniards foon flipped their grapnels, and we were bufy in cutting his tackling, but fo as to keep his yard in our fhrouds; and their fhip at laft got clear, and ventured not near us again, but fired at a diftance, while they repaired their leak.

The other fhip then came up, and the fight continued from noon, till fix in the evening, when darknefs came on, and we made for *Marmora*, the Spaniards purfuing us; and fo flowly did we fail, and fuch fmall way did we make, that next morning we were not three leagues from *Cape Noa*. The two Spaniards outfailed us when they could fee, and in an hour's time came up with us, and commanded us to furrender to the King of Spain upon fair quarter.

But *Merham* only fmiled at them, and, calling for wine, he filled a glafs, and drank to them, having done which, he difcharged his quarter pieces.

This did fo incenfe the Spaniards that they clofed with us and boarded us, and many of them rufhed up the fhrouds and endeavoured to unfling the mainfail; which the mafter, and fome others who were in the round-houfe, perceiving, fhot at them, and caufed them, to their coft, to tumble down. And, indeed, about the round-houfe the Spaniards were fo peftered, that they were forced to the great cabin, which, owing to the firing, blew up, becaufe of the powder there ftored. The fmoke and the fire were fo great, that both they, and we, thought the fhip on fire.

In the forecaftle, too, things were not quite fo comfortable for the Spaniards as they would have liked, for, many of them being on the grating, we blew them up by means of a bag of gunpowder, fo that they cleared themfelves away from us with great fpeed, leaving behind them their dead and wounded and fome few prifoners. *Merham* at once fet about quenching the flames, and after a time fucceeded in fo doing, with the aid of wet cloths and water; and it was near time that fuch fhould be done, for it began to grow apace, too faft, indeed, for our liking.

The Spaniards ftill kept firing upon us, but we managed to ftop the worft leaks by means of old fails, which we warped over the fhot holes, and prepared to fight it out to the laft man. The

F

Spaniards, feeing the fire quenched, and that we ftill were not only able, but very willing to continue the fight, hung out a flag of truce, demanding a parley; but that defperate and brave man, *Merham*, had but one way with him, and would have none of their parleys, and only gave them for anfwer the report of his ordnance, which he did know well how to ufe for his advantage.

Thus we fpent the next afternoon, and half that night, when the fire grew flacker, until at laft it ceafed altogether, and we found that the Spaniards had either loft us, or left us, with either of which we were well content. Next morning we took account of our loffes, and found we had 27 men flain and 16 wounded; whilft we could count in the hull of our veffel the marks of 140 great fhot. But, if we could truft the account of one of our Spanifh prifoners, they had loft 100 men in the *Admiral*, and they much feared that their veffel would fink ere fhe could reach any port, as, indeed, fhe might have done, for I never heard aught more of her. We ourfelves being crippled, not only by reafon of the fhot, but by the fire on board, thought it moft prudent to look after our own fafety, and, accordingly, we fhaped our courfe for *Santa Cruz*, *Cape Goa*, and *Mogador*, until we came again to *Saffee*, and thence I took

fhip and returned to *England*, for I longed once
more to fee my native country.

It was in the year 1604 that I came home, if
not a rich man, yet with good ftore of coin, and,
befides, I had the fmall eftate that had been left
me by my father, fo that I wanted for nothing and
had to fpare. Naturally, for like will cleave to
like, I fought the company of men like myfelf,
who had adventured fomewhat, and had been in
diftant lands. [It was thus I fell in with many who
had been to the *New World*, and all their talk was
of its wonders.] And they told me what had happened fince I had been away. How in the year of
grace 1584, Captains *Amidas* and *Barlow*, who
had been fent out on a voyage of difcovery by that
moft worfhipful nobleman, and worthy knight, *Sir
Walter Raleigh*, did coaft round the *Carolinas*, and
entered *Ocracocke* inlet, where they took poffeffion
of the foil on behalf of their Sovereign, and which
was afterwards called *Virginia*, in honour of our
ever bleffed Virgin Queen *Elizabeth*, of glorious
memory. From them I learned how they tarried
not there at that time, but how *Ralph Lane* (afterwards Sir *Ralph*) went out to found a colony,
how that languifhed, and how Sir *Francis Drake*
brought them home. More by token that *Lane*
brought with him that bleffed herb tobacco, and
was the firft man that brought it to *England*; and

F 2

yet have I heard men say, some that it was *Drake*, others that it was *Raleigh*. Nor are they altogether wrong, for if *Raleigh* had not sent *Lane* out, and *Drake* had not brought *Lane* home, he could not at that time have showed us Englishmen the virtues of that precious herb.

Ay, and I learned how the fifty men left there by Sir *Richard Grenville* had not been heard of, although Sir *Walter Raleigh* had sent five several times to search after them, at his own charges; the last time sending (in 1602) *Samuel Mace*, of *Weymouth*, a very sufficient mariner, and an honest, sober man, who had been to Virginia twice before; and afterwards it was learned that the whole of the fifty had been murdered, and that one little innocent babe had been born, and had been baptized by the name of *Virginia*.

Among others whom I met, was Captain *Bartholomew Gosnold*, who had (in the year 1602) sailed from *Falmouth* in a small bark called *The Concord*, with a crew of thirty-two persons, and had discovered the north part of *Virginia*. His was a venturous voyage, for he went to unknown parts with but a small vessel and crew; but it was ever thus in my time. Sir *Francis Drake's* ship, in which he so worthily sailed round the world, was but of small tonnage, and so were those that sailed with *Frobisher*. What a man had to do he set his whole mind on, and if the enterprife was within the power of man to accomplifh, he did it. The leader chofe his men with great care, and took heed to be ever the chief, and leader, amongft them in all things.

I alfo met with Mafter *John Bereton*, who writ an account of Captain *Gosnold's* voyage; and from them and others, I heard fo much of the marvels of thofe new lands, that my brains were fairly turned; and there feemed great chance of good fortune, for *Gosnold* told me of how he fared in the way of cargo. How the native Indians would give valuable fkins, fuch as beavers, martens, otters, wild cats, black foxes, deer and seal fkins, for next to nought, or for fome trifle fuch as a knife or fo; that they had copper which they valued not; and that he brought home a cargo of furs, cedar, and faffafras, the roots of which he fold in England at 3s. a pound, or £336 the ton; fo that he made much money by his venture.

They defcribed the land as exceeding fair to view, full of high timbered oaks, their leaves thrice as broad as ours, cedars ftraight and tall, beech, elms, hollies, walnut trees in abundance— the fruit as big as ours, as appeared by thofe they found under the trees, which had lien all the year ungathered. Hazel-nut trees, cherry trees, the leaf, bark, and bignefs not differing from ours in

England, but the ftalk beareth the bloffoms or fruit at the end thereof, like a clufter of grapes, forty or fifty in a bunch; faffafras trees in great plenty all the island over, which, as I have told you, is a tree of high price and profit. Alfo divers other fruit trees, fome of them with ftrange barks, of an orange colour, in feeling foft and fmooth like velvet.

There were lakes of water in which were abundance of tortoifes, and divers forts of fhell fifh, as fcallops, muffels, cockles, lobfters, crabs, oyfters and whelks, whilft of other fifh there was plenty, from whales downwards. There were feals, cod, mackerel, bream, herring, thornback, hake, rockfifh, and dog-fifh, with many others; and a great multitude of wild-fowl of larger growth than ours. But not to cloy you with particular rehearfal of fuch things as God and Nature hath beftowed on thefe places, in comparifon with which the moft fertile part of all England is but barren, I will only fay that their relation made me think of nought elfe; fo that when Captain *Gofnold* propofed to found a colony and plantation in *Virginia*, I entered into his plan moft eagerly, with all my heart and foul; and being then, in that year of our Lord, 1604, but twenty-five years of age, I bethought me that I might pafs the remainder of my life in greater eafe, and with far more profit to myfelf than by fighting, as I had hitherto done. So I decided to caft in my lot with Captain *Gofnold*, Mafter *Edward Maria Wingfield*, a merchant of the West of *England*, Mafter *Robert Hunt*, a clergyman, and divers other gentlemen.

CHAPTER V.

THE whole of the next year was fpent in fruitlefs efforts to launch our projeɗ of a plantation; but we had made up our minds to do it, and at length we fucceeded. We had to go from one great man to another, to folicit their intereft in obtaining a charter, and to provide us with money; for though we were all willing to venture a fomewhat, yet did it fall far too fhort of our requirements: we could find the men as colonifts, fome one elfe had to find the money. Some faid nay to the matter at once, others would keep us hanging on from day to day, bearing us up with hopes of help; and then would be exceeding forry, but juft at this prefent, money was fo fcarce with them, they could not; and fo on. But, at length, our perfeverance overcame all obftacles, and on 10th April in the year 1606, his Moft Gracious Majefty *James I.* granted a

Charter* for two Companies to be formed, whereof
one was in *London*, and the other in *Plymouth*.

The *London* Company confifted of Sir *Thomas
Gates*, Sir *George Somers*, *Richard Hackluyt*, *Edward
Wingfield*, and others, and to them was affigned
one portion of the land, and the *Plymouth* Company
had another, with land lying between, common to
both. There were proper claufes which bound each
not to interfere with the other, and the rent we were
to pay our Soverain Lord King *James*, was one-
fifth of all the gold and filver we might get from
the mines, which we, in our ignorance, did fancy
exifted in great plenty, and one-fifteenth of all the
copper. I never heard that his Majefty's treafury
did ever benefit from our gold and filver mines,
but there hath been no voyage of difcovery to
America, but what thefe faid mines have figured
hugely in the brains of thofe who did propofe
them; as *Tacitus* in his *Vita Agricolæ* faith,
"Omne ignotum pro magnifico eft," we all
thought wonderful things of what we knew not of,
yet were we well aware of the great riches feen by
Pizarro, *Cortez*, and *Hernandez de Soto*.

We might coin our own money, but the management of the plantations was left in the hands of a
Council in *England*, who nominated a Council and

---

* See Appendix.

Governor for the Colony. Perhaps it was the beft way at ftarting, but it did not work well. In *England*, they knew nought of what was going on, but what was written to them by the reports of the returned fea-captains; and thofe difaffected, who went, or were fent, back to *England*. They liftened more to thefe latter, than to the reports of the Governor and Council, and, of neceffity, things did not profper as well as they might have done. 'Tis true, the King referved unto himfelf the fupreme control of all, but I never heard that he troubled his head with our affairs : had we found gold and filver, things might have been different, but as what we returned did not pay our expenfes, much lefs yield a profit on the adventure, no great heed was taken of us by our royal patron.

The other benefits we, the firft colonifts, had referved to us, was the right of levying a duty on all veffels trading in our harbours, and this we were to have as our own for twenty years, after which time it went to the King. We were ftill to be accounted as Englifhmen, which might be of ufe when any of our number returned to *England*, but was not a great boon if they stopped where they were.

Think not, that becaufe we had got a Charter, we could therefore ftart at once on our expedition; by no means; there were many difficulties to be

overcome, which took up another year. There
were fhips to be got, and victualled, and manned.
At length we got together three, one of one hundred
tons, one of forty, and a pinnace of twenty tons ;
fo that what with the crews, and the adventurers,
who numbered 100 men, we were fomewhat clofely
packed. We were fortunate in procuring a good
captain, to whom the tranfportation of the company
was committed, one Captain *Chriftopher Newport*,
a mariner well pra&ifed for the weftern parts of
America, as he had voyaged there more than once.
For ourfelves, I think our Englifh Council behaved
foolifhly, not confidering fufficiently the nature of
our undertaking. We had by far too many gentlemen adventurers amongft us, and of a neceffity,
fome of thefe muft needs be not quite all one could
wifh as reliable comrades. Out of our 100 colonifts
there were fifty-two gentlemen adventurers, befides
Mafter *Robert Hunt*, the preacher, and Mafters
Thomas Wotton and *William Wilkinfon*, the chirurgeons. We had four carpenters, twelve labourers,
a blackfmith, a failor, a barber, a bricklayer, a
mafon, a tailor, and a drummer. There were alfo
four boys, and divers others whofe condition I do
not now mind me of, making up 100 in all.

Another thing, too, which bred much mifchief
on the voyage, and afterwards, was that we knew
not when we ftarted, who was to be the Chief of

this our expedition, fo that for a long time there was no head, and things went on any how. For the Council, in what they deemed their wifdom, had given us our orders for government in a box, all fealed up, with ftrict orders that it fhould not be opened, nor the feals broken, till that we had landed in *Virginia*, and then only fhould we know who had been chofen as Governor.

At laft, as all things muft have an end, we were got on board, and on the 19th day of December, in the year of our Lord 1606, we fet fail from *Blackwall* in our little fleet. Alas! even this was but badly managed, for the delay we had been put to had driven off our failing until the worft and moft ftormy part of the year; fo that, although we did fail on the date I have juft faid, we were fo hindered by unprofperous winds, that we were knocking about in fight of *England* for fix whole weeks. It was, indeed, but a forry Chriftmas that we fpent on board. Although, as is the wont of Englifhmen, wherefoever they may be, we made the beft cheer we could in honour of the feafon, yet, by reafon of the roughnefs of the fea and contrary winds, many were helplefs from fea ficknefs. Nay, Mafter *Hunt*, our preacher, was fo weak and fick that few expected his recovery. But, although he was but twenty miles from his own habitation (for at that time we were in the Downs) yet, notwithstanding the stormy weather and the scandalous imputations (of some few, little better than Atheists, of the greatest rank amongst us) suggested against him, all this could not force from him so much as a seeming desire to relinquish the adventure; but he preferred the service of God, in so good a voyage, before contesting with his godless foes, whose disastrous designs (could they have prevailed) would even then have overthrown the whole business of the expedition, so many discontents did then arise.

But Master *Hunt*, with the water of patience and his godly exhortations, quenched those flames of envy and dissension.

I know I had but scant cause to love some of them, for when we stopped at the *Canaries* for water, some of these gentry, envying my repute, spread about a scandalous report that I intended to usurp the government, murder the Council, and make myself King. A fine tale did they make up, how that I had confederates in all the three ships, and that if some of them were arrested they would affirm it to be true. There is no need for me to say that such notions never for a moment, at any time, entered into my head; but, for some reason, I was not popular among a portion of the adventurers, perhaps because, in my life time, I had done some deeds of daring, whereby my name had be-

come known and fomewhat diftinguifhed, whilft
they were nobodies, who never had done, and never
would do, anything above their fellows. Moreover,
I would take no part in their quarrels, but ftood
faft by the godly Mafter *Hunt*, and between us we
chid them, and told them fome home truths fo
plainly that they liked us not. They could not,
and dared not, do anything againft Mafter *Hunt*,
feeing that he was a Minifter of Religion; but on
me they could fpit their venom, and they did fo.
What ufe was it for me to deny their lies? They
only fpake the more. For a time they prevailed,
and it was decided for the quietnefs of the fhip and
the benefit of the expedition that I was to be kept
a prifoner till the end of the voyage. And fo I
was, moft unjuftly, but I will tell the remainder of
this ftory in its proper place.

As I have faid, we watered at the *Canaries*, we
traded with the favages at *Domenica*, and we fpent
three weeks in refrefhing ourfelves amongft thefe
Weft India Iflands. In *Guadalupe* was a fpring fo
hot that we boiled pork therein as well as if it had
been done over the fire; and in the *Virgin Ifles*,
where we fpent fome time, we fed on tortoifes,
pelicans, parrots, and curious and rare fifhes, as alfo
on a loathfome beaft fomewhat like a crocodile,
called an iguana.

After we had failed from thence and were pur-

fuing our way, murmurs began to be heard, which
fwelled louder and louder, that we were altogether
out of our reckoning, and, indeed, this was true,
feeing that the mariners had three days paft their
reckoning and had found no land.   The murmuring increafed almoft to open mutiny amongft fome
of the worft affected of our adventurers, and one
man (I do not think among all our feamen you
could have found another who could have even
thought of doing as he propofed), the captain of
the pinnace, a man named *Ratcliffe*, wanted, forfooth, to bear up his helm, and fo return to *England*,
rather than make further fearch.   This cowardly
conduct was defpifed by all, but there is no knowing
to what extent the murmuring would have grown,
had not God, the guider of all good actions, decided
the matter for us by caufing an extreme ftorm,
during which we drove before the wind under bare
poles all night, and, contrary to all our expectations,
we found ourfelves at our defired port, for never
had any of us feen that coaft before.   This bleffed
event took place on April 26, 1607.

Great was our joy, and as it was new land, never
having been explored before, we chriftened the land
we firft fighted, which is at the entrance of *Chefapeake
Bay*, *Cape Henry*, after the Prince of *Wales*; and
afterwards, the oppofite cape, *Cape Charles*, after
his brother.

With no difcipline among us, each gentleman adventurer being as good as his neighbour, who can wonder that as foon as we anchored fome would go on fhore? And fo they did, fome thirty of them, to their coft, as they afterwards found it, for, foolifhly imagining that the place was uninhabited, they landed unarmed, without taking any precautions againft furprife, and went roaming about, chattering noifily, and making as if they were lords of all. And fo, truly, they were in the end, but not juft then; for, mark you, five poor favages, whom afterwards we would have laughed at, did make thofe thirty fine fellows flee, with two of their number fore hurt. They faid they knew not what power was behind thofe five Indians, and fo hap it was true, for to alter the words I quoted of *Tacitus* his book—" Omne ignotum pro terribili."

That night we fulfilled our orders and opened that myftical box, whofe contents had been a fore puzzle to us in our voyage, for many of us thought, I am to be Governor; or, if he had not fuch ambition, then faid he, I am to be of the Council. However, on opening the box, every man foon knew his fate, for the inftructions were very brief and to the purpofe. Our Mafters (for fo muft I call them) in *London* had named feven of us as Council—namely, Mafter *Bartholomew Gofnold* and myfelf, together with *Wingfield*, Captain *Newport*,

John Ratcliffe, John Martin, and *George Kendall,*
and we, amongſt us, were to chooſe a Preſident for
a year, and he and the Council ſhould jointly govern
the affairs of our little Colony. Matters of moment
were to be examined by a jury, but to be determined
and ſettled by the major part of the Council, in
which the Preſident had two voices. Great was
the diſcuſſion thereon, and alſo on another paper
of inſtructions, which accompanied theſe orders for
our governance. This other paper concerned the
choice of a place of ſettlement, and the manner of
our there ſeating ourſelves, with the neceſſary orders
and methods of diſcovery, and how we were to
behave in our intercourſe with the natives.

Beſides, the Council in *England* ever thought of
making us the vehicle of gathering money for
them, to repay their venture a thouſandfold; ſo we
were ſpecially enjoined to be intent on the diſcovery
of the *South Sea,* as the certain and infallible way to
immenſe riches. Thus, our orders were, that if we
happened to diſcover any navigable rivers, and
among them any that had two main branches, to
make choice of that which tended moſt towards
the north-weſt; ſince they judged that the other
ſea would be ſooneſt found that way. And we
were to diſcover, if we could, whether the river on
whoſe bank we ſhould make our ſettlement ſprang
out of the mountains, or was fed from lakes, for

they judged that fhould it come from a lake, it was
poffible that on the other fide there might be
another river, which by its courfe might render
the paffage to the *Eaft India* or *South Sea* practical
and eafy.

We now knew what we were expected to do,
and our next tafk was to find fome place of
fettlement; fo next day we began to build our
fhallop, which had been fhipped in portions, eafy
to be fitted together, and a party, well armed,
marched eight miles inland without feeing a favage,
although we found a fire where they had been roaft-
ing oyfters. They muft have fled away when they faw
us coming, for they left behind them many oyfters
cooking, which we did eat, and enjoy right heartily.
Next day we went up the bay and coafted along,
when we difcovered a river. The fhallop was
launched and the Captain and some of our
gentlemen went fome diftance up the river. They
alfo found no natives, but a canoe fome forty feet
long made out of the trunk of a tree. They alfo
found great ftore of oyfters, and found pearls in
many of them.

It would weary you to tell of what we did each
day. Suffice it to fay that it was fome time before
we finally fixed on a place of fettlement, and that
each day brought its marvels to us, to whom all
was new. Our people fell in with many of the

favages, but they were friendly, and we gave them many trifles, with which they were much pleafed. The land was beautiful, and one of the moft pleafant in the whole world for large and ufeful navigable rivers. Heaven and earth never agreed better to frame a place for man's habitation, were it fully manured and inhabited by induftrious people; here are mountains, hills, valleys, rivers, and brooks, all running moft pleafantly into a fair bay, compaffed (but for its mouth) with fruitful and delightfome land. There is excellent land full of flowers of divers kinds and colours, and as goodly trees as I have feen, as cedar, cyprefs, and fuch like, as well as beech, oak, walnut, faffafras, and vines in abundance, whofe grapes hang in clufters to many trees, and other trees unknown to us. There are alfo many fruits, as ftrawberries, four times bigger and better than ours in *England*, mulberries, rafpberries, and fruits unknown. In the rivers are great plenty of fifh of all kinds, and as for fturgeon, all the world cannot be compared to it. Alfo in this country are many great and fair meadows, low marfhes, having excellent pafture for cattle. There is alfo great ftore of deer, both red and fallow; whilft of wild animals, there are bears, foxes, otters, beavers, mufkats, and wild beafts unknown.

For feventeen days we thus explored, until on the

13th day of May, 1607, we finally moored our
fhips to fome trees, in fix fathoms water, and fixed
upon that place for our fettlement, which was
a peninfula on the north fide of the river *Powhatan*,
about forty miles from the mouth. Some of us
landed, and the firft act was to fwear the Council,
to which they would not admit me, and *Wingfield*
was chofen Prefident. He and others made an
oration, and the fettlement was formally named
James Town, after the King's moft excellent
Majefty.

CHAPTER VI.

NEXT day all the men were landed, and all were
fet to work hard. The Council contrived the
fort, and fome were fet to work on that, others kept
guard, fome cut down trees for fpace on which to
pitch their tents, fome dug gardens or made nets,
and others were bufy providing clap-board with
which to re-lade the fhip. Ofttimes the favages
vifited us, and were very friendly, fo we received
them well; yet I could not but miftruft them, for
they were very cunning. Still, the Council would
take no precautions, the Prefident would allow of
no exercifing at arms, nor would he admit of any
other fortifications than the boughs of trees caft

together in the form of a half-moon, and for this flight protection we were indebted to the extraordinary pains and diligence of Captain *Kendall.* Our firft Prefident was not only a fool, but a mifchievous fool.

The work allotted to me was to join Captain *Newport* and twenty others, and explore the river to its head. This we did, being very fairly treated by the natives. We paffed by divers fmall habitations, and came in fix days to a town called *Powhatan*, the chief place of thofe parts. Indeed, the river is called *Powhatan*, and so is the chief named, and the people alfo are called *Powhatans.* This town is pleafantly and ftrongly fituated, and the river is not navigable more than a mile higher up, by reafon of the rocks and ifles. On the 24th day of May, 1607, we reached the head of the river, and fet up a crofs there, naming it the *King's River*, and there we proclaimed that *James*, King of *England*, had the moft right unto it. We then returned to *James Town.*

And now mark the folly and imprudence of our Prefident's behaviour. The favages had murmured greatly at our planting in their country, but fome faid, " Why fhould we be offended with them, fo long as they hurt us not, nor take anything away by force ? They take but a little wafte ground, which doth none of us any good." Yet this was but the opinion of a few, the larger number difliking our prefence, fo they determined to get rid of us if poffible. They made an attempt to capture *James Town* whilft we were away up the river, and, on our return, we found them in a forry ftate and in fore ftraits, for had we not arrived then, there had been an end there of the fort, for we found feventeen men hurt and a boy flain by the favages; and had it not chanced that a bar fhot from one of the fhips had ftruck down a bough from a tree amongft the Indians, that caufed them to retire, our men had all been flain, being at the time all at work, and their arms put away in packing cafes.

Now, truly, the Prefident was contented that the fort fhould be palifadoed, the ordnance mounted, and the men armed and exercifed; and, indeed, it was high time that this fhould be done, for many were the affaults and ambufcadoes of the favages, and our men, by their diforderly ftraggling, were often hurt, whilft the Indians, by the nimblenefs of their heels, always efcaped. I leave you to guefs what toil we had, with but fo few men to guard our workmen o' days, watch all night, refift our enemies, and effect our bufinefs, to reload the fhips, cut down trees, and prepare the ground to plant our corn, &c.

Captain *Newport*, though one of the Council,

had only been hired to tranfport us, and, having got his fhip laden with whatever we could find him as a cargo, wanted to return. Now, for thirteen weeks I had been a prifoner, and was ftill under arreft, although, for the general good, I had been allowed to go with Captain *Newport* up the river; but, when he wanted to fail for *England*, my enemies, of whom the chiefeft was *Wingfield*, our Prefident, wanted to fend me back by him to be judged by the Council in *England*. This was cunningly devifed, as it was pretended to be for my good, as they faid they would rather it were fo than that they, by particularifing my pretended defigns, might make me fo odious to my fellow-adventurers as to endanger my life, or elfe utterly overthrow my reputation.

But, as I was perfectly innocent of anything with which they could charge me, I fcorned their pretended charity, and publicly defied the utmoft of their cruelty. They did not dare, for all their defpite of me, to refufe me the trial I afked, and when it came off, all the company did fee my innocency, and my adverfaries' malice; yea, even thofe fuborned to accufe me turned round upon their employers, and accufed them of fubornation; and although many untruths were alleged againft me, yet they were fo thoroughly difproved, that it begat a general hatred in the hearts of the company againſt ſuch unjuſt commanders, inſomuch that the Preſident, *Wingfield*, whoſe hatred of me, and malicious conduct, were made ſo apparent, was adjudged to pay me two hundred pounds as com-penſation for my grievances. This ſum of money he had not by him, ſo that all that he had was ſeized upon, in part ſatisfaction, and given to me. But I had done all that I wanted. I had cleared my character from all ſtain, and had fully eſtabliſhed my innocency, and I cared not to keep *Wingfield's* goods as mine own. Yet, as the award was a righteous one, and it had been given me by the whole of the coloniſts, and, indeed, I did deſerve ſome ſolatium for my injuries, I accepted what was awarded, and preſently returned it to ſtore for the general uſe of the Colony.

Now was it time for that godly man, Maſter *Hunt*, to do his part in healing our ſtrifes, and he went from one to the other with ſweet words of good counſel: how that we ſhould love and forgive our enemies; nay, he uſed more worldly arguments, pointing out that the welfare of our little band depended chiefly upon our union, for that we were in an unknown land, expoſed to the attacks of hoſtile natives, and we needed, therefore, all the ties of brotherly love. His arguments prevailed, for we all loved him for his exceeding goodneſs. I was admitted to take my rightful place as one of

the Council, and the next day we all received the
Holy Communion together, as an outward and
vifible pledge of reconciliation. And, indeed, it
did feem as if the bleffed Spirit of Peace had come
down to dwell among us, for the next day came
an embaffage from the favages, voluntarily defiring
peace, and to dwell in good accord with us, fo that
when Captain *Newport* left us for *England*, sailing
on the 15th of June, 1607, he could take back a
truthful report that he had left our little Colony
of 100 fouls all well.

When Captain *Newport* failed, leaving us very
bare and fcanty of victuals, he promifed to return
with fupplies within twenty weeks, but immediately after his departure we fell into fore ftraits for
food, fo that within ten days there were fcarce ten
of us who could walk, or hardly ftand, by reafon
of the weaknefs and extreme ficknefs that oppreffed
us. The caufe was not far to feek, for whilft the
fhips yet ftayed with us, our allowance had been
fomewhat bettered by a daily proportion of bifcuit,
which the failors would pilfer either to fell, give,
or exchange with us for money, faffafras, furs, or
love ; but when they departed, there remained
neither tavern, beer-houfe, nor place of relief, but
the common kettle, into which was put every
man's daily allowance of half a pint of wheat and
as much barley, which was boiled with water.

This would have been but scant food, even had it been good, but the corn, having fried for twenty-six weeks in the ship's hold, had as many weevils as grains, so that we might truly call it rather so much bran than corn.

Our drink was water, and our lodgings were castles in the air, and, had we been as free from all other sins as we were from gluttony and drunkenness, we might have been canonised for saints, that is, all save our precious President, who quietly took and appropriated to his private use all the oatmeal, sack, aqua vitæ, beef, eggs, and what not, and lived in grand style. He had some small conscience left, however; he meddled not with the common kettle, as indeed no man in his senses would, had he aught else to eat.

With this lodging and diet, and our extreme toil in carrying and driving palisadoes, we were sore bruised and strained, and indeed had we been in England, our continual labour in the heat of the sun would have weakened us as much. Sad, too, was it for us to bury so many of our number, for between May and September fifty were put under the turf. On the 6th day of August, the first man, *John Asbie*, died of a bloody flux, and then they followed one another very fast. On the 22nd day of August, there died Captain *Bartholomew Gosnold*, who was the first to organise our expedition, and we buried him honourably, having all the ordnance in the fort fired off, with many volleys of fmall fhot.

Methinks it was the water which we had perforce to drink, for we had no well, but drew our fupply from the river, which at flood tide was very falt, and at low tide full of flime and filth. Thus we lived for the fpace of five months in this miferable diftrefs, not having five able men to man our bulwarks upon any occafion. If it had not pleafed God to have put a terror into the hearts of the favages, we fhould furely all have perifhed by thofe wild and cruel Pagans, being in the weak ftate we then were, for our men lay night and day groaning in every corner of the fort moft pitiful to hear. It made one's heart bleed to hear the pitiful murmurings and outcries of our fick men, without relief night and day for fix weeks, fome departing out of this world, often three and four of a night, of fwellings, fluxes, burning fevers, fudden deaths, &c. ; but for the moft part they died of fheer famine. In the morning their bodies were trailed out of their cabins like dogs, and so were they buried.

We had other troubles as well, for after Captain *Gofnold's* death, the Council could hardly agree by reafon of the diffenfions wrought by Captain *Kendall,* who afterwards, having committed fome heinous matters which were proved againſt him, was depoſed, and turned out of the Council.

Whilſt we were ſcarce keeping body and ſoul together by means of ſturgeon and ſea-crabs, our cowardly Preſident (who all this time had felt neither want nor ſickneſs) attempted to eſcape in the pinnace, which ſo enraged us, and moved our dying ſpirits, that on the 11th September, 1607, we arraigned him, and depoſed him, not only from the Preſidentſhip, but from the Council, making of him but an ordinary mortal, who had to take his ſhare from the common kettle with the reſt. And we elected *Ratcliffe* in his place.

I was ill, as alſo were *Martin* and *Ratcliffe*, but we ſoon got better, and then the moſt part of the ſoldiers recovered, thanks to the ſkilful diligence of Maſter *Thomas Wotton*, our chirurgeon-general. Yet now was all our proviſion ſpent, even the ſturgeon, and we each hour expected an attack from the ſavages, when God, in that deſperate extremity, ſo changed the hearts of theſe heathen, that they brought, of their own will, ſuch plenty of their fruits and proviſion that no man wanted.

The new Preſident and *Martin*, being but little beloved, were men of weak judgment in danger, and leſs induſtry in peace, and they ſoon found that the beſt way to order matters was to give me the management of all things, and I at once ſet

our people to work at building. I fet them an
example of hard work, always bearing the greateft
tafk for my own fhare, and thus, and with good
words and fair promifes, got fome to mow, others to
bind thatch, fome to build houfes, and others to
thatch them, fo that in a fhort time they were all
provided with lodging, faving myfelf.

This done, I faw that the favages did not bring
in the fame quantity of food as aforetime, fo with
fome of my workmen I fhipped myfelf in the fhallop
to fearch the country for food and trade. There
were fome impediments to this, for we knew not the
language, nor how to manage the boat, nor had
we enough men, nor were they well enough armed,
confidering the multitude of the favages ; yet we
were not difcouraged. With only fix or feven
companions, I dropped down the river, and making
figns to fome Indians for what we wanted, they
derided us, as famifhed men, and offered us a
handful of corn, or a piece of bread, in exchange
for our fwords and mufkets. Seeing I could get
nothing by trade and courtefy, I determined to
act, although contrary to my commiffion, fo I let
fly our mufkets and ran the boat on fhore,
whereat they fled into the woods.

We landed and marched to their village, when
we found great heaps of corn, and I had much ado
to reftrain my hungry men from taking it, as I

expected every moment that the favages would attack us, which they did not long afterwards with a hideous noife. A band of fixty or feventy of them, looking like very fiends, painted as they were, fome of them black, fome red, fome white, fome parti-coloured, came in a fquare order, finging and dancing out of the woods, with their *Okee* (which was an idol made of fkins, ftuffed with mofs, all painted and hung with chains and copper) borne before them, and in this manner, being well armed with clubs, fhields, and bows and arrows, they charged us; but we fo kindly received them with our mufkets loaded with piftol-fhot, that down fell their god, and divers of them lay fprawling on the ground. The reft fled to the woods, and ere long fent one of their number to offer peace and redeem their *Okee*. I told them, as well as I could make myfelf underftood, that if only fix of them would come in unarmed, and load my boat, I would not only be their friend, but would reftore them their *Okee*, and give them beads, copper, and hatchets befides, which on both fides was performed to our mutual fatisfaction. Nay, the favages were fo pleafed, that they brought us venifon, turkeys, wild fowl, bread, and what-ever other food they had, finging and dancing in fign of friendfhip till we departed.

I could inftil no habits of thrift into our fettlers,

for, notwithftanding our late ·mifery, they ufed the fupplies I obtained with no caution whatever, living fimply from hand to mouth ; fo I caufed the pinnace to be got ready, fo that I might get provifions for the following year. Meanwhile, I made three or four journeys, and difcovered the *Chickahominy* river, and brought back fome fupplies; yet what I carefully provided, the reft careleffly fpent.

CHAPTER VII.

MOREOVER, at this time, there was trouble in the Colony, for difcipline was always lax during my abfence, a fact which *Wingfield* and *Kendall*, who were living in difgrace, took advantage of. They faw the Prefident's weaknefs, and *Martin's* perpetual ficknefs, fo they made friends with the failors and fome of the others, fo that they might regain their former credit and authority ; or, at all events, when they were aboard the pinnace—which I had prepared, as I have already told you—they were to alter its courfe and fail for England.

By good luck, I returned unexpectedly, and the plot was difcovered to me. I immediately rallied round me all those that were well affected, and, after appealing in vain to the good sense of the others, we turned the guns of our fort (which were Sakers) upon them, and I swore I would either make them stay, or sink them in the river. This had the desired effect; they knew me full well, and that what I said, that I should do; so, after much grumbling, and many angry speeches, they returned to their duty. But such a gross rebellion could not be passed over without some punishment, so the chief rebel, Captain *Kendall*, was arrested, duly arraigned and tried, and was sentenced to be shot, which sentence was properly carried into effect. One would have thought this would have cured them of such disorders; but no, not long afterwards, the President and Captain *Archer* were minded to have abandoned the country, but I curbed their project and suppressed it.

The chief cause for grumbling, however, was soon removed, for we found plenty of corn along the banks of the *Chickahominy* river, where hundreds of the savages would stand in divers places with baskets full, awaiting the coming of the boat. Besides which, on the approach of winter, the rivers became so covered with swans, geese, ducks, and cranes, that we daily feasted with good bread, *Virginia* peas, and pumpkins, with fish, fowl, and divers sorts of wild animals, as fat as we could eat them, fo that none of our Tuftaffaty* humorifts defired to leave for *England.*

Our comedies feldom lafted long without being followed by a tragedy, and one was making ready for me. Idle exceptions were being muttered againft me for not going and difcovering the head of the *Chickahominy* river, which fome fuppofed would lead to the long-defired *South Sea,* and the Council preffed it upon me, and taunted me with being too flow in fo worthy an attempt. In vain I urged upon them the neceffity of providing a fufficient ftore of food for the winter. This they heeded not; their bellies were now full, and, as it ever was with them, they took no thought for the morrow. So it was fettled I fhould go, and I went.

The voyage was rendered very tedious and painful, by reafon of the many trees which had fallen acrofs the river, and all of which had to be cut in half before a paffage could be made for the boat. At length we reached a place where the barge could go no farther, fo I had it moored in a broad bay out of reach of fhot, whilft I went

---

* An allufion to the *gentlemen* adventurers. It was not an uncommon word, and it is thus given by Dr. John Donne in his fourth Satire (line 31, &c.):—
     " Sleevelefs his jerkin was, and it had been
         Velvet, but 'twas now (fo much ground was feen)
         Become Tuftaffaty," &c.

forward with two Englifhmen and two favages, who were acting as guides, in a canoe, ftrictly charging thofe left in the barge on no account to go on fhore. But I had not been long abfent when, of courfe, they did go afhore, and whilft strollingabout heedleffly—for they would not believe there were favages about becaufe they could not fee them—one of them, named *George Caffen*, was feized by the favages and killed; but not till after they had got out of him by which way I had gone, and then the King of *Pamaunkee*, with 200 bowmen, started on my track, having firft found the other two men, *Robinfon* and *Emry*, who were fitting by their fire, and whom they fhot full of arrows and flew.

I had reached the marfhes at the river head, twenty miles in the defert, and was employed in fowling, in order to procure victual for my men, when fuddenly I found myfelf furrounded, albeit at fome diftance, by favages, whofe dreadful cries and yells were enough to make the ftouteft heart to fink. Although they were fome 200 againft myfelf, I thought not of yielding, but determined to fell my life dearly and to make a brave fight for it. And a happy idea ftruck me that perhaps my favage guide might have had fomewhat to do with the delivering of me thus into the hands of his countrymen, fo I took off my garters and bound

H

him, all trembling, to my arm, thus ufing him as a
buckler.   Thus, by keeping a bold front to them,
I hoped, as they feemed to fear to come very clofe
to me, to reach the fhore, and halloe for affiftance
from the canoe.

At length an arrow ftruck me in the thigh,
although it wounded me not much, as it was fhot
from fome diftance; ftill it ftung me, and I thought
I would repay them to the beft of my power, fo
taking aim, I fired and killed one of their number.
This proceeding ftayed them for a time, they not
being accuftomed to the ufe of fire-arms, and gave
me time to reload.   After a while, however, they
renewed the onflaught, and I had many arrows
ftick in my clothes, but not much hurt.   Yet, me-

thought, I would give them another leffon, and I
fhot at and killed two more of their number. This
made them keep their diftance, and, perchance, I

might have been able to have followed out my
plan, and to have fought my way fuccefsfully to
the boat, had not an evil chance happened unto me;
for keeping my face ever toward my tormentors,
without heeding whither my fteps were going, I
flipped up to the middle in an oozy, miry, and
boggy creek, and my favage, who was bound to me,
with me.

This was a great misfortune, forafmuch as, with
all my endeavours, I could not get out; and, moreover, the creek was deadly cold, and I was getting
benumbed. So there was nothing left but to die
miferably or to furrender myfelf; and I chofe
the latter, hoping to find means to make them
friendly towards me and thus preferve my life. I
called out to them, as beft I could in their language,
and alfo made figns unto them that I was willing
to give myfelf up to them. But they would not
come anigh me fo long as I was armed, which was
no wonder, feeing that I had flain three of them,
and fore galled divers others, fo that there was
nought left for me to do but to throw away my
arms, forely againft my will. Then, according to
our compofition and agreement, they drew us forth
out of the morafs and led me to the fire, where
my men had been treacheroufly flain, and they
diligently chafed my benumbed limbs until I had
recovered the full ufe of them.

When my limbs had regained their accuftomed warmth and fupplenefs I demanded to fee their captain or leader, and they fhowed me *Opechan-kanough*, King of *Pamaunkee*, to whom I at once gave a round ivory double-compafs dial, in order to make him friendly towards me if poffible. And it was, indeed, a marvel to fee thefe poor, ignorant favages, gazing with wonder at the playing of the needle, which they could fee fo plainly and yet could not touch, by reafon of the glafs which covered it. But when, as well as I could, both in their language and by figns, I told them of the roundnefs of the earth, and of the fkies, and of the fpheres of the fun, moon, and ftars, and how the fun did chafe the night round about the world continually ; the diverfity of nations, variety of complexions, and how we were to them *Antipodes*, and many other such-like matters, they all ftood as amazed with admiration.

But this lafted not long, for within an hour the recollection of their flain brethren overcame their curiofity, and their favage natures fo prevailed, that they tied me to a tree, and as many as could ftand about me prepared to fhoot me. Now, indeed, I thought that my laft hour had come, and fo it had, were it not that their king, holding up the com-pafs in his hand, had ordered them to defift ; whereupon they all laid down their bows and arrows, and in a triumphant manner carried me with them to *Orapaks*, one of their towns, where after their manner I was kindly ufed and fed.

They were very proud of having captured me, and carried me along with them, rejoicing after their manner.   They led me along bound by cords to two ſtrong ſavages, whilſt the others danced about me, looking like very devils.   Their town, truly, was not much, for it conſiſted only of thirty or forty hunting lodges, built up of mats, which they remove as they pleaſe, as we do tents; and all the women and children came ſtaring to look at the wonderful white man.   Then did they exalt themſelves greatly, and, ſetting me bound in their midſt, they caſt themſelves into a ring, dancing in ſuch ſeveral poſtures, and ſinging and yelling out helliſh noiſes and ſcreeches; being ſtrangely painted, with every one his quiver of arrows, and at his back a club.   They were clad in fox or otter ſkins, or ſome ſuch matter, their head and ſhoulders painted ſcarlet, which made an exceeding handſome ſhow.   Their bows they carried in their hands, and had the ſkin of a bird, with its wings spread out, dried, with a piece of copper, a white ſhell, a long feather, a ſmall rattle from the tail of one of their ſnakes, or ſome ſuch toy in their hair.

After they had danced three dances they left off, and all departed, and I was conducted to a long houſe, where thirty or forty tall fellows guarded me, and I knew not what was next in ſtore for me; but ere long ſome came with proviſion for me, and of that ſuch great ſtore, both of bread and veniſon, as would have ſerved twenty men. But my ſtomach at that time was not very good, and I but trifled with it, when, feeing that I ate it not all (perchance they thought a white man's appetite was fomething very great), they put it by in bafkets and hung them over my head. About midnight they fet the meal again before me, but I feared to touch it, as none of them would eat a morfel with me, till next morning they brought me as much more, and did eat all the old provifion, and referved the new, as they had done before. This plan of cramming me did forely grieve me, for I furely thought they were about to fat me in order to eat me. Yet even in this ftrait I found a friend, to my aftonifhment, and which was to me a token that a kind action is never loft, for, fuffering as I did with the cold, I was moft heartily glad when one *Maocaffater* brought me his gown to keep me warm, reminding me at the fame time how that, when he was at *James Town*, upon our firft arrival, I had given him fome beads and toys, and this was his manner of requital.

But this only fhows one fide of favage nature, for but two days afterwards a man would have flain me (but that the guard prevented it) for the death of his fon, to whom they had taken me juft when he was breathing his laft. They had an idea that becaufe I could kill them, by means unknown to them, I could alfo bring them to life as eafily, and

fo this poor ignorant favage took me to recover
his fon, and, becaufe I could not do it, forfooth,
he was fain to kill me.   Still, I managed, by craft,
to turn even this evil to good account, for I told
them that I had, at *James Town*, a water which
would have cured him, would they but let me go
and fetch it, but they would not permit that, as
they wanted to affault the town; yea, they
even afked my advice thereon, and offered me as
recompenfe, life, liberty, land, and women.   I had
a table-book with me, by good luck, and, tearing
out a leaf or two, I writ thereon, to them at the
Fort, exactly what was intended, pointing out to
them that the meffengers were in very truth but
fpies, and directing them to affright them well;
but, at the fame time, to fend by them fuch things
as I wrote for, and of which I fent an inventory.
I filled the minds of the favages with ftories of
difficulties and dangers, efpecially of the mines,
the great guns, and other engines, and exceedingly
affrighted them; yet, according to my requeft,
they went to *James Town*, in as bitter weather as
could be of froft and fnow, and within three days
returned with an anfwer.

When they came back they told their ftory,
and, indeed, they were full of amazement at the
wonders they had feen.   Our people at *James
Town* had fallied out at their approach, as I

foretold they would, and the favages had at once fled; yet, in the night, they returned to the place where I had told them they would receive an anfwer, and fuch things as I had promifed them, and fo it fell out, and they found them juft as I had faid, which made them return wondering, as it did all to whom they told it; and, indeed, they could by no means divine how that the paper could fpeak.

CHAPTER VIII

AFTER this I was led in a kind of triumph through divers of their villages upon the rivers *Rapahanock* and *Patawomek*; in fact, I was made a fhow of to the whole nation, and then was brought by another way to the King's habitation at *Pamaunkee*, where I was entertained with ftrange and fearful conjurations—

> " As if neare led to hell,
>   Amongft the devils to dwell."

And it was after this manner. On a morning early, a great fire was made in a long houfe, and a mat fpread on the one fide as on the other, and on one mat they made me fit, and all the guards went out of the houfe, leaving me alone. I had not long been left to myfelf before in came fkipping

a great grim fellow, all painted over with coal,
mingled with oil, and with many fnake and weafel
fkins ftuffed with mofs, having their tails tied all
together, fo as they met like a taffel on the crown
of his head, and round about the taffel was a
coronet of feathers, which covered his face, and
the fkins hung round about his head, back, and
fhoulders; and, to add to all this, he had a hellifh,
difcordant voice, and a rattle in his hand.

With moft ftrange geftures and paffions he began

his invocations, and environed the fire with a circle of meal, which done, three more such devils came rushing in with the same antic tricks, painted half black and half red, but all about their eyes was painted white, whilst they had some red streaks along their cheeks. These three danced around me for a pretty while, and then came in three more as ugly as the rest, only these had red round their eyes and white streaks on their black faces. At last they sat down right against me, three of them on the one hand of the chief priest, and three on the other. Then all with their rattles began a song, which being ended, the chief priest laid down five wheat corns. Then straining his arms and hands with such violence that he sweat, and his veins swelled, he began a short oration, at the conclusion of which they all gave a groan, after which he laid down three more grains of corn.

Soon after, they began their song again, and then there was another oration, ever laying down the same number of corns, till they had twice encircled the fire; that done, they took a bundle of little sticks prepared for that purpose, continuing still their devotion, and at the end of every song and oration they laid down a stick betwixt the divisions of corn. Till night, neither I nor they did either eat or drink, but then we all feasted merrily, with the best provisions they could get. Three days they ufed this ceremony, the meaning whereof they told me was to know whether I meant them well or no; but at that time, as I well remember, I could only fancy that they were fatting me for flaughter, and that thefe ftrange conjurations were but, as it were, the prologue to the play.

To give you an idea of the ignorance of thefe poor favages, I muft tell you that, fomehow or other, they had procured a bag of gunpowder, doubtlefs from fome rogue at *James Town*, which they brought to me, and told me they meant to keep it till next fpring, to plant as they did their corn. I did not undeceive the poor creatures, and I doubt not but they fowed it; but it fhowed me how weak was the government at *James Town*, to permit gunpowder to be trafficked with thefe favages. So far, however, they were friendly to me, and the King's brother invited me to his houfe, where he fed me mightily with bread, fowl, and the flefh of wild beafts; but none of them would eat with me, and all the meat I left, owing to the great profufion provided for me, was put away into bafkets, and when I returned to the King, all his women and children made merry, and feafted thereon.

But there was a mightier king than him of *Pamaunkee*, namely *Powhatan*, their Emperor, of whom I have fpoken before; and he, being at a place called *Meronocomoco*, I was taken thither to be prefented to him. Here, while *Powhatan* and his train were putting themfelves in their greateft braveries, I had to ftand the gaze of more than two hundred of his grim courtiers, who ftood wondering and ftaring at me, as if I were fome ftrange animal, which indeed I was to them.

At laft I was ufhered into the prefence of *Powhatan*, and found him feated before a fire, on a feat fomewhat refembling a bedftead, covered with a great robe made of racoon fkins, with all the tails hanging thereto. On either hand did fit a young wench of fixteen or eighteen years, and along each fide of the houfe were two rows of men, and behind them as many women, all with their heads and fhoulders painted red ; many of their heads were bedecked with the white down of birds, but everyone wore fomething in their hair, and a great chain of white beads about their necks.

When I made my entrance before the King, all the people gave a great fhout, and, to do me honour, the Queen of *Appamatuck* was appointed to bring me water, wherewith I might wafh my hands, and another brought me a bunch of feathers wherewith to dry them, inftead of a towel; and then they feafted me in the beft manner they could, which, after all, was but barbarous.

They then held a great confultation about me,

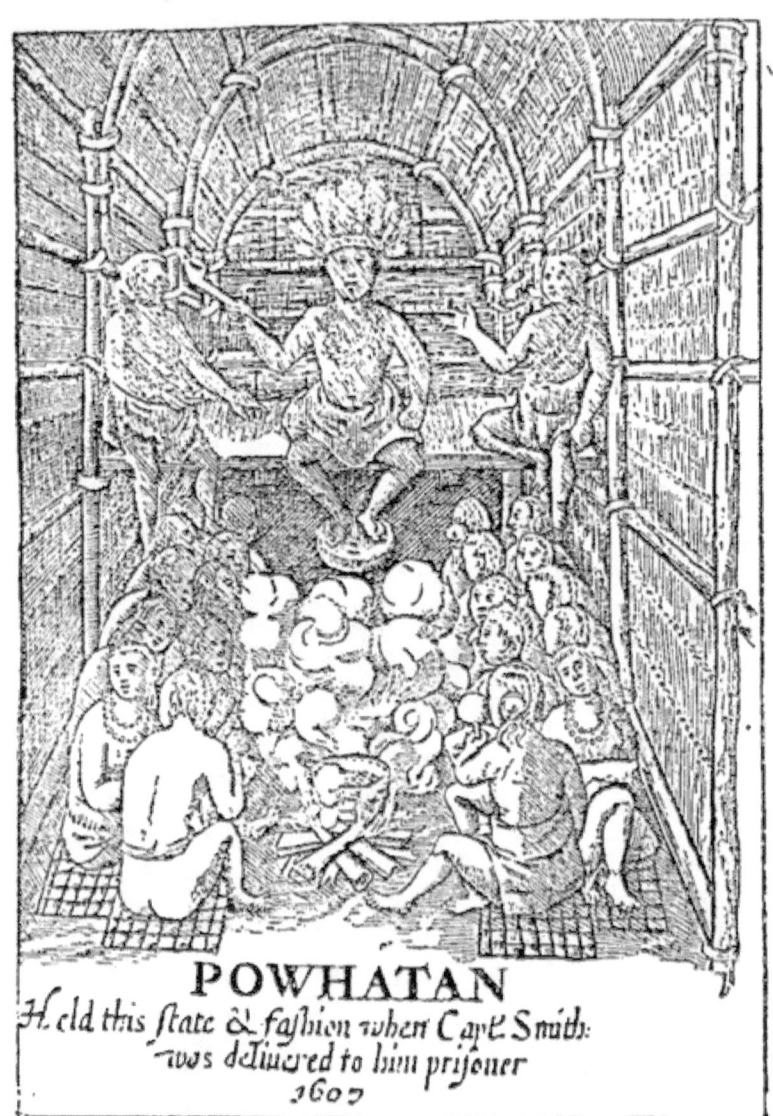

POWHATAN
Held this ſtate & faſhion when Capt. Smith.
was deliuered to him priſoner
1607

which I could not altogether underſtand, but the
concluſion was that I was to die ; a fate which, in
truth, was near coming to paſs, but for God's

The Country wee now call Virginia beginneth at Cape Henry diſtant
from Roanoack 60 miles, where was Sʳ Walter Raleigh's plantation:
and becauſe the people differ very litle from them of Powhatan in any
thing, I have inſerted thoſe figures in this place becauſe of the conveniency.

Kyng Powhatan commands C: Smith to be ſlaine, his
daughter Pokahontas beggs his life his thankfullneſſ
and how he ſubiected 39 of their kings, reade ÿ hiſtory.

printed by Iames Reeve

goodneſs, as you ſhall hear. And, indeed, it did
ſeem as if my laſt hour was at hand, for as many
of the ſavages as could, lay hold of me, and

having brought two great ftones, which they placed before *Powhatan*, they dragged me to them, and laid my head thereon, making ready with their clubs to beat out my brains.

But now, mark the mercy of God towards me when in this evil cafe, for furely it was His handi-work. Their clubs were raifed, and in another moment I fhould have been dead, when *Pocahontas*, the King's deareft daughter, a child of ten years old, finding no entreaties could prevail to fave me, darted forward, and, taking my head in her arms, laid her own upon it, and thus prevented my death. She thus claimed me as her own, and for her fake *Powhatan* was contented that I fhould live, and that I fhould henceforth fpend my time in making him hatchets, and bells, beads, and copper ornaments for *Pocahontas*. They made no manner of doubt but that I could make all thefe things, for in that country the men are of all handicrafts ; nay, even the King himself will make his own robes, fhoes, bows and arrows, or pots, plant, hunt, and do the fame as his fubjects. You will hear more anon of that dear child, the *non-pareil* of *Virginia*, for fortune afterwards threw us much together.

'Tis an old faying that " the night is darkeft juft before dawn," and, furely, fo it was in my cafe, for, having but narrowly efcaped from the fearful jaws of death, a brighter dawn was in ftore for me. Two days afterwards, *Powhatan* caufed me to be taken to a great houfe in the woods, and there, upon a mat by the fire, I was left alone. Not long after, from behind a mat that divided the houfe into two parts, came the moft doleful noife I had ever heard, and then forth came *Powhatan*, moft fearfully difguifed, and looking more like a devil than a man, with fome two hundred more as horrid-looking as himfelf. The King came unto me and told me that now, as we were friends, I fhould prefently go to *James Town*, and from thence fend him two great guns and a grindftone, for he had heard rumours of the terrible effect of the great guns, and he knew well the value of a grindftone. He alfo faid that if I fent him thefe he would give me the country of *Capahowofick*, and for ever efteem me as his fon.

And fo it came to pafs that I was fent to *James Town* with twelve men as guides, and that night we quartered in the woods. I muft confefs I felt not fafe with them, and miftrufted them forely, ftill expecting (as I had done all the long time of my imprifonment) every hour, to be put to one death or another, in fpite of all their feafting ; but Almighty God (by His divine providence) had mollified the hearts of thofe ftern barbarians with compaffion.

I

The next morning betimes, we came to the Fort, where I treated the favages with as much kindnefs as I could. I fhowed one of them named *Rawhunt*, who was *Powhatan's* trufty fervant, two demi-culverins and a mill-ftone to carry to their mafter, but they found them fomewhat too heavy for them ; yet, in order to fhow them what terrible engines were thefe fame big guns, I had them loaded with ftones, and then did difcharge them among the boughs of a great tree loaded with icicles, and the ice, and the branches, did come fo tumbling down, that the poor favages ran away half dead with fear. Yet by degrees was their fright allayed, and I gave them fome toys, and fent by them to *Powhatan*, his women, and children, fuch prefents as gave them general content ; and mighty glad was I once more to recover my freedom.

It was lucky for our little Colony that I came back when I did, for the difcontented amongft them (and there were fome who could, or would, fee no good in anything) had broken loofe, and were all in combuftion ; the ftrongeft, once more, preparing to run away with the pinnace, and fo break up our little community. But I took the law into my own hands, and, feeing them putting their project into execution, I fired at them (not fo as to hurt them, but to fhow that I could do fo, had I fuch a

mind) with fakers,* falcons,† and mufket-fhot, fo
that they came to their fenfes right fpeedily, and
abandoned their refolve. Still, they tried to be
revenged on me, for fome, no better than they
fhould be, had plotted with the Prefident the next
day to have me put to death—and why, think you?
They pleaded that by the Levitical law I was
guilty of the murders of *Robinfon* and *Emry*, as
they faid it was by my fault that had led them to
their deftruction; but I quickly took fuch order
with thefe *lawyers*, that I laid them by the heels
in durance, until fuch time as I fent them prifoners
to *England*, and fo ended this rebellion.

Now, indeed, we were in ftraits for food, and
here again it would feem as if even my dolorous
captivity had been the means of doing good to the
Colony at large; for, moft affuredly, had I not
been made a prifoner, and in danger of death, I
fhould not have known my dear little maid *Pocahontas*, and, therefore, not knowing her, fhe
would not have come to vifit us, as fhe did, every
four or five days, with her attendants, bringing
with her every time fo much provifion as to fave

---

* A faker weighed between 1,400 and 1,600 lb., had a
bore of 3¼ to 4 inches, was charged with 4 to 5½ lb. of
powder, and carried a fhot of from 5 to 5½ lb.

† A falcon weighed 700 lb., had a bore of 2¼ in., was
charged with 2 lb. powder, and carried a fhot of 2½ lb.
("The Gunner," by Robt. Norton, ed. 1628, p. 53.)

many lives, that but for her would have died of
ftarvation. Moreover, my relation of the ftate
and plenty of *Powhatan* (who till that time was
unknown to them) fo revived their dead fpirits,
that they began to hope once more, and all
fear was abandoned. Yet there were fome, even
of the better fort, who would ftill plot, and who
fain would have me join with them in abandoning
the country, in company of fome ten or twelve of
them, leaving behind us to the fury of the favages
Mr. *Hunt*, our Preacher ; Mafter *Anthony Gofnold*,
a moft worthy, honeft, and induftrious gentleman ;
Mafter *Thomas Wotton*, and fome twenty-feven
others of our countrymen. But this I would not
hear of, preferring at all rifks to ftop and fhare
our fortunes (whatever they might be) together.

CHAPTER IX.

I HAVE often noted that when things were very
bad they furely mended, and fo it was with us,
for we had not been forgotten by the Prefident
and Council in *England*, who had defpatched two
good fhips to us, with near a hundred men, well
furnifhed with all things that could be imagined
neceffary, both for them and us. One veffel was
commanded by our old friend Captain *Newport*,

and the other by Captain *Francis Nelfon*, an honeft man, and an expert mariner. But fuch was the leewardnefs of his fhip, that, though he was in fight of *Cape Henry*, he was forced by ftormy, contrary winds fo far to fea, that the next land he faw was the *Weft Indies*, to which he was glad to get, in order to repair his mafts, and procure water. But *Newport* got in fafely, and arrived at *James Town* not long after I had recovered my freedom.

My captivity amongft thefe favages had greatly endeared me to them, and, as I have faid, every few days they brought me fufficient provifions to laft us from hand to mouth, fome being prefents from *Powhatan* or *Pocahontas*, and the remainder that which they brought to trade, over which I made myfelf the Market Clerk, and fixed at a price which I confidered fair to both fides; and they were delighted at the profpect of the arrival of Captain *Newport*, whom I called, to them, my father.

The Prefident and Council, being jealous of my influence with the natives, did all in their power to leffen it, as, for inftance, by giving four times more for their commodities than the fum I had appointed, thus intending to fhow that they had four times my greatnefs and authority; and, indeed, all trading at a fair price was at an end

after the arrival of the fhip, for we were fo over-
joyed with the fupplies they brought us, that we
could not devife too much to pleafe the mariners.
We gave them liberty to truck or trade at their
pleafure, and they fo fpoilt the market, that in a
fhort time it followed, that could not be had for
a pound of copper, which before was fold us for an
ounce.   This lavifhnefs, and the prefents which
were often fent to *Powhatan*, made him think much
of the greatnefs and power of Captain *Newport*,
fo that this great favage defired efpecially to fee
him.

The pinnace was prepared, and Captain *Newport* embarked, accompanied by myfelf and Mr.
Scrivener, a very wife, underftanding gentleman,
newly arrived, and admitted of the Council, and
thirty or forty men.   When we arrived at
Meronocomoco, Newport, who remembered how I had
been ferved, was fomewhat fearfome and fufpicious;
but I knew the favages better than he, and I undertook to encounter the worft that could happen, with
but twenty men, well appointed, and with that
number we went afhore.   We had to pafs over
many creeks, over which were but forry bridges,
made only of a few poles tied together with the
bark of trees, fo that I fufpected they were but
traps, and therefore I caufed divers favages to go
over firft, keeping fome of the chief as hoftages,

until half of our men had paſſed over, ſo that they might form a guard when the reſt of us croſſed. But all things turned out well, and we were kindly conducted to their town by two or three hundred ſavages.

There *Powhatan* received us in great ſtate, and did all that was in his power to entertain us, feaſting us with the moſt plenty of victuals he could provide ; and, beſides, there were about four or five hundred people as a guard for us, through whom we walked. Then a proclamation was made that none ſhould preſume to do us wrong, or diſcourteſy, under pain of death.

We had much feaſting, dancing, and ſinging, and we quartered that night with *Powhatan.* The next day Captain *Newport* came aſhore, and received as much content as thoſe people could give him. A boy named *Thomas Salvage* was then given unto *Powhatan,* whom *Newport* called his ſon ; and, in exchange, *Powhatan* gave him *Namontack,* his truſty ſervant, and one of a ſhrewd, ſubtle capacity. Three or four more days we ſpent in feaſting, dancing, and trading, wherein *Powhatan* carried himſelf ſo proudly, yet diſcreetly (in his ſavage manner), that we could not but admire his natural gifts, conſidering his education. He ſcorned to trade in the ſame manner as did his ſubjects, but ſpake to *Newport* in this manner :—" Captain

Newport, it is not agreeable to my greatnefs, in this peddling manner to trade for trifles, and I efteem you as a great chief. Therefore, lay me down all your commodities together ; what I like I will take, and in récompenfe give you what I think fitting their value."

I told *Newport* that this was only his device to cheat us, but he thought to outbrave this favage in oftentation of greatnefs, and fo to bewitch him with his bounty, as to have what he lifted. But my idea was the right one, as he found when he let *Powhatan* have his way ; for he valued his corn at fuch a rate, that I think we might have got it cheaper in *Spain*, for we had not four bufhels for what we expected to have twenty hogfheads. This bred fome unpleafantnefs between *Newport* and me, for I cared not to fpoil our trade with the natives for all time to come, which faĉt, however, *Newport* regarded not, as it would not affect him, and he preferred appearing very liberal, and oftentatious, in the King's eyes. In this ftrait I had recourfe to a little harmlefs craft, or ftrategy, which was this : I glanced in the eyes of *Powhatan* many trifles, and he fixed his humour upon a few blue beads. For a long time, he importunately defired them, but the more he liked them, the higher I praifed them, and the lefs inclined I feemed to be to part with them. I praifed them up as being

composed of a most rare substance, of the colour
of the skies, and fit only to be worn by the greatest
kings in the world. This so inflamed him, that
he became half mad with the desire of possessing such
strange jewels, and it ended that for a pound or two
of blue beads I bought of the King two or three
hundred bushels of corn, and yet parted good friends.

I may say that I tried the same plan with the
King of *Pamaunkee*, and did as well with him with
my blue beads, which grew by this means of that
estimation, that none durst wear any of them but
these great kings, their wives, and children; and
so we returned all well to *James Town*, where this
new supply was lodged with the rest. Now,
whether it was that this grain was not sufficiently
dried or no, I cannot say, but a fire broke out
in the granary, and so spread to our quarters,
and to the town, which, being but thatched with
reeds, was soon burnt; yea, so fierce was the fire,
that even the palisadoes were burnt, though eight
or ten yards distant. It destroyed our arms,
bedding, and apparel, and much private provision.
Good Master *Hunt*, our preacher, lost all his
library, and, indeed, all that he had, save only the
clothes which he wore upon his back; yet none
ever heard him repine at his loss. This great
mischance happened in the winter of 1607, which
was noted for its extreme frost.

Now the ship loitering, lying idle, was a great source of vexation to me; altogether it lay fourteen weeks, when she might have discharged her cargo, loaded again, and have sailed in as many days. And the cause of my vexation was this, that our people would part with their corn, or money, spare clothes, gold rings, furs, or even give bills of payment, in order to get luxuries and drink from that floating tavern. This delay not only impoverished the colonists by draining them of all their resources, but, as the seamen must be fed for the whole of that time, they consumed the food that was intended for the supply of us all.

Both myself, and *Scrivener*, did our best to amend what was amiss, but the major part went with the President, and we were out-voted. What was wanted at home, it seemed, and what Captain *Newport* so particularly wished to take home, was gold; but although they washed the sand, yet found they no gold, for the best of reasons, that there was none to find. At last the ship did sail, and we, not having any use of Parliaments, Plays, Petitions, Admirals, Recorders, Chronologers, Courts of Plea, nor Justices of Peace, sent Master *Wingfield*, and Captain *Archer*, home with Captain *Newport*, and thought ourselves well rid of such evilly disposed companions.

After the sailing of Captain *Newport* with our

difaffected brethren, things fettled down a little; but, although our Prefident was nominally our ruler, yet he was ftill fickly, and was quite content to confine his energies to the fale of the ftore commodities, whereby he maintained his eftate, and got a confiderable revenue. But as the fpring was approaching, Mr. *Scrivener* and I thought that it was high time that fomething fhould be done towards the rebuilding of the town; and, dividing our labours, we each fuperintended a portion of that work, together with repairing our palifadoes, the cutting down of trees, preparing our fields, planting our corn, rebuilding our church, and re-roofing our ftore-houfe; which tafks kept us all bufy and content.

Whilft we were thus hard at work, judge of our aftonifhment at the arrival of Mafter *Nelfon* in the *Phœnix*, which, truly, we had judged as loft. He was a man of a different ftamp from Captain *Newport*, and he behaved towards us right well. He landed all his men fafely, and he had fo managed his ftores (caufing the *Weft Indian Ifles* to feed his crew, whilft he was there) that he brought us a goodly quantity of victual; which, when we had added to it that we had gotten, was near fuffi-cient to laft us half a year. He had not anything but he freely imparted it, which honeft dealing (being a mariner) caufed us to admire him: in truth, we could not have wifhed more than he did for us. Now, in order fomewhat to repay him, it was propofed that I (for the Prefident held that it ftood not with his dignity to leave the Fort) fhould ftart with an expedition to difcover and fearch the country of the *Monacans* beyond the *Falls*. Sixty able men were allotted me, whom I trained fo diligently in their arms, fkirmifhing, and fuch like, that within fix days we little feared whom we might by hap encounter.   I was fomewhat averfe to this expedition, which was undertaken at the fuggeftion of Captain *Martin*, whofe head was always running on gold.   I would fain have fraught the fhip with cedar, which could be got readily, and was a prefent difpatch, rather than re-lade her with dirt, or go a feeking after *Martin's* fantaftical gold; and indeed, without our help, things fo fell out that they happened juft as I would wifh, and we ftarted not on our expedition.

It came to pafs in this wife.   When Captain *Newport* departed, *Powhatan*, in order to exprefs his love for him, prefented him with twenty turkeys, on the condition that he fhould return him twenty fwords, which *Newport* was weak enough to do.   Of courfe it was foolifh policy thus to arm the favages, and to put weapons in their hands, to be ufed againft ourfelves, but *Newport* thought little about that; he had his turkeys, and that was all he cared for. *Powhatan* having once fucceeded fo eafily in obtaining arms, thought to purfue the fame plan with me, and fent me alfo twenty turkeys on the fame terms, but he was difappointed ; for although I was quite willing to pay for them in any lawful manner, yet would I not be fo foolifh—or more juftly speaking, fo culpable—as to fupply him with weapons.

This fomewhat annoyed *Powhatan*, who was not ufed to being thwarted ; and, not finding his humour obeyed, he caufed his people to obtain weapons by any device. They would lie in wait at our very gates, and take them perforce, furprife us when at work, or by any means whatfoever, which was fo long permitted, that they became fo infolent that there was no holding them. The command from *England*, not to offend the natives, was very ftrait, and our authorities, who never left their houfes, would rather be anything than peace-breakers. This charitable humour prevailed till it chanced that they meddled with me. I would brook no nonfenfe from them, and without farther deliberation, gave them fuch an encounter as they had never had before. Some of them I hunted up and down the ifland, fome I terrified as they had never been in their lives, by whipping, beating, and imprifoning ; fo much fo, that in revenge they furprifed two of our diforderly foraging foldiers, and having affembled their forces, boldly threatened at our gates that they would force me to releafe feven favages, who for their villanies I had kept prifoners, or they would kill us all.

This might affright the Prefident, but it had no effect on me, fo that to try what they were made of I fallied out amongft them, and in lefs than an hour had fo mauled, and hampered them, that they brought me our two men, and begged for peace, without faying one word about their feven brethren who were my prifoners. Thefe men I examined, and got a confeffion from them by ftratagem, for I took one of them away and caufed feveral volleys of fhot to be fired. This, I told them, was their companion being fhot, becaufe he would not confefs who were the plotters of thefe villanies. This brought them to their fenfes, and they all agreed in one point, that they were directed by *Powhatan* to obtain for him our weapons, wherewith he might cut our throats; and they told us of the manner, how, where, and when, which we plainly found moft true and apparent.

Yet did this old fox fend us meffengers, as well as his deareft daughter *Pocahontas*, with prefents, in order to excufe him of having any fhare in the injuries done, which, he faid, was the fault of fome rafh, untoward captains, his fubjects; defiring us to fet them at liberty for this time, with the affurance of his love for ever. After this I gave the prifoners what correction I thought fit, and then used them well for a day or two, after which I delivered them to *Pocahontas*, for whofe fake only, I feigned to have faved their lives, and gave them their liberty. The patient Council, that nothing would move to war with the favages, would gladly have wrangled with me for my cruelty, yet to any man's knowledge was none of them flain. It had this good effect upon the favages, that it brought them into fuch fear and obedience that my very name would fufficiently affright them; whereas before, we fometimes had peace and war twice in a day, and very feldom did a week pafs, but we had fome treacherous villany or other.

At length the idea of fearching for gold, where-with to lade the *Phœnix*, was abandoned, and the far more fenfible arrangement arrived at, to freight her with cedar, which I foon accomplifhed, thanks to the diligence of her mafter, and Mafter *Scrivener*, at the Fort, who did his duty well. The fhip being ready to fet fail, Captain *Martin* (who was always very fickly and unferviceable, and who was always hankering after finding that gold, which did not exift, thereby creating great difunion amongft us) took a fancy that he fhould like to return to *England*, where he might enjoy the credit of having found his fuppofed gold; and leave was readily granted, for we were all right glad to be well quit of him.

CHAPTER X.

NOW the *Phœnix* brought us out many
colonifts, amongft whom were thirty-three
gentlemen adventurers, twenty-one labourers, fix
tailors, one chirurgeon and two apothecaries, one
jeweller, two refiners, two goldfmiths, one gunfmith,
one blackfmith, one cooper, one tobacco-pipe maker,
and one perfumer !   This will fhow you what the
Council at home thought of our colony—fending us
out fo many gentlemen (as if we had not enough of
them already, forfooth) and fo few labourers. Perhaps
Richard Belfield, the perfumer (!) was fent out to
compound fweet fcents for thefe fine gentlemen ;
we could find no other reafon for his coming to us.
But had he not turned his hand to other things, he
would not have made a living by his trade.   And,
again, fee how the luft of finding gold, was apparent
in their fending out refiners and goldfmiths, who
never had occafion to exercife their craft ; as alfo
the jeweller, for there were no precious ftones nor
jewels, fave only fuch few pearls as might be found
in the oyfters, of which there were great plenty.

Our weak-minded Prefident kept a fort of ftate,
out of all proportion to our humble means, fo that
Scrivener and I, finding our remonftrances of no
avail, had to treat the matter in a rougher manner,

and we tied him, and his parafites, down to certain allowances; fomewhat according to the rules of proportion. But no fooner had I got ready to ftart on my expedition of discovery, than the Prefident's authority fo overfwayed Mr. *Scrivener's* difcretion, that our ftore, our time, our ftrength and labours, were idly confumed to fulfil his fantafies.

On June 2, 1608, I left the Fort on my voyage, in order to explore the Bay of *Chefapeake.* I had been forced to abandon my idea of an inland expedition, for which I had fpent time and trouble in drilling my men, and now was fain to be content with a far fmaller following than was at firft allotted to me, having only with me *Walter Ruffell,* Doctor of Phyfick, fix Gentlemen adventurers, and feven foldiers. With this little band of comrades, I embarked in an open barge of not quite three tons burden, and accompanied the *Phœnix* as far as *Cape Henry,* where, bidding her God fpeed, we parted company, and croffed the bay to the eaftern fhore, where we fell in with fome ifles which we chriftened *Smith's Ifles,* after my name.

The firft people we faw were two grim and ftout favages, with long poles like javelins, headed with bone. They boldly demanded who we were, and what we wanted. I replied in a manner which fatisfied them, and they then feemed very kind,

K

directing us to *Accomack*, the habitation of their
chief, where we were kindly entreated.   This king
was the comelieft, propereft, and moft civil favage
we encountered.   His country is a pleafant, fertile
clay foil, with fome fmall creeks; good harbours
for fmall boats, but not for fhips.   He told us of a
ftrange accident which lately happened unto his
people, which, if true, is indeed remarkable.   It
feemed that two children had lately died, and for
fome reafon or other, whether moved by extreme
paffions or dreaming vifions, fantafies or affection,
an ardent longing feized upon the parents to revifit
their dead carcafes.   To their aftonifhment they
found no figns of death upon them (although they
were really dead), but their countenances were
cheerful and ruddy, as though they had regained
their vital fpirits.   Many came to behold this
ftrange appearance, as if it had been a miracle,
amounting to the greater part of the people, and
(here is the marvel of the ftory) all that looked
upon them died not long after, fo that few efcaped.

We could underftand them very well, for they
fpoke the language of *Powhatan*, and from the
defcription they gave of their country it muft be
very charming.   Leaving them, we failed along
the coaft, fearching every inlet and bay, to fee if
any were fit for harbours and habitations.   Seeing
many ifles in the midft of the bay, we bore up for

them, but ere we could reach them we encountered such an extreme guft of wind, which was accompanied by rain, thunder, and lightning, that we changed our courfe, and with great difficulty efcaped fafely from the raging of the elements. The higheft land on the main, which, indeed, was but low, we called *Keale's Hill*, after *Richard Keale*, one of our foldiers; and thofe ifles which we tried in vain to reach, we called *Ruffell's Ifles*, after our worthy phyfician. Next day we tried after frefh water, but, finding none, we were forced to follow the next eaftern channel, which brought us to the river of *Wighcocomoco*.

The people here were, at firft, inclined to affault us, but we reaffured them, and then they welcomed us with fongs and dances, and much mirth; and, indeed, they became very tractable, fo that they allowed us to fearch their houfes for water; but all we could obtain would fill but three barricoes,* and that fuch puddle ftuff, that never till then did we know the value of good water. We digged and fearched in many places, but without avail, and in good footh, before two days had expired we would gladly have given two barricoes of gold, had we them, for one of that puddle water of *Wighco-comoco*. The iflands round about were numerous,

---

* Small firkins.

K 2

but good for nought for habitation ; but we fell in
with a high land upon the main, where was a great
pond of frefh water, but fo exceeding hot, that we
fuppofed it to be fome fort of bath.   That place I
called *Point Ployer*, in honour of the eftimable
Count of that name, who, as you will remember,
relieved me fo nobly when I was in dire want in
Brittany.   So did this place relieve our neceffities
when we were in fore ftraits for water.

The weather grew very ftormy, with thunder,
lightning, and rain, and the waves fo beat in upon
our little boat that we had great difficulty in keeping her afloat, by conftantly bailing, and for two days
we were forced to live on thofe uninhabited ifles.
Whilft there, we repaired our fail, which had been
fplit and torn away by the force of the wind, with
our fhirts, for we had no canvas ; and when the
weather moderated, we again fet fail for the main,
and fell in with a pretty convenient river on the
eaft coaft of the bay, called *Cufkarawaok*, where
the people ran, as if amazed, in troops from point
to point, and divers of them got into the tops of
trees, from whence they employed themfelves in
fhooting at us.   They were not fparing of their
arrows, and made the moft angry geftures to fhow
what a rage they were in.   Long time they fhot at
us, but they did us no harm, feeing we were riding
at anchor out of bow fhot ; but we, all this time,

were making to them all the moſt friendly geſtures we could think of.

Finding we were not to be frightened by them, they tried, the next day, what fraud and cunning would do. So they came down to the ſhore, every one unarmed, and each carrying a baſket, dancing in a ring in order to entice us on ſhore ; but ſeeing there was nothing in them but villainy, we diſcharged a volley of muſkets, loaded with piſtol-ſhots, whereat they all fell tumbling on the ground, ſome creeping one way, ſome another, into a great cluſter of reeds hard by, where their companions lay in ambuſcade. Towards evening we weighed anchor, and approached the ſhore, diſcharging five or ſix ſhots among the reeds. On landing we found many baſkets and ſome blood, but ſaw not a ſavage.

However, we left them ſome pieces of copper, beads, bells, and looking-glaſſes, which gave them ſuch belief in us, and we became ſuch good friends, that they abſolutely contended one with another, who ſhould fetch us water, ſtay with us for hoſtage, ſhow our men the way to any place, and in every way to give us the beſt content.

We afterwards ſailed along the eaſtern coaſt, but found nothing of much note, all along being well watered, but very mountainous and barren ; the valleys very fertile, but extremely thickly ſet with underwood, as well as trees, and much frequented with wolves, bears, deer, and other wild beafts. We paffed many fhallow creeks, but the firft we found navigable for fhips we called *Bolus*, for the clay there in many places under the cliffs which were made by the high water, did grow up in red and white knots, like gum out of trees, the reft of the earth all round being hard, fandy gravel; the red clay was fo like Bole Armenian, that we therefore chriftened the creek by the name of *Bolus*.

When firft we fet fail fome of our gallants doubted not but that I fhould be in too great a hurry to get home again, but when they had been in the bay fome twelve or fourteen days, ofttimes tired at the oars, our bread fo fpoilt with wet that it was rotten (yet fo good were their ftomachs that they could digeft it), they did, with continual complaints, fo importune me to return, that I was obliged to befpeak them in this manner: "Gentle-men, if you will remember the memorable hiftory of Sir *Ralph Lane*, how his company importuned him to proceed in the difcovery of *Moratico*, alleging that they had yet a dog, that being boiled with Saxafras leaves, would richly feed them on their return; then what a fhame would it be for you (that have been fo fufpicious of my tendernefs) to force me to return, with fo much provifion as we have, and fcarce able to fay where we have been;

nor have we yet heard of that we were fent to feek. You cannot fay but I have fhared with you in the worft, which is paft; and for what is to come, of lodging, diet, or whatfoever, I am contented that you allot the worft part to myfelf. As for your fears that I will lofe myfelf in thefe unknown large waters, or will be fwallowed up in fome ftormy guft, abandon thefe childifh fears, for worfe than is paft is not likely to happen, and there is as much danger to return as to proceed. Regain, therefore, your old fpirits, for return I will not (if God pleafe) till I have feen the *Maffawomeks*, found *Patawomek*, or the end of this water you conceive to be end-lefs."

This fpeech fomewhat calmed them, but for two or three days after, we experienced bad winds and weather, whofe adverfe extremities caufed fuch difcouragement that three or four fell fick, whofe pitiful complaints caufed us to return, and leave this bay, which was fome nine miles broad, with a depth of water of from nine to ten fathoms.

On the 16th June we fell in with the river *Patawomek*, and, as by this time our men had re-covered their health, and at the fame time had loft fome of their fear, we were content to take fome pains to explore that noble river, which was feven miles broad. We failed up it for thirty miles with-out feeing an inhabitant; when we met with two

favages in a canoe, who conducted us up a little
bayed creek towards *Onawmament*, where the woods
were filled with ambufcades of favages to the number of three or four thoufand, fo ftrangely painted,
grimed, and difguifed, fhouting, yelling, and crying,
fo that as many fpirits from hell could not have
looked more terrible.

By their geftures and bravado they feemed to be
longing to attack us, fo I thought it as well to fhow
a like feeming willingnefs on our part to encounter
them. But, when they faw the grazing of our
bullets on the water, (many guns being fhot on
purpofe that they might fee the effect,) and heard
the echo the firing made in the woods, they threw
down their bows and arrows, and became friendly.
We exchanged hoftages, and *James Watkins*, one
of our foldiers, was fent fix miles into the woods
to their king's habitation. We were then very
kindly ufed by thefe favages, and they made us
underftand that they were commanded to betray us
by the direction of *Powhatan*, and that he had been
inftigated fo to do by the difcontented ones at *James
Town*, becaufe I did caufe them to ftay in the
country againft their wills.

We found the fame kindnefs at other places we
vifited, where the people did their beft to content
us, and we made our way far up the river. At
one part we found that the water, which had fallen

from the high rocks, was highly charged with
metal, fo that the clay fand, which we dug at their
foot, was fo mingled with yellow fpangles, that it
looked as if it were half made of pin duft. When
we returned, we inquired of *Matchqueono,* the King
of *Patawomeke,* about this metal, and he gave us
guides who conducted us up a little river called
Quiyough, up which we rowed as high as we could.
Leaving the boat with fix of our company well
armed, I marched fome feven or eight miles before
we reached the mine, taking with me my hoftages,
who were coupled together and led by a fmall chain,
of which they were mighty proud, inafmuch as
they were promifed to have it given to them for
their pains, and they thought themfelves richly
adorned indeed.

The mine was a great rocky mountain like antimony, in which they had digged a great hole with
their fhells and hatchets. Hard by ran a fair brook
of cryftal-like water, in which they wafhed away
the drofs and kept the remainder, which they put
in little bags and fell all over the country, where
it is ufed to paint their bodies, faces, or their idols;
which makes them look like blackamores dufted
over with filver. We carried away as much as we
could, and returned to our boat, and when we got
back we rewarded this kind king and his friendly
people with fome prefents, and took our leaves

with mutual good will.   I was glad to have found this mine, for *Newport*, when he went home after bringing us to *Virginia*, took a few bags of this metal with him, and he did affure us that he had had it affayed, and that it was half filver; but all that we got proved of no value.

In the courfe of our journeyings we alfo met with a few beavers, otters, bears, martens, and minks; and in divers places there was fuch an abundance of fifh, lying quite thick, with their heads above water, as our barge drove through them, that for want of a net we attempted to catch them with a frying-pan, but we found it a bad inftrument to catch fifh with.   Neither better fifh, nor in more plenty, nor more variety for fmall fifh, had any of us ever feen in any place, but they are not to be caught with frying-pans.   Some fmall cod alfo did we fee fwim clofe in fhore by *Smith's Ifles*, and fome we found dead upon the fhore.

You muft not think that all our journeying was quiet and peaceful; far from it.   We had many quarrels, encounters with, and treacheries from the favages, but we always furmounted the difficulties, and fo encountered them, and curbed their infolence, that they invariably concluded with prefents to purchafe peace; yet we had the exceeding good hap not to lofe a man.   In my dealings with thefe people, I ever obferved the precaution, at our firft meeting, to demand their bows and arrows, fwords, mantles and furs, with a child or two for a hoftage, whereby we could quickly perceive, by their agreeing to the demand, or the reverfe, whether they intended any villany or no. And now, as our provifions were getting low, we thought of returning.

I muft not omit to tell you of an accident which happened to me on our return. At the mouth of the river *Rapahanock* are a many fhoals, and it chanced, by reafon of the ebb tide, that our barge grounded on one of them, and there we muft needs abide until the next tide came to float us. As I was looking in the water, I efpied many fifhes lurking in the reeds, and for very fport and paftime, to while away an hour, I amufed myfelf by nailing them to the ground with my fword. This fet all my crew following my example, and by this means we caught more fifh in one hour than we could eat in a day. It came to pafs that I had pierced a very curioufly-fhaped fifh, and knowing nothing about it, was taking it off the point of my fword as I had done others. It was much of the fafhion of a thornback, with a long tail like a riding-whip, in the midft whereof is a moft poifonous fting of two or three inches long, bearded like a faw on either fide. This the fifh ftuck into my wrift, to the depth of near an inch and a half; no blood iffued forth, nor could any wound be feen, except a little blue fpot, but the torment was inftantly extreme, by reafon of its poifon, and in four hours' time my hand, arm, and fhoulder had fwollen to fuch a fize, and my agony was fo great, that I concluded that my death was indeed nigh, and this, my. opinion, was fhared by the whole company.

Forefeeing my death, I directed my grave to be dug on a neighbouring ifland, a tafk which was dolefully carried out by my forrowful companions, and I alfo ordered my funeral; yet it fell out, as you all know, that I did not die, for it pleafed God that by virtue of a precious oil, which Doctor *Ruffell*, our phyfician, applied to the wound, after he had founded it with a probe, the tormenting pain was, ere night, fo well affwaged, that I began to be an hungered, and longed for my fupper, and then did, with a good heart, have mine enemy cooked, and did eat a portion of him, to my great delight, and to the joy and content of the whole company. And the next day, when we left that memorable place, by one confent we called it *Sting Ray Ifland*, after the name of the fifh.

I was, however, ftill unwell, and having neither chirurgeon or any medicaments with us, fave only the precious bottle of prefervative oil, I gave orders to fet fail at once for *James Town*. When we arrived at *Kecoughton*, at the mouth of *Powhatan* river, the simple savages there, seeing me ill, and one of our men somewhat bloody from a hurt he had received in his leg, and that we had with us quantities of bows, arrows, mantles, and furs, would needs imagine we had been at war, and impatiently importuned us to tell them with whom. Finding they would not believe the truth, to please them we romanced a bit, and told them, as a great secret, that we had got much spoil from the *Massawomeks*; and this rumour went faster up the river than did our barge, so that we were told of it when, on the 20th July, we reached *Waraskoyack*, which would be our last place of call before reaching *James Town.* We were in most excellent spirits, so much so that some of our wags begged my permission to play off a merry jest on those at *James Town*, and as it was a harmless one, I said yes. So we trimmed our barge with painted streamers, and such other devices as we could, and made her look exceeding brave, and our device succeeded to our heart's content, for they at *James Town* surely thought, as we meant them to do, that we were a boat from some Spanish frigate, and were, in consequence, greatly perturbed in their minds respecting us. And so, God be thanked, we all arrived safely on the 21 July, having been absent seven weeks.

CHAPTER XI.

IT is needlefs to fay, that, as was my wont, I
found the colony in a wretched plight on my
return. The whole of the company which had been
left by the *Phœnix* was fick, and of the reft, fome
were lame, fome bruifed, and all unable to do anything but complain of the pride, and unreafonable,
needlefs cruelty of the Prefident, who had riotoufly
confumed our ftore, and, to crown his follies, had
made them build him an unneceffary building for
his pleafure in the woods. Had we not arrived as
we did, faid they, they would have been revenged
on him, but the good news of our difcovery, and
the hope we had, according to what the favages
had told us, that our bay ftretched into the South
Sea, or fomewhere near it, appeafed their fury
fomewhat. But they would be fatisfied with nothing
lefs than that *Ratliffe* fhould be depofed, and that I
fhould take the government upon myfelf, as by
rotation it fhould have come to my turn. It was
certain that if *Ratliffe* remained as Prefident, the
colony would be in open rebellion, and probably
be broken up; and, truly, he had brought his fate
upon himfelf by his folly; fo that for the common
weal I agreed, but fubftituted as Prefident my dear

and very good friend Mr. *Scrivener*. I equally
diftributed thofe private provifions which *Ratliffe*
had taken unto himfelf; I appointed more honeft
officers to affift Mafter *Scrivener* (who then lay
exceeding fick of a burning fever), and, having
regard to the weaknefs of the company, and the
heat of that feafon of the year, which rendered
them unable to work, I left them to live at eafe,
fo that they might recover their healths; but I,
myfelf, embarked to finifh my difcovery.

No one can fay that I dallied long at *James
Town*, for three days after my return—that is, on
July 24—I fet out with twelve companions to finifh
my difcovery. I had with me Mafter *Anthony
Bagnall* as chirurgeon, five other gentlemen, and
fix foldiers, and they were nearly all the fame as
accompanied me on my laft expedition. The wind
being contrary, caufed our ftay at *Kecoughton*,
where the King feafted us, his people being fatisfied
that we were on our way purpofely to be revenged
on the *Maffawomeks*. In the evening we fired a
few rockets, which, flying in the air, fo terrified
the poor favages, that they imagined nothing was
impoffible to us, and they were very eager to
affift us, but I would not accept their help. We
revifited *Sting Ray* Ifland and the river *Bolus*. Soon
after that, when croffing the bay, we encountered
feven or eight canoes full of *Maffawomeks*. Seeing

they were preparing to attack us, we left off rowing, and made way with our fail to encounter them : not that I particularly wifhed fo to do, if I could avoid it, for there were but four of us, befides myfelf, who could ftand; for, two days after we left *Kecoughton*, the reft were fick almoft to death, until they got feafoned to the country.

Hiding them under our tarpauling, we put their hats upon fticks by the barge's fide, and betwixt two hats, a man with two guns, fo as to make us feem many in number, and I fancy the Indians did take thofe hats to be men, for they fled with all poffible fpeed to the fhore, and there ftayed, ftaring at the failing of our barge, till we anchored right againft them. It was long ere we could draw them to come unto us, but at laft they fent two of their number, unarmed, in a canoe, and the reft followed to help them if they needed it. I gave to each of thefe two a belt, and they were fo delighted that they foon brought their fellows on board, who prefented me with venifon, bears' flefh, fifh, bows, arrows, clubs, targets, and bears' fkins. We could not underftand a word they fpoke, but, by figns, they fignified unto us that they had been at war with the *Tockwoghes,* which they confirmed by fhowing us their wounds, which were quite recent. They went away at nightfall, leaving us under the impreffion that they would come again on the morrow morning; but after that we never ſaw them.

When we entered the river *Tockwogh*, we found the ſavages in a fleet of boats, all armed after their barbarous manner, and they environed us. I thought, of courſe, that we ſhould have to fight them, but it chanced that there was one of them who could ſpeak the language of *Powhatan*, who perſuaded the reſt to a friendly parley. But when they ſaw we were in poſſeſſion of *Maſſawomek* weapons, they believed, as did thoſe of *Kecoughton*, that we had taken them perforce, ſo that they honoured us highly, and took us to their paliſadoed town, where their men, women, and children met us with dances and ſongs, and with preſents of fruits, furs, and whatever they had, ſpreading mats for us to ſit on, and expreſſing their love for us to the beſt of their ability. We ſaw among theſe people many knives, hatchets, and pieces of braſs, which they ſaid they had from the *Saſqueſahanocks*, a mighty people, and mortal enemies to the *Maſſa-womeks*. I aſked them to prevail on ſome of theſe Indians to pay me a viſit, and in about three or four days' time ſixty of theſe giant-like people came, bringing with them preſents of veniſon, tobacco-pipes, three feet in length, baſkets, targets, and bows and arrows.

We had uſe daily to have prayer, with the

L

finging of a Pfalm, at which folemnity the poor
favages much wondered.   One day, after we had
finifhed our devotions, they began in a moft paffionate manner to hold up their hands to the fun,
at the fame time finging a moft fearful fong, after
which they embraced me, and adored me in the
fame manner.   I was compelled to rebuke them
for this, but they took no heed, and proceeded
with their fong until it was finifhed; then, with a
ftrange and moft furious action, and with a voice like
that of devils, they began an oration as to their affection for me.   When that was done, they covered
me with a great painted bear's fkin, then one hung
a great chain of white beads, weighing at leaft fix
or feven pounds, about my neck, and others
brought mantles of divers forts of fkins fown
together.   These, with many other toys, they laid
at my feet, and, ftroking my neck with their hands,
they created me their governor and protector,
promifing their aids, victuals, or whatfoever they
had, fhould be mine, if I would only ftay with
them, to defend and revenge them of the *Maffawomeks*.   But as we could not ftay, we left them
forrowing for our departure, and we promifed the
next year again to vifit them.

As we went along, a new world opened up unto
us, and I had to be like unto *Adam*, and give names
to all the places we faw : to wit, the higheft moun-

tains we faw northward I called *Perigrine Mount*, and a rocky river, *Willoughby River*, both in memory of the village in which I was born, and of my moſt honoured good friend, the Lord *Wil-loughby*; but the greater part of the names, as was meet, I took from thoſe who accompanied me and ſhared my adventure. And in every place thus named, and at the fartheſt points we reached going up the rivers, we cut in trees as many croſſes as we had a mind to, and, in many places, made holes in trees, wherein we put notes which we wrote, and, in ſome places, croſſes of brafs, to ſignify to thoſe who might come after us that Engliſhmen had been there.

Having explored the end of the bay, we returned to go up the river *Rapahanock*, where the people were very friendly, and we met with an old acquaintance, one *Moſco*, a luſty ſavage of *Wigh-comoco*, who had an exceeding love for us. We ſuppoſed him to be ſome Frenchman's ſon, becauſe he had a thick, black, buſhy beard, and the ſavages ſeldom have any at all, and of this beard he was not a little proud. He would do anything for us. Wood and water would he fetch us, guide us any-whither; nay, cauſe divers of his countrymen to help us tow our barge againſt wind and tide from place to place, till we came to *Patawomek*; there he reſted till we returned from the head of the rivers,

and then he guided us to the mine we had fuppofed
to be antimony.   And he never failed to do us all
the good he could, perfuading us, in any cafe, not
to go to the *Rapahanocks*, for they would kill us
for being friends with another tribe that, but lately,
had ftolen three of the King's women.   This, we
did think, was but that only his friends might have
our trade ; and fo, being mighty wife in our own
conceit, we croffed the river to the *Rapahanocks*.

There we faw fome twelve or fixteen men ftanding on the fhore, who directed us to a little creek,
where was good landing ; but before we would land,
according to our cuftom, we afked to exchange
a man in fign of love and friendfhip.   After they
had confulted together for a little while, four or
five of them waded up to their middles in the
ftream to fetch our man, and leave us one of them ;
and, as if to fhow we need not fear them, they
had with them neither clubs, nor bows and arrows.
Notwithftanding all this fair feeming, *Anas Todkill*,
one of our foldiers, being fent on fhore to fee if he
could difcover any ambufcadoes, and, generally, to
look about him, defired to go over the plain to
fetch fome wood, but they were unwilling to do fo,
except we would come into the creek, where the
boat might come clofe afhore.

Todkill, having by degrees got fome two ftone's-
throws up the plain, perceived, as he thought, fome

two or three hundred men behind the trees, and
when he attempted to return to the boat to inform
us of what he had beheld, the ſavages eſſayed to
carry him away by force, ſo he called out to us that
we were betrayed ; and hardly had he ſpoken, when
the Indian hoſtage which we had in the boat leaped
overboard, but *Watkins*, his keeper, was too ſharp
for him, and ſlew him in the water. It was not a
time for heſitation, and we let fly amongſt them,
ſo that they fled, and *Todkill* eſcaped ; yet they
ſhot at him ſo faſt that he fell to the ground ere he
could recover the boat.

Here, too, we found the value of *Moſco's*
counſel, for he adviſed us to ſet the *Maſſawomek*
targets about the fore part of our boat, like a fore-
caſtle, and they ſtood us in good ſtead, for, from
behind them, we could fire at the ſavages and beat
them off the plain, without any hurt to ourſelves ;
yet they ſhot more than a thouſand arrows, and
then fled into the woods. Arming ourſelves
with theſe light targets (which are made of ſmall
ſticks, interwoven with ſtrings of their hemp and
ſilk graſs), we reſcued *Todkill*, who was beſmeared
with the blood of thoſe who held him, who had
been ſhot by us, but, as God pleaſed, he had no
hurt ; and, following them up into the woods,
we found ſome ſlain, and in divers parts much
blood. It would ſeem that all their arrows were

fpent, for we heard no more of them. Their canoes we took, and the arrows we found we broke, fave thofe we kept for *Mofco*, to whom we gave the canoes as fome reward for his kindnefs.

———

CHAPTER XII.

HAVING had this warning, and not knowing when we might expect another vifit from the favages, we fpent the reft of the day in fortifying our boat with our *Maffawomek* fhields, and our friend *Mofco* followed us along the fhore ; but after a while he came into the boat. After we had paffed three or four towns, we came to a place where, feemingly, on the fhore were thirty or forty bufhes growing among the fedge. We thought nothing of them until arrows came from that direction, fhot by unfeen foes. They did us no harm, as they only ftruck the fhields and dropped into the river, but *Mofco* fell flat on his face in the boat, and fhouted out that the *Rapahanock* were there, fo we fired a volley, and lo ! all the little bufhes fell down, and when we had got about half a mile away, up jumped a lot of Indians, who fhowed themfelves, dancing and finging very merrily.

As we went higher up the river, some of the
kings used us very kindly, and their people
brought us whatsoever *Mosco* told them to do.
And here we had a great loss to our little expedition, for it pleased God to take one of our
company, Mr. *Fetherstone*, who, all the time he
had been in this country, had behaved himself
honestly, valiantly, and industriously. We buried
him in a little bay, which we called *Fetherstone's
Bay*, and over him we fired a volley of shot. He
had never got over the sickness that had afflicted
the greater number of our company ; but the rest,
notwithstanding their ill diet and bad lodging,
crowded in so small a barge, and by reason of
ever-present danger, never resting, but always
vigilant, had all well recovered their healths. The
day after we got as high up the river as our boat
would float, and there we followed our usual
practice of setting up crosses, and graving our
names in the trees.

Whilst thus engaged, our sentinel saw an arrow
drop by him, but we could not find who shot it ;
although we spent an hour in ranging up and
down, digging in the earth, and examining all
large stones, bushes, or springs, yet could we see
no place where a savage could hide. However,
we thought it wise to profit by the warning, and
we recovered our arms, which we had laid down ;

and luckily we did fo, for fcarcely were we once more armed, when we perceived about a hundred nimble Indians fkipping from tree to tree, letting fly their arrows as faft as they could, but they hurt us not, as the trees ferved us as barricadoes. But *Mofco* did us good fervice, for he jumped from tree to tree, fhooting at them, and when his arrows were fpent, he ran to the boat for more, fo that they thought we had many favages with us.   And in about half an hour they vanifhed as fuddenly as they appeared.

As we returned, we found a favage who was wounded in the knee, and lay as if dead; but we found on examining him that he was alive, which *Mofco* feeing, was as furious as a dog is at a bear, and wanted to beat out his brains.   But this we would not fuffer, and we carried the Indian to our boat, where our chirurgeon dreffed the wound, and fo affuaged the pain, that in an hour's time the favage looked fomewhat cheerful, and did eat and fpeak, and through *Mofco* we queftioned him, and found out what nation he was of.   We demanded of him why they came in that hoftile manner to us, who came to them in peace and friendfhip, and he anfwered that they had heard we were a people come from under the world, to take their world from them.   And many things he told us of their country, and its inhabitants, for which information I gave him many toys, and tried to perfuade him to go with us, and he as earneftly begged us to ftop where we were, and he would fee that we were friends with his people.

But *Mofco*, in whom I had great confidence, advifed us to be gone prefently, for that thefe Indians were very naughty. As we went along, we were continually being fhot at, but no hurt was done, becaufe of our fhields, and the favages followed us all through the night, about the diftance of twelve miles, and when day broke, we found ourfelves in a broad bay, out of danger of their fhot; fo we anchored, and had our breakfaft, after which our prifoner held a long difcourfe with his countrymen, and told them how good we were, and how well we had ufed him; that we had another Indian with us, who loved us as his life, who would have taken his life had we not have prevented him. This talk, and more like it, did fo prevail with his countrymen, that they all hung their bows and quivers on the trees, and one came fwimming to our boat with a bow tied on his head, and another with a quiver of arrows, which were fent me as a prefent. We afterwards landed, and gave up our prifoner to the four kings of that place. They were loft in admiration of us, and refufed us nothing that we defired; they

took our piftols for pipes, and much defired to
poffefs them, but that we could not accede to, but
I contented them with other commodities, and we
parted excellent friends, for I left some five
hundred of them laughing, dancing, finging, and
making very merry.

On our return, we vifited all our friends, who
rejoiced with us exceedingly, and would fain have
us friends alfo with the *Rapahanocks;* but I told
them they had twice affaulted me, that had come
but in love to do them good, and therefore I
would now burn all their houfes, deftroy their
corn, and ever hold them for mine enemies, unlefs
they made me fatisfaction.   They defired to know
what they fhould do, fo I told them they muft
bring me their king's bow and arrows, and muft
never prefume to come armed wherever I was;
that they muft be friends with my friends, and
give me their king's fon in pledge to perform
what I required of them.   Upon this they
prefently fent to the *Rapahanocks* to meet me at
the place where we firft fought, and there, in
prefence of two other kings, their chief did give
me his bow and arrows, and confirmed all I
defired, except his fon, for having no more but
him, he could not live without him; but inftead
of his fon, he would give me three women.   This
I accepted, and fo in three or four canoes we went

to *Moraughtacund*, where *Mofco* told fuch wonderful tales of us, and gave fo many bows and
arrows to his friends, that they no lefs loved him
than they admired us. The three women were
brought to me, and to each I gave a chain of
beads ; and then, calling the three chiefs before
him, I bade *Rapahanock* take her he loved beft, and
Moraughtacund choofe next, and to *Mofco* I gave
the third.

The next day were fix or feven hundred of
them, all dancing and finging, and not a bow to
be feen amongft them, all promifing ever to be
our friends, and to plant corn purpofely for us ;
and on our part I promifed, if they did fo, to
provide them with hatchets, copper, and beads.
And fo we parted, we giving them a volley of
fhot as a falute, and they fhouting loudly, and
crying with all their ftrength.

Methought, now that I knew fo many nations
who lived at a diftance from us at *James Town*,
it would be as well if I knew fomewhat of thofe
who were our neighbours near home ; fo, fetting
fail for the fouthern fhore, we failed up a narrow
river into the country of the *Chefapeakes*. This
we afcended for fome fix or feven miles, but,
although we faw many of their houfes and garden
plots, we neither faw nor heard any people, fo
that we returned to the great river *Powhatan*,

making our way to *James Town.* Coafting the
fhore towards *Nandafumund*, which is moftly
compofed of oyfter banks, we efpied, at the mouth
of that river, fix or feven favages making their
weirs, who prefently fled; afhore we went, and
where they had been working we threw divers
toys, and fo departed.

Far we had not gone ere they came again, and
began to fing and dance, and to recall us, and
thus we began our firft acquaintance. At laft, one
of them defired us to go to his houfe up the
river, and he came voluntarily into our boat, and
the reft ran after us by the fhore with all the fhow
of love that could be. Seven or eight miles we
failed up this narrow river; at laft, on the
Weftern fhore, we faw large cornfields, and in the
midft of the river was a little ifle, whereon was
abundance of corn. Our favage told us the people
were all a hunting, but in the ifle was his houfe,
to which he invited us with much kindnefs. We
entered, and there found his wife and children, and
we left them all much contented with the prefents
we gave them.

The others being now come up, defired us alfo to
go up the river yet a little higher, to fee their
houfes; here our hoft left us, the reft rowed by us
in a canoe till we were far paft the ifle, and the
river had become very narrow. Here we defired

fome of them to come aboard us, whereat, paufing a little, they told us they would but fetch their bows and arrows, and all go with us; but once afhore, and armed, they perfuaded us to go forward, but we could not by any means get them to go either into their own canoe, or our boat. This I liked not, and fo, miftrufting them, I gave orders to put up the fhields, and prepare for the worft.

It was lucky I did fo, for thefe favages meditated a notable treachery. There were now woods on either fide of us, and I noticed we were followed by feven or eight canoes. Prefently from each fide of the river came arrows as faft as two or three hundred men could fhoot them, whereupon we turned round fo as to get once more into the open. Thofe that were in the canoes let fly alfo as faft, but we could foon account for them, for amongft them we beftowed fo many fhot that the moft of them leaped overboard and fwam afhore, but two or three efcaped by rowing. They foon found our mufkets carried farther than their bows, and, in truth, we had not fired twenty fhots before they had all retired behind the trees. Having thus got out of their trap, we feized on all their canoes and moored them in the midft of the open water. More than a hundred arrows ftuck in our targets, and about the boat, yet none hurt, only our chirurgeon, Mafter *Anthony Bagnall*, was fhot in his hat, and had another arrow in his fleeve. But feeing their multitudes, and fufpecting, as it turned out to be, that both the *Nandfamunds* and the *Chefapeakes* were together, I thought it better to ride by their canoes awhile, to bethink whether it were better to burn all in the ifle, or draw them to a compofition till we were in a pofition to take all they had, which was fufficient to feed all our colony; but, after taking counfel together, it was decided to burn the ifland at night.

In the interim we began to cut their canoes in pieces, which was a fight that fo grieved them that it brought them to their fenfes, and they prefently laid down their bows, making figns of peace. Peace, I told them, I would accept, provided they did bring me their king's bows and arrows, and a chain of pearls; and that when we came again they muft give us four hundred bafkets full of corn, otherwife we would break all their boats, burn their houfes and corn, and all that they had. To perform all this they faid they only wanted a canoe, so I ordered one to be fet adrift, and bad them fwim to fetch her, and told them that they had better haften, for that until their promife was performed I fhould but continue to break their canoes. They cried out piteoufly for us not to do fo, for all fhould be as we wifhed, which prefently they performed. Away they threw their bows and arrows, and all of

them came as faſt as they could with their baſkets
of corn. We took as many as we could carry, and
ſo, departing good friends, we returned to *James
Town,* where we ſafely arrived on September 7,
1608, having been abſent between ſix and ſeven
weeks.

CHAPTER XIII.

THERE we found Maſter *Scrivener,* and divers
others whom we left ſick, well recovered ;
many dead, ſome ſtill ſick—the late Preſident was
a priſoner for mutiny—and, thanks to the honeſt
diligence of Maſter *Scrivener,* the harveſt had been
gathered, but the proviſion in ſtore had been much
ſpoiled by the rain. So that all our colony had
done was to have waſted that ſummer altogether
(owing to the government, or rather, miſgovern-
ment, of Captain *Ratliffe*); a fact only partially
redeemed by the diſcoveries I had made.

And now an event happened unto me which
made me feel very proud and joyful, and thankful
unto God, for that He had raiſed me, once a poor
friendleſs boy, to ſuch an high eſtate. For
Captain *Newport,* who had juſt returned from
England, brought out with him Letters Patent
appointing me Preſident of *Virginia,* and on

September 10, 1608, by the election of the Council, and at the request of the Company, I accepted the honourable position, which I would in no wise have done before—though I had often been importuned thereunto.   The first thing I did was to put a stop to the building of *Ratliffe's* palace, as being a needless labour ; but I had the church thoroughly repaired, the store-house provided with a new roof, and buildings prepared for the supplies we expected. The fort was made of a five square form, the order of the watch renewed, the squadrons (each setting of the watch) trained, the whole company every Saturday exercised on the plain by the west bulwark, which I had made smooth and level for the purpose. This martial parade-ground we called *Smithfield*, and there sometimes more than a hundred savages would stand in amazement, to behold how a file of musketeers would batter a tree against which was set a mark for them to fire at, and this inspired those savages with a wholesome dread of our power.

Now, Captain *Newport* had brought out with him some private instructions from the Council, which were very foolish, and showed how little they knew of the country they had to govern and colonize.   He was not to return without a lump of gold, when there was none in existence ; he was to make certain of the existence of a way to the *South*

Sea, and for that purpofe he had brought with him a barge built in five pieces, which was propofed to be carried on men's fhoulders over the mountains about which I wrote to the Treafurer and Council of *Virginia.** "And for the quartered boat to be borne by the foldiers over the Falles, *Newport* had 120 of the beft men he could chufe. If he had burnt her to afhes, one might have carried her in a bag, but as fhe is, five hundred cannot, to a navigable place above the Falles." He alfo was inftructed to bring back with him one of the loft company fent out by Sir *Walter Raleigh,†* which was about as likely a tafk as either of the others. He alfo brought out with him a crown and fcarlet robe, wherewith to crown *Powhatan,* together with an ewer and bafin, a bedftead and clothes. Thefe prefents were moft ill-judged, for we had his favour much better when we only ufed to give him a plain piece of copper, than after he had received thefe ftately gifts, which made him fo overvalue himfelf that he refpected us as much as nothing at all.

He alfo brought out with him eight Poles and

---

* See Appendix.

† That taken out by Captain John White, in 1587. When he revifited it 1589, the colony was deftroyed and overgrown with weeds, and he winds up his defcription thus : "And thus we left, feeking our colony that was never any of them found, nor feen, to this day, 1622."

Dutchmen, to make pitch, tar, glafs, mills and foap afhes; which might have been all very well when the country was more replenifhed with people and neceffaries, but to fend them, and feventy more, without victuals, to work, was not fo well advifed and confidered of, as it fhould have been. Not that this would hurt us had they been 200, though we were then 130 of ourfelves, for we had the favages in that *decorum,* (their harveft being nearly gathered,) that we feared not to get victuals for 500; but this, as in all elfe, the Council at home evidently relied more on what *Newport* told them, than on our reports fent home.

Among thofe whom he brought out, were two who were to be added to our Council, one Captain *Richard Waldo,* the other Captain *Winne,* two ancient foldiers, and valiant gentlemen, but as yet, being fo newly arrived, quite ignorant of the bufinefs. With thefe on the Council, and *Ratliffe* being alfo permitted to have his voice, and Mafter *Scrivener* being very defirous to fee ftrange countries, it did fo fall out that, although I was Prefident, yet the major part of the Council had the authority, and ruled it as they lifted. Captain *Newport* was anxious to take the pinnace of twenty tons, and go and deliver his prefents, and crown *Powhatan,* and he would fain have 120 chofen men for a guard. He furthermore argued that the pinnace could be made ufeful on the return voyage by being freighted with corn. I laughed at his fears of the defperate favages, and undertook to go myfelf to *Powhatan*, and afk him to come to *James Town* and fetch his prefents. And fo was it fettled, and where *Newport* durft not go with lefs than 120 men, I only took with me four, and with them went over land to *Weromocomoco*, fome twelve miles, and there croffed the river *Pamaunkee* in a canoe. There I abode, and fent for *Powhatan*, who was thirty miles off, and in the mean time *Pocahontas* and her women entertained me after this manner.

In a fair plain, we had made a fire, which I, on a mat, was fitting before, when, fuddenly, among the woods, was heard fuch a hideous noife and shrieking, that we betook ourfelves at once to our arms, and feized on two or three old men who were near us, fuppofing that *Powhatan*, with all his power, was coming to furprife us. But prefently *Pocahontas* came, making me underftand that I might kill her if any hurt were intended, but 1 was foon fatisfied that there was none, for there was now a crowd of fpectators, of men, women and children. And in truth it turned out to be a Mafque, after the Virginian manner, with which my dear friend, *Pocahontas*, would fain amufe us; and as you may never have heard of one, I will tell you the manner of it, and how it was performed. Thirty

young women came naked out of a wood, only
covered before and behind with a few green leaves,
but their bodies were all painted, fome of one
colour, fome of another, but all differing; their
leader had a fair pair of buck's horns on her head,
and an otter's fkin at her girdle, and another on
her arm; at her back fhe had a quiver of arrows,
and in her hand fhe carried a bow and arrows. The
next had in her hand a fword, another a club,
another a pot ftick: they were all horned alike,
and all the others carried fomething or other. They
looked like fiends, as with loud fhouts and cries,
they rufhed from among the trees, and, cafting
themfelves in a ring round about the fire, they fang
and danced after their fafhion, oft breaking out
into loud yells, and then again folemnly finging
and dancing. Having spent near an hour in this
Mafcarado, they departed in like manner as they
entered.

After they had removed from their perfons all
traces of their mafking, they reappeared, and
folemnly invited us to their lodging, where I was
no fooner within the houfe, but all thefe nymphs
began moft prettily to teafe me, crowding round,
preffing on, and hanging about me, continually
crying " Love you not me? Love you not me?"
When this falutation was ended, the feaft was fet
forth, confifting of all the favage dainties they

could devife; fome of them waiting upon us, fome finging, and others dancing before us, which mirth being ended, with firebrands, inftead of torches, they conducted us to our lodgings.

Powhatan came the next day, and to him I delivered my meffage, how that fome prefents had been fent him, and defired him to come to *James Town* and receive them, as well as to fee Father *Newport*, and, at the fame time, we would help him to conclude his revenge upon the *Monacans.* But the fubtle favage was puffed up with pride at the idea of having prefents fent him from our King, and fancied himfelf of great importance : fo he replied, "If your King has fent me prefents, I alfo am a king, and this is my land; eight days I will ftay to receive them. Your Father is to come to me, not I to him, nor yet to your Fort, neither will I bite at fuch a bait. As for the *Monacans,* I can revenge mine own injuries; and with regard to any falt water beyond the mountains, the relations you have had from my people are falfe." Whereupon he began to draw plans upon the ground of all thofe regions. I had many other difcourfes with him, in which each rendered to the other many complimental courtefies, but I could get no other anfwer from him, fo was fain to be content with it, and return.

So the prefents were fent by water, which was

near an hundred miles, and *Newport* and I went
by land with fifty good fhots, as a guard of
honour. When the boat arrived, we fettled the
next day for the Coronation, and then, with as
much ftate as we could, the prefents were brought
to the King; and we delivered to him his bafin
and ewer, and fet up his bedftead with its furniture.
We explained to him their different ufes, and them
he could comprehend; but he could not underftand
the fcarlet cloak and apparel, with which we would
indue him, and we had much ado before we could
put them upon him; but, being perfuaded at laft
that they would not hurt him, he fuffered himfelf
to be clothed after our will.

But, if he rebelled againft putting on the robe,
how much more did he kick againft having the
crown placed upon his head. In very truth, the
poor favage did have no idea of what was meant by
it, he knowing nothing, either of the majefty, or
meaning, of a crown. Nor could we induce him to
bend his knee and kneel; nor would he do it in
fpite of the many perfuafions, examples, and
inftructions we gave him, even until we were all
fairly tired out. But we had not come there
fpecially to crown him, and then go away with our
tafk unfinifhed, fo that the crown had to be put on
him fomehow. And at laft we accomplifhed it,
for *Newport* and I, by leaning on his fhoulders,

did make him ſtoop a little, and then three others of our number, who had the crown ready in theii hands, did put it on his head, which being done, a piſtol was fired, as a warning to thoſe in the boats, who were prepared, and they poured forth ſuch a volley of ſhot that the King ſtarted up in a horrible fear, which was not allayed till that he ſaw that all was well. When he had recovered himſelf, in order to requite our kindneſs, he gave his old ſhoes and mantle to Captain *Newport ;* but he would not help us in any way againſt the *Monacans ;* and, after ſome ſmall complimental kindneſſes on both ſides, he preſented *Newport* with a heap of wheat ears, which might contain ſome ſeven or eight buſhels, and with about as much more, which we bought in the town, we returned to the Fort.

CHAPTER XIV.

THE ſeventy coloniſts, which the ſhip brought over, were now all landed, and among them were the firſt gentlewoman, Miſtreſs *Forreſt,* and the firſt woman ſervant, to wit, *Anne Burras,* her maid, that ever we had amongſt us. But they were, as all ſuch cargoes that we had ſent to us, unſuitable to our market ; for beſides the two captains, who were to be of our Council, there was

Mafter *Francis Weft*, brother to Lord *De la Warre*, and twenty-five other gentlemen, fourteen tradefmen, and but twelve labourers, which, with fome boys, Dutchmen,* Poles, and others, made up the number. The fhip, then, being empty, Captain *Newport*, with 120 chofen men, led by Captain *Waldo*, Lieutenant *Percie*, Captain *Winne*, Mafter *Weft*, and Mafter *Scrivener*, fet forward for the difcovery of *Monacan*, leaving me at the Fort to relade the fhip, with about eighty or ninety men, fuch as they were.

Now the *Monacans* lived at the head of *Powhatan* river, upon which, as you know, *James Town* was fituate, and the expedition having got to the Falls, marched about forty miles` inland in two days and a half, and then returned by the fame way. They difcovered but two towns of the *Monacans*, and by them were ufed neither well nor ill, although they took prifoner one of the petty kings, and led him, bound, to fhow them the way. On their return, they fearched many places for fuppofed mines, and, having a refiner with them, they fpent fome time in refining the ores, but to no good account, although he endeavoured to perfuade them to believe that he had extracted fome fmall quantity of filver; and that (which was not unlikely) better ftuff might be had for the digging.

* Deutfches, or Germans.

The favages would not trade with them, and they could not find where their corn was, for they had hid it in the woods, fo that, thus deluded, they returned to *James Town*, half of them fick, all complaining, and tired with toil, famine, and dif-content, their journey having been perfectly fruit-lefs, as I foretold it would be; and, indeed, I was not forry that it fhould fo be, for it was a good leffon for them to learn, not to go running after marfh fires, but to truft to fteady labour.

I knew full well what mifchief idlenefs wrought, and of that they had had their fill of late, fo I fchemed work for all. Some I fet to make glafs, others tar, pitch, and potafhes, and thefe I left at the Fort under the orders of the Council, and in their overfight, for it was but meet that the Coun-cil fhould have fome tafk to perform, as well as the reft of the company. For myfelf, I fully per-ceived how it would be for the good of us all, if fome of the fine gentlemen of our company, were hardened by fome little labour with their hands. I well knew the characters of all, and chofe my men accordingly, among them two proper gentle-men of the laft fupply, *Gabriel Beadle* and *John Ruffell*, and with a band of about thirty, I moved down the river fome five miles from *James Town*, to teach them how to cut down trees, make clap-board, and lie out in the woods; thus inuring them to the life they would have to lead, did they want to make the Colony a fuccefs.

At firft the hard work, cooking their own food, and lying upon the ground, was very ftrange to them, but they could fay nought in difparagement thereof, for they faw that in all things, in lodging, eating and drinking, working or playing, I, their Prefident, fared but as they did : nay, in order to encourage them, it haply might be, that I worked harder and fared worfe than they.   All thefe things, therefore, were carried on fo pleafantly, that, within a week, they became mafters of their craft ; making it their delight to hear the trees thunder as they fell ; but the axes fo oft bliftered their tender fingers, that many a time every third blow had a loud oath to drown the echo.   For the remedy of which fin, and for the good of their fouls, as the work was benefiting their bodies, I devifed how to have every man's oaths numbered, and at night time, when we had a little pleafant recreation, the culprit was duly arraigned, and for every oath that was recorded againft him; he did have a can of water poured down his fleeve.   This was the caufe of much merriment, yet fomehow thofe who were punifhed, liked it not fo well, as to care ofttimes to have it repeated, and fo became more guarded of his tongue, and foon it came to pafs that a man fhould fcarce hear an oath in a week.

For he who scorns and makes but jests of cursings, and his oath,
He doeth contemn, not man but God, nor God, nor man, but
   both.

But in all this, let no man think that I and those gentlemen spent their time as common wood-haggers at felling trees, or such like labours, as if we had been pressed to it as hirelings, or common slaves; but what they did, after they were once somewhat inured to it, seemed (and some really thought so) only as a pleasure and a recreation, and thirty or forty of such voluntary gentlemen would do more work in a day, than one hundred of the rest that must be pressed to it by compulsion ; still I say not, but that twenty good workmen had been better than them all.

When I returned from the woods, I found that Master *Scrivener*, Captain *Waldo*, and Captain *Winne*, had each, in like manner, carefully looked after their charge, but seeing the time consumed, and how that no provisions had been secured (the ship all this time lying idle at a great charge), I presently embarked myself in the discovery barge, giving orders to the Council to send Lieutenant *Percie* after me with the next barge that arrived at the Fort. I had with me two barges, and eighteen men, and went up the *Chickahominy* river. Arriving at a spot I had determined on, I found that this dogged nation was well acquainted with our

wants, and refufed to trade, with as much fcorn
and infolency as they could exprefs.   Seeing that
it was *Powhatan's* policy to ftarve us, I told them
that I came there not fo much for corn, as to
revenge myfelf on them for my imprifonment, and
the murder of our men, and fo I landed my men,
and made as if I would charge them, upon which
they immediately fled.   But prefently they fent
their Ambaffadors to me with corn, fifh, fowl, and
whatfoever they had, in order to make their peace.
They complained extremely of their own wants
(for their corn that year was but bad), yet they
freighted our boats with an hundred bufhels of
corn, and alfo Lieutenant *Percie's*, who arrived
foon after, in like manner; and, having done the
beft they could to content us, we parted good
friends, and I returned to *James Town.*

My thus returning laden with provifions, much
contented the company, for they feared nothing
more than ftarving: yet there were fome among
them that fo envied my good fuccefs, that they
would rather have run the hazard of ftarving, than
that my efforts for the benefit of the community
fhould prove fo much more effectual than theirs.
Both *Newport* and *Ratliffe*, who were always to
the fore in my difpraife, had, in my abfence, in-
vented fome projects, not only to have depofed
me, but to have kept me out of the Fort, for that

I, being Prefident, had left my place, and the
Fort, without their confent, but their envious con-
fpiracy came to nought, and had not Captain
Newport cried *Peccavi*, I would have difcharged
the fhip, and caufed him to ftay one year in
Virginia, to learn to fpeak of his own convenience.

All this time, our old tavern, the fhip, made as
much out of all them that had either money, or
ware, as could be defired : indeed, on all fides,
both foldiers, failors, and favages, there was ten
times more pains taken to keep up their private,
and damnable trade, than to provide the Colony
with things that were neceffary. No wonder that
Newport and the mariners reported in *England*
that we had fuch plenty, and brought us out fo
many men without victual, when they had fo many
private factors in the Fort, that within fix or feven
weeks, of two or three hundred axes, chifels, hoes,
and pickaxes, fcarce twenty could be found : and
pike-heads, fhot, powder, and anything they could
fteal from their fellows was vendible, and they
knew well enough how to trade fecretly with the
favages for furs, bafkets, young beafts, and fuch
like commodities, or exchange them with the failors
for butter, cheefe, beef, pork, aqua vitæ, beer,
bifcuit, oatmeal, and oil. We could get no furs,
in all *Virginia*, for our ftores, yet one mafter got

fo many by this indirect means, that he confefled having fold them in England for £30.

I fent Mafter *Scrivener* with the barges and pinnace to *Werowocomoco*, where he found the favages more ready to fight than to trade, but owing to his vigilance no hurt was done, and he fucceeded in getting three or four hogfheads of corn. I was glad to be able to difpatch Captain *Newport* with famples of pitch, tar, glafs, frankin-cenfe, and potafhes, with as much clap-board and wainfcot as could be provided, and he failed for *England*, we that remained being in number about two hundred.

Now this was a large number to feed, and we were all fomewhat affrighted at the profpect of famine, fo that I minded me of the promife I extorted from the *Chefapeakes*, at *Nandfamund*, in September laft, of providing me with four hundred bafkets of corn, or I would burn and deftroy their place. I took three boats, and was accompanied by Captain *Winne* and Mafter *Scrivener*. However, when we came to *Nandfamund*, the favages not only refufed to deliver me the corn they had promifed, but would not trade with us in any way; excufing themfelves that they had fpent the moft part that they had gotten, and that they were commanded by *Powhatan* to keep that they had, and not to let us come into their river; fo that I

was conftrained to deal with them per force, and
fhow them I was not to be trifled with, but would
make them keep their promife. I gave orders to
our company to fire, and at the found of the
mufkets they all fled, and fhot not an arrow at us.
The firft houfe we came to we fet on fire, which
when they perceived, they defired we fhould make
no more fpoil, and they would give us half they
had. How they collected it I know not, but
before night they loaded our three boats.

After thus teaching them this ufeful leffon, we
dropped down the river to our quarters for the
night, which were fome four miles diftant. This
was an open wood under the lee of a hill, where all
the ground was covered with fnow, and hard frozen.
We digged away the fnow, and made a great fire in
its place, and when the ground was well dried and
warm, we turned away the fire to another place,
and covering the warm earth with a mat, there we
lay very warm. To keep away the wind, we made
a fcreen of another mat ; if the wind fhifted, we
fhifted our fcreen, and when the ground grew cold,
we moved the fire again, and once more had a
warm bed. And thus, many a cold night, have we
lain in this manner, yet thofe that went commonly
upon all like occafions, were always in health, lufty
and fat. Another good refult of our expedition
was, that the favages promifed that becaufe I had

fpared them this year, they would plant purpofely for us.

It was about this time that we had our firft marriage in *Virginia*, and it was between *John Laydon*, a labourer who came out with me, and *Anne Burras*, Miftrefs *Forreft's* maid, and we did not fail to do it all honour and proper courtefy; we faw them bedded, and gave them the caudle, but as we had no bridefmaids, we could not throw the ftocking.

CHAPTER XV.

THE corn I had gotten would laft a little while, but more muft be procured, at any coft, from fomewhere; fo I refolved, with Captain *Waldo* (who I knew I could depend on in time of need), to furprife *Powhatan* and all his provifion. Captain *Winne*, however, oppofed my idea, as did alfo Mafter *Scrivener*, who, for fome private purpofe, was plotting in *England* to ruin me, and, together, they did their beft to hinder my project. But no perfuafion of theirs could induce me to ftarve, or to allow thofe under my care to do fo, could I prevent it, and I had made up my mind for the expedition, when a meffage came from *Powhatan*, faying he would load my fhip with corn if I would but fend him fome men to build him a houfe, give him a grindftone, fifty fwords, fome guns, a cock and a hen, together with much copper and beads.

I was not ignorant of his devices and fubtlety, yet I was unwilling to neglect any opportunity; fo I prefently fent him four Dutchmen and one Englifhman, and then, with Captain *Waldo* and forty-fix men in the pinnace and two barges, we ftarted. I would only take with me fuch as offered themfelves voluntarily, for the expedition was looked upon as being very dangerous, for they all knew that I would not return empty, were there any corn to be got; however, as I fay, I would only take volunteers, for I found fo many that I appointed, make excufes to ftay behind. *Scrivener* I left as my deputy at *James Town*, but I took with me Lieutenant *Percie*, brother to my Lord the Earl of *Northumberland*, and alfo Mafter *Francis Weft*, brother to the Lord *De la Warr*.

The company being victualled but for three or four days, we lodged the firft night at *Warafkoyack*, where I managed to get fufficieut provifion; but the King there, who was a very kind friend to us, did his beft, by all manner of argument, to divert me from going to *Powhatan*; when, however, he perceived he could not prevail, he advifed in this manner: "Captain *Smith*, you fhall find *Powhatan* to ufe you kindly, but truft him not, and be fure

N

he have no opportunity to feize on your arms, for
he hath fent for you only to cut your throats." I
thanked him for his good and friendly counfel; yet
I put his love to yet a further proof, for I defired
of him guides to *Chawwonock*, to the king of
which place I would fain fend a prefent to bind
him as a friend to me. I entrufted this expedition
to Mr. *Sicklemore*, a very valiant, honeft, and
painftaking foldier: he took with him two guides,
and I gave him inftructions to feek for the loft
company of Sir *Walter Raleigh's*, and alfo to look
about him and fee if there were any filk grafs.
Then we departed thence, parting very excellent
friends, for I did affure the King of my perpetual
love, and I left my page, *Samuel Collier*, with him
to learn the language.

The next night we lodged at *Kecoughton*, and
here we were conftrained to abide for fix or feven
days, by reafon of the extreme wind, rain, froft, and
fnow, fo that it caufed us to keep our Chriftmas
among thefe favages. Wherever an Englifhman
may be, and in whatever part of the world, he
muft keep Chriftmas with feafting and merriment.
And, indeed, we were never more merry, nor fed
on more plenty of good oyfters, fifh, flefh, wild
fowl, and good bread; nor never had better fires
in *England* than in the dry, fmoky houfes of
Kecoughton.

But when we departed thence, when we found no houfes, we took not fo much pleafure in lying out, three or four nights together, and in any weather, under the trees by a fire, as we had ufed to do, as I told you. There was fuch plenty of wild fowl that I, *Anthony Bagnall*, and Sergeant *Pifing*, did kill, at three fhots, one hundred and forty-eight fowls.

At *Kifkiack*, the froft and contrary winds forced us to take up our abode with the favages, and, indeed, we never wanted fhelter when we found any houfes. It was on the 12th of January when we arrived at *Werowocomoco*, where we found the river frozen for near half a mile from the fhore ; but I, being unwilling to wafte any time, broke the ice with my barge, as far as I could, and had got fomewhat nearer the land, when the ebbing of the tide left the boat aground among the oozy fhoals. Yet rather than lie there for another tide and be frozen to death, I encouraged my companions to follow my example and jump into the river, wading up to our middles in that muddy, frozen ooze. But in this march, Mafter *Ruffell* (whom none could perfuade to ftay behind), being fome- what ill, and exceeding heavy, fo overtoiled himfelf that the reft of us had much ado (ere he got afhore) to regain life into his benumbed limbs. So we quartered ourfelves in the firft houfes we came to, and fent to *Powhatan* for provifions, who fent us plenty of bread, turkeys, and venifon.

The next day we vifited him, and, having feafted us after his ordinary manner, he turned round to me and ftraitly afked me when I would begone? Such was the wilinefs of this favage, that he feigned that he fent not for us, neither had he any corn, and his people much lefs; yet, faid he, for forty fwords he would procure us forty bafkets full. I fhowed him the very men there prefent that brought me the meffage and conditions, and I afked *Powhatan* how it chanced he became fo forgetful? To that he made no anfwer, but concluded this portion of our difcourfe with a merry laughter, afking for our commodities, but he liked none without guns and fwords, valuing a bafket of corn as more precious than a bafket of copper, faying he could rate his corn but not the copper.

Now I, feeing the intent of this fubtle favage, began to deal with him by telling him that I had many ways by which I could have procured my provifions; yet, believing his promifes to fupply my wants, I came to him—that I had no fwords nor guns to fpare, and that what I had would keep me from want, but I wifhed to be friendly with him.

The King having attentively liftened to this

difcourfe, promifed that both he and all his country would fpare me what they could, the which we fhould receive within two days, but he wifhed us to lay our weapons afide, as the people thought we had come to invade and poffefs their country.

With many fuch difcourfes we fpent the day, being quartered that night in the King's houfes, and the next day he went on again with his building, which he little intended fhould proceed. For the Dutchmen, finding *Powhatan's* great plenty, and knowing our want, and perceiving alfo his preparations to furprife us, little thinking we could efcape both him and famine, had, in order to obtain his favour, revealed to him as much as they knew of our eftates and projects, and how to prevent them. One of them, efpecially, was a man of fo great fpirit, under-ftanding, judgment, and refolution, a man that was certain of his wages for his labour, and one whom we ever ufed well, as, indeed, we did all his countrymen. Now I, knowing well this man, and knowing no one whom I could better truft, nor that was fitter for that employment, had fent him as a fpy to difcover *Powhatan's* intent ; at that time little doubting his honefty, nor truly was I certain of his villany till nearly half a year after.

Whilft we were awaiting the coming of fupplies

from the country, the King and I wrangled over a
bargain for ten quarters of corn for a copper
kettle; for which, as I faw he much affected it,
I wanted much more, but having regard to our
prefent fcarcity, I agreed to take it, provided he
gave me the fame quantity next year, or elfe the
country of *Monacan*, with which bargain both
feemed well contented; but *Powhatan*, with great
guile, ftrove to argue that, being good friends, it
would be better for us to vifit him without arms,
as nought could perfuade his people but that we
were come to invade them, and he added, " Think
you I am fo fimple as not to know that it is better
to eat good meat, lie well, and fleep quietly with
my women and children, laugh and be merry with
you, have copper, hatchets, or whatever I want,
being your friend, than be forced to fly from all,
to lie cold in the woods, feed upon acorns, roots,
and fuch trafh, and be fo hunted by you that I
can neither reft, eat, or fleep; but my tired men
muft watch, and if a twig but break, every one
crieth, ' There cometh Captain *Smith* ;' then muft
I fly, I know not whither; and thus with miferable
able fear end my miferable life, leaving my
pleafures to fuch youths as you."

Herein *Powhatan* fhowed his fubtlety, but I
replied to him that had we intended him any hurt,
we could have effected it long ere this; that his

people coming to *James Town* were entertained
with their bows and arrows without any exception,
we efteeming it with them, as with us, to wear their
arms as their apparel. And I added, that I feared no
threats of withholding provifion, for we had a rule
by which we could find it without his knowledge.

Many other difcourfes of the like fort did we
have together, and at laft we began to trade.
But I would order things fomewhat after my own
fafhion, and not altogether as *Powhatan* liked,
fo that he foon began to perceive that his will
would not be admitted as a law, nor would we
difperfe our guard, nor difarm our men; and then,
with a figh, he addreffed me thus: " Captain
Smith, I never treated any Chief fo kindly as
yourfelf, and yet from you I receive the leaft
kindnefs of any. Captain *Newport* gave me
fwords, copper, clothes, a bed, towels, or what I
defired, ever taking what I offered him, and would
fend away his guns when I entreated him. Captain
Newport you call father, and fo you call me, but
I fee that in fpite of us both, you will do what
you lift, and we muft both feek to content you.
But, if you intend fo friendly as you fay, fend
hence your arms, that I may believe you, for the
love I bear you doth caufe me thus nakedly to
forget myfelf."

But I could plainly fee what *Powhatan's* object

was, namely, but to trifle away the time, so that he might securely cut our throats; so I got some of the savages to break the ice, so that my boat might come to fetch both the corn and myself, and I also gave orders for more men to come on shore, for indeed I did mean to surprise the King, and in the meanwhile to keep him from suspicion. I dissembled with him, beguiling him after this manner : " *Powhatan*, you must know, as I have but one God, I honour but one King ; and I live not here as your subject, but as your friend, to pleasure you with what I can. By the gifts you bestow on me, you gain more than by trade ; yet, would you visit me as I do you, you should know it is not our custom to sell our courtesies as a vendible commodity. Bring all your country-men with you for your guard, I will not dislike it as being over jealous. But, to content you, to-morrow I will leave my arms, and trust to your promise. I call you father, indeed, and as a father you shall see I will love you, but the small care you have of such a child caused my men to persuade me to look to myself."

This crafty savage, however, was but speaking and acting falsely all the time, and took the opportunity, whilst the ice was being broken, and before I could receive any reinforcements, to flee with all his women, children, and luggage. Yet, to avoid fufpicion, did he leave two or three of the women talking with me, fo that I might hear nought of their removal, until they had gotten far away, and his men had fecretly furrounded and befet the houfe. I found, however, that fome-thing unufual was afoot, and feizing my piftol, fword, and target, I very foon cleared a road for myfelf among thofe naked devils. At the very firft fhot thofe next to me tumbled one over another, and the reft quickly fled, fome one way, fome another; fo that without any hurt, and only accompanied by *John Ruffell*, I reached the main guard.

When the favages perceived that I fo eafily efcaped, and that I and my eighteen men (for I had no more) cared nought for them, they ufed the uttermoft of their fkill to make excufes, and diffemble the matter, and *Powhatan*, to excufe his flight, and the fudden coming of this multitude, fent me a great bracelet and a chain of pearls, which were brought by an old man, who made an oration to this effect: "Captain *Smith*, our chief is fled, fearing your guns; and knowing that when the ice was broken, there would come more men, he has fent this number of men to guard his corn from being ftolen, which might happen without your knowledge. Now, although fome of them be hurt by you, yet *Powhatan* is your friend, and fo will for ever continue. Since the ice is open, he would have you fend away your corn, and, if you would have his company, fend away alfo your guns, which fo affright his people, that they dare not come to you, as he promifed they fhould."

Then, having provided bafkets for our men to carry our corn to the boats, they kindly offered their fervices to guard our arms, that none fhould fteal them. There were a great many of them, and moft of them goodly, well-proportioned fellows, as grim as fiends, yet were they fo timid at the very fight of our cocking our matches and preparing to let fly, that a very few words caufed them to leave their bows and arrows in our keeping, and carry down our corn upon their backs; and they did this with fuch a will, that we needed not to importune them to make difpatch, they did fo earneftly want to fee our backs. But we could not gratify them in this matter as fpeedily as they wifhed, for, it being ebb tide, our barges were left on the ooze, and we were obliged to ftay till the next high water, fo that we returned again to our old quarters.

CHAPTER XVI.

IN the meantime, *Powhatan*, and the Dutchmen I had lent him, were burfting to have my head, for they thought, furely, could they but kill me, all would be theirs, and they neglected no opportunity to effect their purpofe. And the Indians craftily kept up a femblance of friendfhip, and, with all the merry fports they could devife, fpent the time till night; but then they all returned to *Powhatan*, who, all this time, was making ready his forces with intent to furprife the houfe, and all of us, while we were at fupper. Notwithftanding, the eternal, all-feeing God did prevent him, and by a ftrange means, for *Pocahontas*, the King's deareft jewel and daughter, who beforetimes had faved my life, in that dark night came through the irkfome woods, and told me of all their deceitful plots. How that *Powhatan* would fend us great cheer for our fuppers, by and by; but that he, and all the power he could affemble, would afterwards come and kill us all, if they that brought us the food could not kill us with our own weapons while we were at fupper. Therefore, this dear little maid weepingly begged me prefently to begone, did we wifh to live. I thanked her for her kindnefs, and would fain have given her fuch things as fhe

delighted in ; but, with the tears running down her
cheeks, fhe faid fhe muft not take them, and durft
not be feen to have any of them, for, if *Powhatan*
fhould know it, fhe were but dead ; and fo
fuddenly fhe left me, and ran away by herfelf as fhe
came.

Things fell out even as fhe had faid, for within
lefs than an hour came eight or ten lufty fellows,
with great platters of venifon and other victual,
and they were very importunate to have us put out
our matches (for, being forewarned, we were fore-
armed, and kept our guns in readinefs) faying that
the fmoke from them made them fick, and they
much preffed us to fit down to our victual.   But I,
knowing their fubtlety, made them tafte of every
difh, left it fhould contain poifon, and when they had
done fo, I fent fome of them back to *Powhatan* to
bid him make hafte and attack us, for I was prepared for his coming ; and, as for them, I told them
I knew they came to betray me at fupper, but I
would take care to fruftrate all their other intended
villanies, fo they might take themfelves off and be
gone.   They departed, but not long after came more
meffengers to fee what news, and not long after them
came others.   Thus we fpent the night as vigilantly
as they, till it was high water, yet we feigned, and
did feem to be friendly to the favages, as they to us ;
and to fhow that I was defirous to give *Powhatan*

content, I did leave him *Edward Brynton* to kill him fowl, and the Dutchmen to finifh his houfe; but at the fame time I thought I would vifit *Pamaunkee*, and would return here after the froft was gone, when I might find a better opportunity, if neceffity did occafion it. But I little dreamed of the Dutchmen's treachery, of which you fhall hear.

We had no fooner fet fail than *Powhatan* returned, and he forthwith fent *Adam* and *Francis* (two ftout Dutchmen) to *James Town*. At their coming thither they feigned to Captain *Winne* that all was well, and that I had need of their arms, and was ufing them, wherefore they afked for new ones, which were given them. They alfo told him that the reafon of their coming was for fome more tools and fhift of apparel. Then they went among fome of their confederates in the Fort, fuch expert thieves that they prefently furnifhed them with a great many fwords, pike-heads, guns, fhot, powder, and fuchlike; favages they had at hand to carry the ftolen goods away, and the next day they returned unfufpected, leaving their confederates to follow them at their convenience, and in the interim to convey to them fuch things as they could; for doing which fervice they promifed they fhould live with *Powhatan* as his dear friends, free from thofe miferies which were fure to happen to the Colony. *Powhatan* kept *Samuel*, the other Dutchman, as a hoftage, and kept him hard at work as a blackfmith, and fuch was his diligence that he made three hundred of their kind of hatchets ; and the other two Dutchmen got, in all, fifty fwords, eight guns, and eight pikes. *Brynton* and *Richard Savage*, feeing the Dutchmen fo diligent to accommodate the favages with weapons, attempted to leave the country, and reach *James Town*, but they were apprehended, and expected every moment to be put to death.

It took us but two or three days to reach *Pamaunkee*, and when we had got there, the King entertained us as many days with feafting and much mirth ; and on the day appointed to begin our trade, I, accompanied by Lieutenant *Percie*, Mr. *Weft*, and thirteen others, went up to *Opechancanough's* houfe, which was about a quarter of a mile from the river ; but, to our great furprife, we found no one there but a lame fellow, and a boy ; and all the houfes round about abandoned. However, we ftayed not long ere the King arrived, and after him came divers of his people armed with bows and arrows. But they brought little or no corn with them, and even that they efteemed at fuch a coft that I had to addrefs the King in this manner :

" *Opechancanough*, the great love you profefs with your tongue feems mere deceit by your actions.

Laſt year you kindly freighted our ſhip, but now you have invited me to ſtarve with hunger. You know my want, and I your plenty; of which, by ſome means, I muſt have part : remember, it is fit for kings to keep their promiſe. Here are my commodities, whereof take your choice; the reſt I will proportion fit bargains for your people."

The King ſeemed kindly to accept this offer, and, the better to colour his project, promiſed that the next day, he would come with a greater company, better provided. I committed the charge of the barges and the pinnace to Mr. *Phetiplace ;* and I with my little band of fifteen marched up to the King's house, where we found four or five men newly arrived, each with a great baſket. Not long after came the King, who with a ſtrained cheerfulneſs held us in diſcourſe, dwelling much upon the pains he had taken to keep his promiſe. Suddenly, in ruſhed Mr. *Ruſſell,* crying out that we were all betrayed. And ſo it proved ; for, at leaſt ſeven hundred ſavages, well armed, had environed the houſe, and were in the fields round about. The King evidently gueſſed what *Ruſſell* had ſaid, as we could well perceive by his geſtures and behaviour.

Some of our company, too, ſeemed to be greatly diſmayed, ſo to encourage them, I made a ſpeech to the following effect : " Worthy countrymen, were the mischiefs of my seeming friends no more than the danger of these enemies, I little care were there as many more, did you dare do but as I. But this is my torment ; that if I escape them, our malicious Council, with their open-mouthed minions, will make me such a peace-breaker (in their opinions in *England*) as will break my neck. I would wish those here, that make these seem saints, and me an oppressor. But this is the worst of all, wherein I pray you aid me with your opinions. Should we begin with them, and surprise the King, we cannot keep him and defend well ourselves. If we should each kill our man, and so proceed with all in the house, the rest will all fly ; then shall we get no more than the bodies that are slain, and so starve for victual. As for their fury, it is the least danger, for well you know, being alone, and assaulted by two or three hundred of them, I made them, by the help of God, compound to save my life. And we are sixteen, and they are but seven hundred at the most ; and assure yourselves, God will so assist us, that if you dare stand but to discharge your pieces, the very smoke will be sufficient to affright them. Yet, howsoever, let us fight like men, and not die like sheep : for by that means you know God hath oft delivered me, and so I trust will now. But first, I will deal with them, to bring it to pass that we may fight for fomething, and draw them to it by conditions. If you like this notion, promife me you will be valiant."

It was lucky that time did not permit any argument or debate upon my fpeech, the neceffity for prefent action being manifeft, fo all vowed to execute whatever I fhould attempt, or die. Whereupon, in plain terms, I thus addreffed the King: "I fee, *Opechancanough*, your plot to murder me, but I fear it not. As yet your men and mine have done no harm, but by our direction. Take therefore your arms, you fee mine, my body fhall be as naked as yours: the Ifle in your river is a fit place, if you be contented: and the conqueror, of us two, fhall be lord and mafter over all our men. If you have not enough, take time to fetch more, and bring what number you will: fo every one bring a bafket of corn, againft all which I will ftake the value in copper; you fee I have but fifteen men, and the game at which you and I will play, is the conqueror takes all."

This open challenge was not to the King's tafte, nor was it after their manner, for they are accuftomed to do nothing openly, they can do by craft; and here, had I not been on the alert, they might have fucceeded. For the King, who was guarded by fifty or fixty of his chief men, feemed to wifh to appeafe my fufpicion of unkindnefs, and fpake to

o

me of a great prefent he wifhed to give me, which
was waiting for me at the door. But this feeming
kindnefs was only to draw me out of the door,
where the bait was guarded by at leaft two hundred
men, and thirty under a great tree (that lay athwart
as a barricado) each having his arrow fitted to the
bow-ftring ready to fhoot. I commanded one of
our party, whom I will not name, to go and fee
what manner of deceit they were about to practife,
and to receive the prefent, but he was afraid, and
refufed to go: on which the gentlemen of my
little band, and, indeed, all the reft of them, were
importunate to go, but I would not permit them,
being vexed at that *Coward.* . I commanded
Lieutenant *Percie*, Mafter *Weft*, and the reft to
make good the houfe, and Mafter *Powell*, and
Mafter *Behethland* I told off to guard the door,
and then, being in a great rage, I fnatched .the
King by his long lock, which he wore after their
fafhion, and in the midft of his men, and had my
piftol ready bent againft his cheft. And thus
I led the trembling King, who was near dead with
fear, amongft all his people, and there he delivered
up to me his vambrace, bow, and arrows, after
which it was but a fmall matter to get all his men
to throw down their arms, they being utterly
aftounded, little dreaming that any one durft, in
that manner, have ufed their King, who, to efcape,

beftowed his prefents with good earneft, albeit
with fadnefs. Then I caufed a great number to
come before me unarmed, and, ftill holding the

C. Smith taketh the King of Pamaunkee prifoner 1603

King by the hair of his head, I fpake to them to
this effect:

"I fee (you *Pamaunkees*) the great defire you

have to kill me, and my long fuffering your injuries 'ath emboldened you to this prefumption. The reafon why I have forborne your infolencies, is the promife I made you (before the God I ferve) to be your friend, till you give me juft caufe to be your enemy. If I keep my vow, my God will keep me; you cannot hurt me; if I break it, He will deftroy me. But if you fhoot but one arrow, or fhed but one drop of blood of any of my men, or fteal the leaft of thefe beads or copper, I fpurn you here before me with my foot. You fhall fee I will not ceafe revenge (if once I begin), fo long as I can hear where to find one of your nation that will not deny the name of *Pamaunk.* I am not now at *Raffaweak,* half drowned with mire, where you took me prifoner; yet then, for your keeping your promife, and your good ufage and faving my life, I fo affect you, that your denials of treachery do half perfuade me to miftake myfelf. But if *I* be the mark you aim at, here I am; fhoot he that dare. You promifed to freight my fhip ere I departed, and fo you fhall, or I mean to load her with your dead carcafes; yet, if as friends you will come and trade, I once more promife not to trouble you, except you give me the firft occafion, and your King fhall be free and be my friend, for I am not come to hurt him or any of you."

Upon this, away went their bows and arrows, and men, women, and children brought in their commodities. For two or three hours they fo thronged about me, that they over-wearied me, fo that I retired to reft, leaving Mafter *Behethland* and Mafter *Powell* to receive their prefents ; and now mark the treachery of thefe favages, for fome of them perceiving me faft afleep, and the guard fomewhat careleffly difpofed, about forty or fifty of their chief men, armed either with a club or an Englifh fword, began to enter the houfe, followed by two or three hundred others, who preffed to fecond them. The noife and hafte they made did fo fhake the houfe, that they awoke me from my fleep, and being amazed at this fudden fight, I ftraightway betook myfelf to my fword and target. Mafter *Crafhaw* and fome foldiers came at that moment to my affiftance, and charged them in like manner, whereat they thronged fafter backward than before they did forward. Having cleared the houfe of them, it was not long before the King, who was aware that his treacherous plan had failed, came with fome of his chiefs, and with long oration tried to excufe the intrufion. It was the beft policy for me to pretend to believe him, and fo I did, and the reft of the day was fpent with much kindnefs, the Indians again renewing their prefents with their beft provifions,

and whatfoever I gave them they feemed there-
with well contented.

———

CHAPTER XVII.

NOW in the meantime, after our departure, a
great event happened at the Fort, which was
this : Mafter *Scrivener*, whom I ever regarded as
myfelf, having received letters from *England*,
telling him to make himfelf either Cæfar or
nothing, began to decline in his affection for me,
and would fain have croffed my defire to furprife
Powhatan. A few days after my departure, he
would needs go vifit the *Ifle of Hogs*, and took
with him Captain *Waldo* (although I had efpecially
appointed him to come to my affiftance in cafe of
need,) together with Mafter *Anthony Gofnoll* and
eight others ; but fo violent was the wind, for it
was then the depth of winter, and an extremely
frozen time, that the boat fank, but where, or how,
none ever knew ; the fkiff was much over-laden,
and could fcarce have lived had fhe been empty,
in fuch an extreme tempeft, but he could be
diverted of no perfuafion, although *Waldo* and an
hundred others thought how it would turn out.
Their bodies were firft found by the favages, and it
greatly encouraged them in their conduct toward us

in after-time. It was needful that I fhould know
of this mifhap, but although all were aware of its
neceffity, none could be found to undertake it, the
journey being refufed by all in the Fort, fave only
Mafter *Richard Wyffin*, and he alone undertook
the performance thereof.

In his journey to meet me, he was encountered
with many dangers and difficulties in all parts, as
he went on his way ; and on the night he lodged
with *Powhatan*, he perceived fuch preparations
for war, that, not finding me there, he did affure
himfelf that fome mifchief was intended. *Pocahontas* hid him for a time, and fent thofe that
purfued him the clean contrary way to feek him,
and by her means, by extraordinary bribes, and
much trouble, after three days' travel, he found us
at length, when we were in the midft of thefe
turmoils. Knowing the effect this unhappy news
would have upon our men, I fwore him to conceal
it from the company, and I diffembled my forrow
with the beft countenance I could, and when the
night approached, I went fafely aboard with all
my foldiers, leaving *Opechancanough* at liberty,
as I had promifed, and then went to vifit *Powhatan*.

Now *Powhatan* had breathed forth fire and
fury, and had fo extremely threatened his men
with death if they did not kill me, that the next

day they appointed that all the country fhould come to trade unarmed; yet even thefe poor favages were unwilling to be treacherous, fave that they were fo conftrained, hating fighting with me as much as they did hanging—fuch fear had they of good fuccefs. The next morning the fun had not long appeared before the fields appeared covered with people carrying bafkets to tempt us on fhore, but they would not trade nor fell us anything except that I was prefent; feeing which, I would not go afhore, or, if fo, it would be be in company of fome well armed, and they could not endure the fight of a gun.

Failing to lure me afhore, they began to depart, which when I faw, being unwilling to lofe fo great a booty, I made moft of the men in the pinnace and the barges hide themfelves, as an ambufcado, and only accompanied by Lieutenant *Percie*, Mafter *Weft*, and Mafter *Ruffell*, all well armed, I went on fhore; and others I appointed to receive what was brought, but they were unarmed. The favages came down in large numbers, and, knowing that I could ufe the bank of the river as a trench, I drew them well within reach of my ambufcado. As I was not to be perfuaded to vifit the King, he, know-ing the moft of us to be unarmed, came to vifit me with two or three hundred men, in the form of two half-moons, and with fome twenty men, and many

women, with painted baſkets. But when they
approached ſomewhat near us, their women and
children fled, for when they had thus environed
us, they thought their purpoſe ſure, yet they ſo
trembled with fear, that they were ſcarce able to
fit their arrows to their bow-ſtrings. There I
ſtood with my three companions, with our guns
ready to fire, looking at them till they were well
in reach of my ambuſcado, who, upon the word
being given, diſcovered themſelves, and we retired
to the barge. Which, when the ſavages perceived,
away they fled, ſhowing the uſe of their heels to
the beſt advantage.

That night I ſent Maſter *Craſhaw* and Maſter
Ford to *James Town* to warn Captain *Winne* how I
was ſituated, and as they journeyed, they met four
or five of the Dutchmen's confederates who had
left the Fort, intending to join *Powhatan*. Theſe
rogues were ſore aſtoniſhed at being thus con-
fronted, and, ſtammering out an excuſe that they
were but roaming about, and to diſarm the ſuſ-
picion of the gentlemen that they intended to run
to the ſavages, they returned to the Fort, and
there continued.

The ſavages hearing our barge go down the
river in the night, were ſo terribly afraid that we
had ſent for more men (we having ſo much threatened their ruin, to burn their houſes, and to de-

ftroy their boats and weirs) that the next day the King fent me a chain of pearls, in order to get me to change my mind and ftop, promifing, although they were fhort of provifions themfelves, to freight our fhip and bring the corn on board, fo that we could have no fufpicion of their conduct. And in . five or fix days after, from all parts of the country within the compafs of ten or twelve miles, although it was extreme froft and fnow, they brought us provifions on their naked backs.

Yet even now muft they needs be treacherous, and, had their fkill been equal to their foul intentions, both I, Mafter *Weft*, and fome others, had been poifoned. As it was, it did but make us fick, and thus expelled itfelf. *Wecuttanow*, a ftout young fellow, knowing he was fufpected of bringing this poifoned prefent, and feeing that I had but a few followers, whilft he had forty or fifty companions, bragged fo proudly about it, as it feemed as though he expected to encounter a revenge. Which, when I perceived, I took him out of the midft of his company, and did not only beat him foundly, but fpurned him like a dog, as if I fcorned to do him any worfe mifchief. Whereupon all of them fled into the woods, thinking they had done a great matter to have fo well efcaped, and the townfmen remaining, prefently freighted our barge to be rid of our company, making many

excufes for *Wecuttanow* (who was *Powhatan's* fon),
and they told us that if we would fhow them him
that brought the poifon, they would deliver him to
us to punifh as we pleafe.

. Men may think it ftrange that there fhould be
fo great a ftir about a little corn, but had it been
gold, we might more eafily have gotten it,
and had I not obtained it, the Colony would
have ftarved. We may be thought very patient
for enduring all thofe injuries, yet it was only by
frightening them we got all we defired, and all they
had; whereas, had we revenged ourfelves, then by
their lofs, had we been loft. We fearched alfo the
countries of *Youghtanund* and *Mattapannent,* where
the people imparted the little they had, with fuch
complaints, lamentations, and tears from the eyes
of women and children, that there is no man,
calling himfelf a Chriftian, but what would have
been fatisfied and moved with compaffion. But
had this happened in October, November, or
December, we might have freighted a fhip of forty
tons, and twice as much might have been had from
the rivers of *Rapahannock, Patawomek,* and *Paw-
tuxum.*

Still, and this was the main occafion of our thus
temporizing, I wifhed to part friends with them, fo
as to give *Powhatan* the lefs caufe to fly, for I ftill
intended to carry out my plan, and furprife him

and take his ftore of provifion. So we returned by
his way, and, when we came to his town, the better
to effect my purpofe, I fent Mafter *Wyffin* and
Mafter *Coe* afhore to difcover how things were, and
to make way for my intended project. But what
think you? They found thofe curfed, treacherous
Dutchmen had caufed *Powhatan* to abandon his new
houfe, and his town, and carry away all his corn and
provifion; and not only fo, but even the people
were fo ill affected, that they were in great doubt
whether they fhould have efcaped with their lives.
So, finding my intent fruftrated, that there was
nothing now to be had, and that it was an unfit
time to revenge my injuries, I fent one whom I
could truft, Mafter *Michael Phettiplace*, by land to
James Town, whither we failed with all the fpeed
we could. And, indeed, when I came to reckon
up, we had not done badly, for at the coft of only
25 lbs. of copper, and 50 lbs. of iron and beads, we
had got enough provifions to have kept our forty-
fix men for fix weeks, befides giving to every man,
as a reward, a month's provifions over and above.
Yet did we deliver into ftore at *James Town*, after
our arrival, near 200 lbs. weight of deer's fat and
479 bufhels of corn.

After the departure of the fhips, all the provifion in ftore (fave that which I had got) was fo
rotten by reafon of laft fummer's rain, and alfo that

it was eaten by rats and worms, that the hogs
would ſcarce eat it. Yet it was the ſoldiers' diet
until our return, when we found nothing done, ſave
that our victual was ſpent, and that the moſt part
of our tools, and a good part of our arms, had
been conveyed to the ſavages. But when we came
to reckon up our ſtore, I found ſufficient to laſt
till the next harveſt, ſo that we thought no more
of ſtarving, and the company was divided into
tens, fifteens, or ſuch numbers as the buſineſs
required. We ſpent ſix hours a day in work, and
the reſt in paſtime and merry exerciſes, in order
to keep up the ſpirits of our men, but ſtill the
greateſt number were froward, and their untowardneſs cauſed me to addreſs them as followeth :— ·

"Countrymen, the long experience of our late
miſeries, I hope, is ſufficient to perſuade everyone
to a preſent correction of himſelf, and think not
that either my pains, or the Adventurers' purſes, will
ever maintain you in idleneſs and ſloth. I ſpeak
not this to you all, for divers of you, I know,
deſerve both honour and reward. Better, then, is
yet here to be had ; but the greater part muſt be
induſtrious, or ſtarve, no matter however you have
been heretofore tolerated by the authority of the
Council, differently from that I have often commanded you. You ſee now that power reſteth
wholly in myſelf. You muſt obey this now for a

law, that *he that will not work fhall not eat* (except
by ficknefs he be difabled), for the labours of thirty
or forty honeft and induftrious men fhall not be
confumed to maintain an hundred and fifty idle
loiterers. And though you prefume that the authority here is but a fhadow, and that I dare not
touch the lives of any of you, but mine own muft
anfwer for it; the Letters Patent fhall each week
be read to you, whofe contents will tell you the
contrary. I would wifh you, therefore, without
contempt, feek to obferve thofe orders fet down
for there are no more Councillors to protect you,
nor to curb my endeavours. Therefore, he
that offendeth, let him affuredly expect his due
punifhment."

By degrees I got them into better ways, for I
made a lift or table, which was a public memorial,
and eafy of accefs, and for every man to fee, of each
man's deferts, and the amount of work he had done,
in order to encourage the good, and with fhame, to
fpur on the reft to amendment. By this means
many became very induftrious, yet were there more
who, by punifhment, performed their bufinefs,
for all were fo tafked that no excufe could prevail
to deceive me. And yet all this time the Dutchmen's friends and confederates, who were within
the Fort, fo clofely and privately conveyed them
powder, fhot, fwords, and tools, that though we

could find out the defect, we could not find by whom it was taken till too late.

CHAPTER XVIII.

NOW thefe accurfed traitors, the Dutchmen, were not content with fimply robbing us, they plotted to take away my life, as you fhall hear. *Powhatan* kindly entertained them, fo that they might inftruct his favages in the ufe of our arms, and finding their friends and conforts not following them as they expected, in order to find out the caufe, they fent one of their number, named *Francis*, a ftout young fellow, difguifed like a favage, to the *Glafs Houfe*, a place in the woods, near a mile from *James Town;* which place they ufed as a rendezvous for all their unfufpected villany. Well, they got forty men to lie in ambufcado for me, but I no fooner heard of this Dutchman than I fent to apprehend him, but he was gone; yet, to prevent his return to *Powhatan*, I prefently defpatched twenty armed men after him, and I myfelf returned from the *Glafs Houfe* alone.

And here I fell in with another adventure, which had gone nigh to have coft me my life, for as I was walking home alone, mufing on the affairs of the

Colony, I perceived a moft ftrong and ftout favage, the King of *Pafpahegh*, who with many lures and fubtle devices ftrove to entice me into his ambufh, but when he found that all his perfuafions were of none effect, and feeing me all unarmed, fave with my faulchion, he attempted to have fhot me, but this I prevented, by at once grappling with him.

C: Smith takes the King of Pafpahegh prifoner. A° 1609.

But if I prevented him from fhooting me, he alfo hindered me from drawing and ufing my faulchion, fo there was nothing for it but to fairly wreftle for our lives. His great height and ftrength were greatly in his favour, fo that by fheer force he bore me into the river to have drowned me: and in the water did a fearful ftruggle enfue.   More than once I thought that furely I fhould have the worft of it, and fo, in good truth, do I think even now, had it not have been that I got fuch a good hold and fair grip of his throat, that I had near ftrangled the King, and then was able to draw my faulchion, with which I was going to cut off his head, but he begged his life fo pitifully, that I fpared him, and leading him prifoner to *James Town*, had him put in chains.

The Dutchman, ere long, was alfo brought in, and though all this time his villany was fufpected, yet nothing could be abfolutely proved againft him, and he feigned a pretty tale to Captain *Winne*, who, however, could not underftand him rightly, by reafon of his not knowing the language well. The ftory that he told was, that in order to fave their lives, they were obliged to accommodate themfelves to *Powhatan*, and were conftrained by him to teach the favages the ufe of our arms. He complained bitterly of having been detained perforce, and faid he had made this efcape at the hazard of his life, and had not meant to return, but was only walking in the woods to gather walnuts. Yet for all this fair tale, there was fo fmall an appearance of truth in it, and *Pafpahegh* did fo plainly tell us of the man's treachery, that without more ado I laid my knave by the heels.

Now, I was minded to fave the poor favage's life

on condition that my Dutchmen were returned to me, and, truly, the King did his beft towards that end, fending daily meffengers to *Powhatan*, but they one and all returned with the fame ftory, that the Dutchmen would not return, and that *Powhatan* neither ftayed, nor hindered them: yet were they not able to bring them fifty miles on men's backs. I treated *Pafpahegh* with kindnefs, and allowed his wives, children, and other people to come and vifit him. They came laden with prefents, which he liberally beftowed to make his peace. Indeed I think he muft have needs given his guard fomething of more value than ordinary, for they grew negligent and guarded him not aright, fo that although he was fettered, he efcaped. I was away at the time, but Captain *Winne* purfued after him, yet he found fuch troops of favages, who had come to refcue their King, that they hindered his paffage, although they exchanged many volleys of fhot, and flights of arrows.

When I returned to the Fort, I heard of this, and at once took two favages prifoners, called *Kemps* and *Tuffore*, who were the two moft exact villains in all the country. I then fent thefe two in charge of Captain *Winne*, and Lieutenant *Percie*, together with fifty chofen men to revenge the injury; and fo had they done, if they had followed my inftructions, or had been advifed by thofe two villains, whom I

purpofely fent with them ; they would have
betrayed both King and kindred for a piece of
copper. But Captain *Winne* trifled away the
night, and the favages, next morning, at the rifing
of the fun, taunted him, and braved and dared him
to come afhore to fight. Both fides let fly at each
other for a good time, but I heard of no hurt that
happened to either ; all they did was to take two
canoes, burn the King's houfe, and having done
this, they returned to *James Town.*

Now I liked not this child's play, and fearing that
thefe bravados, which came to none effect, would
but encourage the favages, began again myfelf to
try conclufions with them, and killed fome fix or
feven of them, taking as many others prifoners. I
burnt their houfes, took their boats, and all their
fifhing weirs, planting fome of them at *James Town*
for my own ufe, and now I refolved to be in earneft,
and not to ceafe till I had revenged myfelf on all
them that had injured me. In my journey for this
purpofe I paffed by *Pafpahegh* going towards
Chicahomania, and the favages did their beft to
draw me into their ambufcados, and feeing that I
cared not for them, but was difregardingly paffing
by their country, they waxed exceeding courageous,
and fhowed themfelves in their braveft manner.
This was as much as I could ftand, fo to try their
valour, I could not but let fly, and, ere I could land,

they recognifed me, and no fooner did they know me, but they threw down their arms and defired peace. Their orator was a lufty young fellow named *Okaning*, whofe worthy difcourfe deferveth to be remembered. And thus it was :

"Captain *Smith*, my mafter is here prefent in the company, thinking it to be Captain *Winne* (of whom he intended to have been revenged, having never offended him), and not you. If he hath offended you in efcaping your imprifonment, the fifhes fwim, the fowls fly, and the very beafts ftrive to efcape the fnare and line. Then blame not him, being a man. He would entreat you to remember, you being a prifoner, what pains he took to fave your life. If, fince, he hath injured you, he was conftrained to it: but, howfoever, you have revenged it with our too great lofs. We perceive, and well know, how you intend to deftroy *us*, that are here to entreat and defire your friend-fhip, and to enjoy our houfes, and plant our fields, of whofe fruit you fhall participate; for we can plant anywhere, though with more labour, and we know you cannot live, if you want our harveft, and that relief we bring you. If you promife us peace, we will believe you; if you proceed in revenge, we will abandon the country."

Upon thefe terms I promifed them peace, till they did us an injury, upon condition they should bring in provision. Thus we all departed good friends, and so we continued till I left the country. This shows pretty plainly the proper course to be pursued towards savages : to suffer no injury from them, but to repay it, and then from fearing, they will get to love you.

And now, after all this severity and slaughter I must needs tell you of a somewhat laughable thing that happened after my return to *James Town*, by which you will see what simple folk these savages were. When I returned, complaint was made to me that the Indians of *Chickahomania*, who all this while traded with us and seemed our friends, were, under colour thereof, only thieves. Amongst other things, a pistol had been stolen, and the thief had fled, so two proper young fellows, that were brothers, and who were known to be his confederates, were apprehended. Now in order to regain this pistol, one of them was imprisoned, and kept as a hostage, whilst the other was let loose, and sent to return the pistol again within twelve hours, or his brother would be hanged.

I pitied the poor naked savage in his cold, damp dungeon, and sent him some victual, and some charcoal for a fire. Ere midnight came, his brother returned with the pistol, and then we went together to see the prisoner, but, to my grievous horror, I found the poor savage so smothered and fuffocated by the fmoke of the charcoal, that he lay on the floor of the dungeon as if he were dead, befides which he was piteoufly burnt by reafon of falling into the fire. The other moft lamentably bewailed his death, and broke forth into fuch bitter agonies that I, to quiet him, told him that, if hereafter they would not fteal, I would bring him to life again, yet little thought I, he could be recovered. Yet we did our beft with aqua vitæ and vinegar, and at length it pleafed God to reftore him again to life, but fo drunk and affrighted that he feemed lunatic, the which as much tormented and grieved the other, as before to fee him dead.

However, upon folemn promife of their good behaviour, I promifed to recover him of his malady ; and directed he fhould be laid by a fire to fleep, and in the morning, having well flept, he recovered his perfect fenfes. His wounds from the burning then having been dreffed, and each a piece of copper given them, they went away fo well contented that it was fpread among all the favages for a miracle, that Captain *Smith* could make a man alive that was dead.

Another ftory will fhow their fimplicity. An ingenious favage, one of *Powhatan's* tribe, having gotten a great bag of powder, and a foldier's iron back-plate, was at *Werowocomoco*, amongft a many of his companions, and, to fhow his extraordinary

fkill, he did dry it over the fire in the iron back-
plate, as he had feen the foldiers do at *James Town.*
But he dried it too long, and whilft fome of his
friends were peeping over it to fee his fkill, it took
fire, and blew him and one or two more to death,
and fo fcorched the reft that they had little pleafure
to meddle any more with powder.

Thefe and many other fuch pretty accidents, fo
amazed and affrighted both *Powhatan* and all his
people, that from all parts, with prefents, they
defired peace ; returning many ftolen things which
we never demanded, nor thought of ; yea, fuch good
effect had they, that they made rogues ingrain,
honeft men, for after they happened, thofe who
were taken ftealing, were fent back, both by
Powhatan and his people, to *James Town,* to receive
whatever punifhment might be adjudged them.
And fo all the country became quiet, and abfolutely
as free for us as for the favages themfelves.

CHAPTER XIX.

NOW were we able greatly to follow our bufinefs, and every man was fet his tafk, and
having, as we thought, plenty of food, all worked
with a will, fo that in three months' time, we had
made three or four lafts* of tar, pitch, and foap
afhes; had made an effay, and produced fome glafs,
dug a well in the Fort, which yielded us excellent
fweet water, which till then was wanting; built fome
twenty houfes; put a frefh roof on to our church,
provided nets and weirs for fifhing; and to put a
ftop to the rafcality of our diforderly thieves, and
alfo as a check upon the favages, I had a block-
houfe built in the neck of our Ifle, and kept by a
garrifon, who regulated the trade with the favages,
and none were allowed to pafs, either Chriftian or
native, without an order from me. We digged
and planted fome thirty or forty acres of land, and
all went well with us. Yea, even our live ftock
increafed to marvel, for our three fows, in
eighteen months, had come to number 60 odd pigs,
and we had near 500 chickens, who gave us no
trouble, but found their own living and brought
themfelves up; but the hogs we tranfported to

---

* A laft is a corn meafure of ten quarters.

Hog Ifland, where alfo we built a block-houfe, with a garrifon, whofe duty it was to give us timely notice of any fhipping, and their fpare time was employed in making clap-board and wainfcot, and cutting down trees.   We alfo built a fort for a retreat, near a convenient river upon a high commanding hill, very hard to be affaulted and eafy to be defended, but ere it could be finifhed, fomething happened which caufed the work to be ftayed.

Which was none other than this.   In going over our ftores of cafked corn, we found it half rotten, and the reft confumed by thoufands of rats (which had fo increafed from thofe left by the fhip, that their numbers were incredible), that we knew not how to keep the little we had got left.   This did drive us all to our wits' ends, for there was nothing in the country but what nature afforded.   Until this time we had kept the two roguifh Indians *Kemps* and *Tuffore* as fettered prifoners, and made them do double tafks, and teach us how to order and plant our fields ; but now, for want of victual, we were fain to fet them at liberty, but, marvellous to fay, they fo liked our company, that they did not defire to go from us.   And the country people round about, to teftify their love for us, did, for fixteen days' continuance, bring us, at the very leaft, 100 a day of fquirrels, turkeys, deer, and other wild beafts.   But this want of corn put a

ftop to all our works, it being work enough to
fupply ourfelves with victual.

I fent 60 or 80 men under Enfign *Laxon* down
the river, to live upon oyfters, and twenty under
Lieutenant *Percie* to try for fifhing at *Point Comfort;* but they did no good, for in fix weeks they
did not once caft out the net, for *Percie* was fick,
having been forely burnt by gunpowder. Mafter
Weft with twenty men went up to the Falls, but
found nothing but a few acorns; whilft of what
we had in ftore, every man had an equal fhare.
_Till this prefent time, the Colony had been fed by
the exertions of fome thirty or forty of us; but
now each man had to work hard to get victual.
_Fortunately we caught more fturgeon than man or
dog could devour, and the induftrious amongft us
dried and pounded it, mixing it with caviar, and
with forrel and other wholefome herbs, fo that it
made a good food in the place of bread and meat.

Others would gather as much *Tockwogh* roots
in a day as would make them bread to laft a week.
This root is the chief food of the favages, and it
groweth like a flag in marfhy places. The roots
are of the greatnefs and tafte of potatoes. And
the manner the Indians prepare it for food is as
follows. They cover a great many of them with
oak leaves and fern, and then cover all with earth,
after the manner of a coal pit; on this they burn a

great fire for twenty-four hours before they dare eat it. Raw, it is no better than poifon, and even if roafted, except it be tender and thoroughly cooked, or fliced and dried in the fun, mixed with forrel and meal or fuch like, it will prickle and torment the throat extremely, and yet in fummer they ufe this ordinarily for bread. So that what with this provifion, and the wild fruits we could obtain, and what we caught, we lived very well, having regard to fuch a diet.

You would think that in fuch a ftate of things all would have turned to, with a will, to procure victual, but fuch was the ftrange condition of some 150 of our company, that had they not been forced, *nolens, volens,* to gather and prepare their victual, they would have all ftarved, or have eaten one another. Yea, thefe diftracted, gluttonous loiterers would, had I not have ftopped it, and ftrictly forbidden it, have fold not only our kettles, hoes, tools, and iron, but fwords, guns, and the very ordnance and houfes, if they could only have been fed and been idle. They would have given the favages all they had for the fruits they did bring in; efpecially for one bafket of corn which they heard of as being at *Powhatan's,* fifty miles from our Fort. Though I bought near half of it to fatisfy their humours, yet to have had the other half they would have fold their fouls, though it

would not have been fufficient to have kept them
for a week. Perpetually were they worrying me,
and thoufands were the fuggeftions and devices, to
get me to abandon the country. I was conftrained,
through want, to endure their amazing follies,
until I found out the author, one *Dyer*, a moft
crafty fellow, and my ancient maligner, whom I
worthily punifhed, and then I argued the cafe with
the reft in this manner :

" Fellow foldiers, I did little think any fo falfe
to report, or fo many to be fo fimple to be perfuaded, that I either intend to ftarve you, or that
Powhatan at this prefent hath corn for himfelf,
much lefs for you ; or that I would not have it, if
I knew where it was to be had. Neither did I
think any fo malicious, as I now fee a great many ;
yet it fhall not fo paffionate me, but that I will do
my beft for my worft maligner. But dream no
longer of this vain hope from *Powhatan*, not that
I will longer forbear to force you, from your idlenefs, and punifh you if you rail. But if I find
any more runners for *Newfoundland* with the
pinnace, let him affuredly look to arrive at the
gallows. You cannot deny but that by the hazard
of my life, many a time I have faved yours, when
(if your own wills had prevailed) you would have
ftarved : and will do ftill, whether I will or not ;
but I proteft by that God that made me, fince

neceffity hath not power to force you to gather for yourfelves, thofe fruits the earth doth yield, you fhall not only gather for yourfelves, but thofe that are fick. As I never yet had more from the ftore than the worft of you, and all my Englifh extraordinary provifion that I have, you fhall fee me divide among the fick. And the rough food you fo fcornfully repine at, when it is put into your mouths, your ftomachs can digeft it ; if you would have better you fhould have brought it. Now, therefore, I will take a courfe by which you fhall provide what is to be had. The fick fhall not ftarve, but equally fhare of all our labours ; and he that gathereth not every day as much as I do, the next day fhall be fent beyond the river, and be banifhed from the Fort as a drone, till he amend his conditions, or ftarve."

Many murmured at this order as being very cruel, but it caufed the greater part fo well to beftir themfelves, that of 200, which was the total number of us (except they were drowned), there died not over feven : for Captain *Winne* and Mafter *Leigh*, they were dead ere this want happened, and the reft died not for want of that which preferved the others. Many I billeted amongft the favages, whereby we got the knowledge of all their paffages, fields, and habitations, and how to gather and ufe their fruits as well as themfelves ;

for they did know we had fuch a commanding power at *James Town* that they durft not wrong us of a pin.

As a fact, thofe poor favages that were thus billeted, ufed our men fo well, that divers of our foldiers ran away to fearch for *Kemps* and *Tuffore*, our old prifoners. Glad were thefe favages to have fuch an opportunity to teftify their love unto us, for when they came unto them, inftead of entertaining them, and fuch things as they had ftolen, with all their great offers, and promifes to revenge their injuries upon me, *Kemps* firft made himfelf fport, by fhowing his countrymen (in their perfons) how he was ufed, girding at them with this law, that thofe who would not work muft not eat, till they were near ftàrved to death, and, befides, they continually threatened to beat them to death ; neither could they get away from him, till that (he and his conforts having fufficiently fported with them) they brought them perforce to me, which well contented me. I fo punifhed them, that many others who alfo intended to follow them, were rather contented to labour at home, than adventure to live idly among the favages (of whom there was more hope to make better Chriftians, and good fubjects, than the one half of thofe that counterfeited themfelves both). For fo afraid were all thofe kings and the better fort of the people to difpleafe us, that fome of the bafer fort that we have extremely hurt and punifhed for their villanies, would beg of us that we fhould not tell it to their kings or countrymen, who would alfo repunifh them, and afterwards return them to *James Town,* to fhow me the teftimony of their love for us.

And now Mafter *Sicklemore,* whom you may remember I fent on an expedition, returned from *Chawwonoke ;* but found little hope and lefs certainty of them who were left by Sir *Walter Raleigh.* His report was that the river was not great, and the people but few, the country moftly overgrown with pines, and here and there did grow ftragglingly, *Pemminaco,* which we call filk grafs. But by the river the ground was good, and exceedingly fertile.

Mafter *Nathaniel Powell* and *Anas Todkill* went in fearch of them, and were conducted to the *Mangoags* to fearch for them there ; but nothing could they learn, fave that they were all dead. The King of the *Mangoags*' was an honeft, proper, promife-keeping king, and of all of them did ever beft affect us ; and though to his falfe gods he was very zealous, yet he would confefs our God as much exceeded his, as our guns did his bows and arrows ; and he would oft-times fend me many prefents, begging of me to pray to my God for rain, or his corn would perifh, for that his own gods were angry. They conducted my embaffage for three days through the woods, into a high country towards the fouth-weft, where they faw here and there a little cornfield, by fome little fpring or fmall brook, but no river could they fee. The people were in all refpects like others, fave in their language; they live moftly upon roots, fruits, and wild beafts, and trade with thofe that live towards the fea and in more fertile countries for dried fifh and corn, whilft they themfelves barter fkins.

Now I never ceafed in my endeavours to recover the fcoundrel Dutchmen, and alfo one *Bentley*, another fugitive, and I thought I was doing well to that intent when I employed one *William Volday*, a *Switzer* by birth, as a go-between; empowering him to ufe promifes of pardon, fo that we might regain them. Little did we then fufpect this double-dyed villain of any treachery, but he plainly taught me the leffon that oft-times where there was the moft truft, there was the greateft treafon; for this wicked hypocrite, who impofed upon me by the feeming hate he bore to the lewd conditions of his curfed countrymen, took advantage of this opportunity of his employment to regain them to convey to them everything they defired to effect their projects, which were to deftroy the Colony; and they would have welcomed even the Spaniard with much devotion, or any other, and intended to do them good fervice if they could only get rid of us.

They took full advantage of the firft opportunity, for, feeing that neceffity had compelled us to difperfe ourfelves, they importuned *Powhatan* to lend them his forces, and they would not only deftroy our hogs, fire our town, and betray our pinnace, but they would bring to his fervice and fubjection the greater part of our company. With this plot they had acquainted many of the difcontented amongft us, and many were agreed to join with them in their devilifh enterprife. But there were thofe of us whofe Chriftian hearts relented at fuch un-Chriftian acts, and *Thomas Doufe* and *Thomas Mallard* voluntarily revealed their plans to me. I caufed them to conceal it, and perfuaded them to continue as if they joined in the plot, only fo to manage things as to bring the irreclaimable Dutchmen and the favages in fuch a manner among the ambufcadoes I would prepare, that not many of them fhould return from our peninfula.

But a rumour of this coming to the ears of the impatient multitude, they importuned me to deal ftraitly with thofe Dutchmen, and many amongft them offered to go and cut their throats before *Powhatan's* face. Of thefe two were Lieutenant *Percie* and Mafter *John Cuderington*, two gentle-

Q

men of as bold, refolute fpirits as could poffibly be found. However, I had occafion of other employ- ment for them, but I allowed Mafter *Wyffin* and Sergeant *Jeffrey Abbot* to go, and ftab, or fhoot them wherever they might be found. They departed, and found the villains with *Powhatan;* but they had fuch oily tongues, and made fuch plaufible excufes, laying all the blame on *Volday,* whom they thought had betrayed them, that *Abbot* was convinced of their innocence, and would do nought againft them, but *Wyffin* was willing, as he could perceive only deceit in them. The King underftanding their miffion, and why they had been fent, prefently fent meffengers to me, to fignify that it was not his fault, he neither detained them, nor hindered the two I had fent from executing my commands; that he did not, nor would he, maintain them, or any one elfe, who gave occafion to my difpleafure.

CHAPTER XX.

BUT whilft this bufinefs was in hand there came a fhip, commanded by one Captain *Argall,* fent by Mafter *Cornelius* to trade with the Colony and fifh for fturgeon. This veffel was well furnifhed with wine and much other good provifions, and though this was not fent to us for our ufe, fave in the way of trade, our neceffities were fuch as enforced us to take it. *Argall* brought us news of a great fupply, and preparation, being made for Lord *De la Warr*, together with letters taxing me with hard dealing with the favages, and not returning the fhips freighted. We kept this fhip till the fleet arrived, by which *Argall* loft a voyage, but we re-victualled him and fent him back to England, with a true relation of the caufes of our fhortcomings, and how impoffible it was to return the wealth they expected, or obferve their inftructions as to enduring the in- folencies of the favages, or, indeed, to do anything to any purpofe, except they would fend us men and means by which we could produce that they fo much defired, otherwife all they did was loft, and the whole could not but come to confufion.

I diffembled, and took no public note of the villany of *Volday*, and one of the Dutchmen named *Adam* returned and came home, relying on his promife of pardon, but *Samuel* ftill ftayed with *Powhatan*, thinking to hear fome news he could avail himfelf of when that the fleet fhould arrive. However, I knew all their plots, and cared not for them, for all furrounding people were friendly with me, and feared me more than *Powhatan*, and many of them, for the love they bore me, would have done anything I would have had them, had any commotion happened, though the fugitives had done all they could to perfuade *Powhatan* that King *James* would kill me for ufing him and his people fo unkindly.

Not knowing the truth, and being led away by the falfe reports of the difaffected, the Treafurer, Council, and Company of *Virginia*, not finding that return and profit from their adventure that they expected, and that thofe who were in the Colony, not having the means to fubfift of themfelves, were but a drag on them, they moved his Majefty to call in their commiffion, and iffue a new one. This was done; the old commiffion was annihilated, and a new one was made in which Sir *Thomas Weft*, Lord *De la Warr*, was to be General of *Virginia*, Sir *Thomas Gates*, his Lieutenant; Sir *George Somers*, Admiral; Sir *Thomas Dale*, High Marfhall; Sir *Ferdinando Wainman*, General of the Horfe; and other offices to many other worthy gentlemen, for their lives (though not any of them had ever been in *Virginia* excepting Captain *Newport*, who was alfo by Patent made Vice-Admiral). Thefe noble gentlemen brought in fuch great fums of money that they fent Sir *Thomas Gates*, Sir *George Somers*, and Captain *Newport*, with nine fhips, and five hundred men. Each of thefe captains carried a copy of this new commiffion, to the intent that whofoever fhould firft arrive, fhould call in the old, without the knowledge or confent of thofe who had borne all the brunt of the work, and prepared the way for them; and, indeed, no regard whatever was paid to us.

All things were ready, and the fhips fet fail from *England* in May, 1609. But, curioufly enough, thofe three captains quarrelled for place and precedency, fo that to end the matter, they concluded that they fhould all go in one fhip, which was called the *Sea Venture*. A hurricane came on, in which a fmall Catch perifhed, and the *Sea Venture*, with an hundred and fifty men, the three captains, and their new commiffions, their bills of lading, with all manner of directions, and the moft part of their provifions on board, was a miffing. But feven fhips arrived fafely, and amongft them that they brought, were my old friends *Ratliffe* (whofe true name was *Sicklemore*), *Martin*, and *Archer*, befides many worthy gentlemen of good means and great parentage. Thefe three, however, as you may well imagine, bore me no love. I had fent them to *England*, and, as they were now returning, they made ufe of the voyage to poifon all men's minds againft me, fo that the moft part mortally hated me, ere ever they faw me.

My fcouts having informed me of this fleet being in fight, I, little dreaming of any fuch fupply, fuppofed them to be Spaniards, and I foon fo put things in order, that I little feared their arrival, nor the fuccefs of our encounter; nay, even the favages were not negligent, on their parts, to aid and affift us to the beft of their power. Had it have been the Spaniard, it would have been better for us all, for we fhould not have trufted him, but treated him as a foe; whereas, when we found out who they were, we received them as friends and country-men, which they repaid by doing all in their power to murder me, furprife the ftore, the Fort, and our lodgings, to ufurp the government, and make us all their fervants and flaves. To a thoufand mif-chiefs did thofe three, *Ratliffe, Martin,* and *Archer,* lead this lewd company, wherein were many unruly gallants, packed thither by their friends to efcape ill deftinies, and thofe would difpofe and determine of the government, fometimes to one, the next day to another; to-day the old commiffion muft rule, to-morrow the new, the next day neither; in fine, they would rule all, or ruin all. Happy had we been had they never arrived, and we for ever abandoned, and, as it were, left to our fortunes; for on earth, taking the number of us, was never more confufion, or mifery, than their factions occafioned.

Now I, feeing the defire that thefe bravos had to rule, and how my authority was fo unexpectedly changed, would willingly have left all and have returned to *England:* but, feeing alfo that there was ſmall hope that this new commiſſion would arrive, (for there had been a hurricane ſuch as ſeldom hath been ſeen) I would no longer ſuffer theſe factious ſpirits to have things their own way. It would be tedious for you to hear of the infinite dangers, plots, and practices I daily eſcaped among this unruly crew, but this I will ſay, that I took [ſuch order, as quickly laid the chief of them by the heels, till my leiſure better ſerved to do them juſtice. Maſter *Percie*, being very ſick, had his requeſt granted to return to *England*; I ſent *Weſt*, with a hundred and twenty of the beſt he could chooſe, to the Falls, at the top of our river, there to ſettle, and *Martin* with near as many to *Nandſamund*, which was on the oppoſite ſide of the river, and both companies had their due proportion of all proviſions according to their numbers.

Before they went, however, my year as Preſident being near expired, I made Captain *Martin* Preſident, in order to follow the order by which a Preſident ſhould be elected every year. But he, being fully aware of his own inſufficiency to fill that poſt, and knowing full well the untowardneſs of the company, and their little regard for him, within three hours afterwards reſigned it to me, and I took up the weary burden once more, only becauſe I felt that there was no one elſe with ſo ſtrong a hand, which was needful, nor with ſo good a knowledge of the favages and their ways ; and fo *Martin* went on his way to *Nandfamund.*

But he managed things there very badly; the people there being friendly to us, and having to give us a certain quantity of corn yearly as a contribution, ufed him kindly ; yet fuch was his foolifh, jealous fear, that in the midft of their rejoicing and mirth, he did furprife this poor naked king, with his monuments, houfes, and the ifle he inhabited, and there fortified himfelf. Yet, being but a poor, weak creature, and fhowing fo openly that he was diftracted with fear, he emboldened the favages to affault him, kill his men, releafe their king, and gather and carry away a thoufand bufhels of corn, he not offering once to interrupt them ; but, inftead, fent whining to me (who was then at the Falls) for thirty good fhots, which were immediately fent him from *James Town.* And when he had them, he fo well employed them that they did juft nothing, but returned again, complaining bitterly of his tendernefs : and he came away with them to *James Town*, leaving his company to their fortunes.

Yet the men he had with him were of good ftuff, for I may tell you as an inftance, that one, *George Forreft*, who was a man of great courage, and had fought well, had feventeen arrows fticking into him, and one fhot through him, yet lived he fix or feven days, as if he had fmall hurt, but then, fad to tell, for want of chirurgery he died.

CHAPTER XXI.

I TOLD you how that I fent Mafter *Weft* up to the Falls, there to found a fettlement; he did fo, and prefently returned to *James Town.* I had my mifgivings, and quickly followed him, after his firft ftart, to fee how the company fared, and, on my way thither, I met him, which made me wonder at his fo quick return. I went on, and found his company planted moft inconfiderately, in a place not only fubject to the river's inundation, but all round environed with many intolerable inconveniences. For remedy whereof, I prefently fent to *Powhatan* to fell me the place called *Powhatan,* promifing to defend him againft the *Monacans.* And I offered him thefe conditions, that he and his people fhould refign me the Fort and houfes, and all that country for a proportion of copper; that all ftealing offenders fhould be fent to me to receive their punifhment; that every houfe fhould pay as a cuftom a bufhel of corn for an inch fquare of copper, and a certain quantity of *Pocones** as a yearly tribute to

---

* Pocones is a fmall root which groweth in the mountains, which, being dried and beat in powder, turneth red. And

King *James* for their protection as a duty; and what other commodities they could fpare, they were to barter at their beft difcretion.

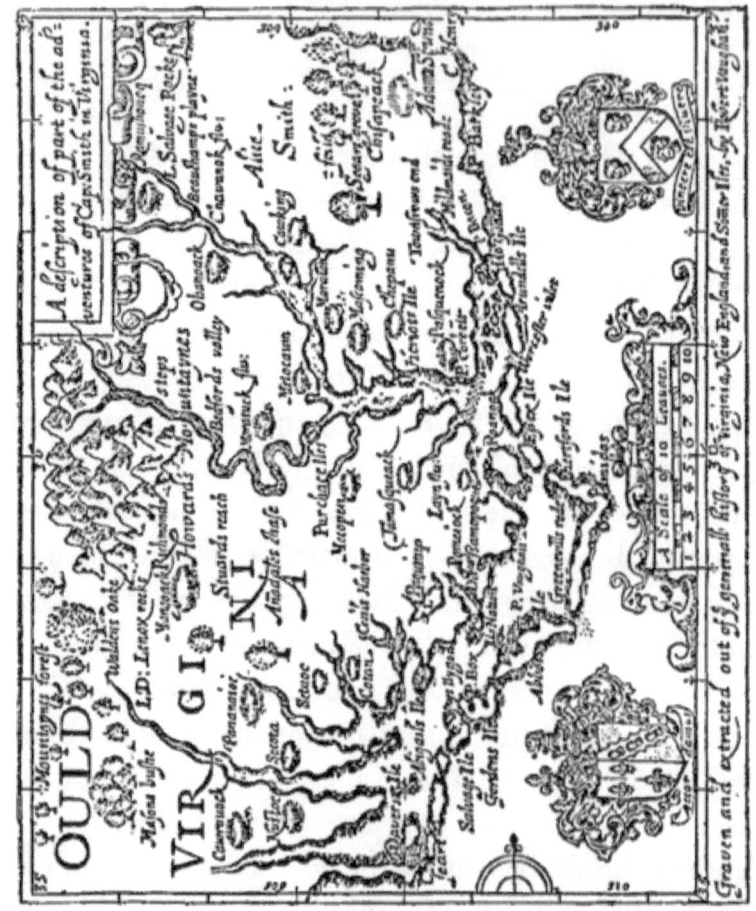

Can you imagine that thofe furies refufed both this excellent place, and thefe good conditions! Not

this they ufe for fwellings, aches, anointing their joints, and painting their heads and garments. They account it very precious, and of much worth.

only did they fo, but they contemned me, my kind
care, and my authority. They thought fo much
of the Lord General's new commiffion, that they
regarded no one. They fuppofed all the *Monacans'* country to be full of gold, and made out that
none fhould come there but whom they pleafed. I
do now wonder to think how that I, with only five
men, durft adventure among them as I did,
(knowing how greedy they were of my blood), or
to land among them, and imprifon the chief leaders
of thefe mutinies; but their number, being an
hundred and twenty, forced me to retire. Yet, in
the interim, I furprifed one of their boats, where-
with I returned to their fhip, where was their provifion, which I alfo took ; and well it chanced that
I found the mariners fo tractable and conftant, elfe
there had been fmall poffibility that I ever efcaped.

But their conduct muft not be taken as that of
the whole company, for there were many among
them who perceived the malice of *Ratliffe* and
Archer and their faction, and would not confort
with them, but ever refted my faithful friends. The
worft was that thofe poor fouls, the favages, who
daily brought their contribution to me, were fo
tormented by that diforderly company, who ftole
their corn, robbed their gardens, beat them, broke
into their houfes, and made fome of them prifoners,
that they daily complained to me that I had

brought them as protectors, men worse than the *Monacans* themselves; and they added that for love of me they had till then endured it, yet they desired my pardon, if, hereafter, they defended themselves, since I did not correct them, as they expected I should have done. Indeed, they importuned me so much to punish their misdemeanours, and were so ready to help, that they offered, if I would but lead them, to fight for me against them; but this, of course, I could not suffer. I liked not to leave them as they were, looking upon them as my charge, even if they were froward, so I spent nine days trying to reclaim them, showing them the folly of their dreams, and gilded hopes of *South Sea* mines, advantageous trading, and easy victories, which they had so madly conceived; but then, seeing I could nothing prevail, I set sail for *James Town.*

Now, no sooner was the ship under sail, and scarcely out of sight, than a little band, of but twelve savages, assaulted those hundred and twenty valiant boasters in their Fort, and, finding some straggling in the woods, they slew many, and so affrighted the rest that their prisoners escaped, and they safely retired with the swords and cloaks of those they had slain. By a lucky chance, as it happed, we had not sailed but half a league when our ship grounded, and this gave us another chance of fummoning them to a parley; and we found them all fo ftrangely amazed with this poor filly affault of twelve favages that they fubmitted themfelves upon any terms to my mercy. When they had thus humbled themfelves, I took action to prevent fuch happening again, and prefently put by the heels fix or feven of the chief offenders. The reft I took to *Powhatan*, and there eftablifhed them right gallantly, for they had a Fort ready built, prettily fortified with poles and bark of trees, fufficient to have defended them from all the favages in *Virginia*. There were dry houfes for lodging, and near two hundred acres of ground cleared, and ready to be planted, and truly none of us know of any place in *Virginia* fo delightful, fo ftrong, or fo pleafant; fo much fo, indeed, that we called it *Non Such*. Then, as I would not leave them at enmity, I appeafed the favages, and each party gave back what had been taken from the other; fo that all were friends.

I had appointed new officers in command, and was again ready to depart, when at that inftant Captain *Weft* arrived, and thofe men, whofe fubmiffion to me had lately been fo humble, now began once more to ftrut and fume, and fo worked upon his gentle nature that new turmoils arofe. For now that they were mafters once more of all their victual, munition, and other things, their factions grew to fuch a height that I fairly gave them over to their own devices, and left them to their fortunes, when the fools at once abandoned *Non Such* and returned again to the open air, at *Weft's Fort*. Sick at heart, and hopelefs of doing any good with fuch wrong-headed affes, I left for *James Town*, and what happened to me on that journey fhall I never forget.

I was quietly fleeping in the boat (for the fhip had returned two days before), when either by accident, or malicioufly of purpofe (which I know not, nor will prefume to judge, but the good God, He knows), fomeone fired my powder pouch, which tore the flefh from my body and thighs, nine or ten inches fquare, in a moft pitiful manner. Awakened from my fleep in this rude way, being dazed and yet in intolerable agony, to quench the tormenting fire, which was frying me in my clothes, I leaped overboard into the deep river, where I was near drowned ere they could recover me. It was a very grievous wound, and I was in the foreft pain, yet in this eftate, without either chirurgeon or chirurgery, I had to go near a hundred miles.

When I arrived at *James Town* I caufed all things to be prepared, either for peace or war, in order to obtain provifion, and whilft thefe things were providing, I fettled that *Ratliffe*, *Archer*, and the reft of their confederates, fhould come to their trials.

But their guilty confciences fearing a juft reward
for their deferts, and feeing me unable to ftand,
and nigh bereft of my fenfes by reafon of the
torment of my pain, the villains plotted to have
me murdered in my bed. But God fo protected
me, that the heart of him that fhould have given
fire to that mercilefs piftol (I will not give his
name, for I have forgiven him the injury he
would have done me), did fail him at the laft
moment, and he could not do the treacherous deed.
They, finding themfelves thwarted in this their
villanous defign, did join together to ufurp the
government, thinking thereby to efcape their
punifhment.

I had notice of their projects, and my old foldiers,
my trufty friends, who had ftood by me in many
an evil cafe, importuned me to let them cut off
the heads of thofe that would refift my command,
yet would I not fuffer them. Fierce pain, and
conftant worry and anxiety, had conquered me,
and I made up my mind to leave the place altogether : fo I fent for the mafters of the fhips, and
took order with them for my return to England.
What elfe could I do ? There was neither chirurgeon nor chirurgery in the Fort of fkill or effect
enough to cure my hurt, and, as the fhips were to
depart next day, the opportunity was not to be
miffed. My commiffion as Prefident was to be

suppreffed, I knew not why, my foldiers and myfelf to be rewarded I knew not how, and a new com- miffion (which difabled the authority I had, and made them prefume fo oft in their mutinies as they did) granted, I knew not to whom. Befides which, fo grievous were my wounds, and fo cruel were my torments, fo that few expected I could live, that I was unable to follow my bufinefs, and regain what we had loft, fupprefs the factions, and range the countries for provifions as I intended.

However, I went about trying to find fome one whom I could truft, to fill my place, but I could find none I thought fit, who would accept the poft. In the meantime, feeing me going, they prevailed on Mafter *Percie*, who was then ready to go to *England*, to ftop with them and be their Prefident. Within lefs than an hour this change had begun, and ended, and the new Prefident and Councillors were already beginning to be fawned upon—but I gave not up my commiffion. Had I not been fo grievoufly wounded by that unhappy blaft, I would quickly have qualified the heat of thofe humours and factions, had the fhips once left them and us to our fortunes, and I would have made that pro- vifion from among the favages, that we fhould have feared neither Spaniard, favage, nor famine. But boafting is unmanly, and unfeemly. I will fay no more of my own deeds, but I think it may

be lawful for me to read you what one who knew
me well, worthy Mafter *Richard Pots*, Clerk of
the Council, wrote concerning me, and to which I
can refer with no little pride, as it is the honeft
expreffion of one who knew well about all the
things whereof he wrote. He faith, fpeaking of
me : "What fhall I fay but thus, we left him, that
in all his proceedings made Juftice his firft guide,
and experience his fecond, ever hating bafeneffe,
floath, pride, and indignitie, more than any dangers ;
that never allowed more for himfelfe, than his
fouldiers with him ; that upon no danger would
fend them where he would not lead them himfelfe ;
that would never fee us want, what he either had,
or could by any meanes get us ; that would rather
want than borrow, and ftarve than not pay ; that
loved action more than words, and hated falfhood
and covetoufneffe worfe than death ; whofe adventures were our lives, and whofe loffe our deaths."

It was in the autumn of the year of grace 1609
that I was carried on board fhip, and failed from
Virginia, which it feems fated I fhall never again
behold. The day before I failed, there arrived
Captain *Davis* in a fmall pinnace, with fixteen
proper men more. And this is how I left them.
They had three fhips, feven boats, commodities
ready to trade with, the harveft newly gathered,
ten weeks' provifion in the ftore, four hundred,

R

ninety and odd perfons, twenty pieces of ordnance, three hundred mufkets, fnaphaunces and firelocks; fhot, powder, and match fufficient, pikes, fwords, and morions more than men. The language and habitations of the favages well known to an hundred well trained and expert foldiers; nets for fifhing, tools of all forts for work, apparel for their wants, fix mares and a horfe, five or fix hundred fwine, as many hens and chickens, fome goats, fome fheep. Yet it came to pafs that as foon as I had left them, they regarded nothing but from hand to mouth, and did confume all they had; nay, they took care for nothing but to perfect fome colourable complaints againft me; to perfect which they even delayed the return of the fhips for three weeks.

Befides all this I left *James Town* ftrongly palifadoed, and it contained fome fifty or fixty houfes, befides which, I left five or fix other forts and plantations, which, although they were not fo fumptuous as the new arrivals expected, they were better than we had at our firft coming. All that time we had but one carpenter in the country, and three others that could do but little, but defired to be learners; two failors, two blackfmiths, and thofe I have called labourers were for the moft part footmen, and fuch as the adventurers had brought out to attend upon them, or fuch as they could perfuade to go with them; that never did know what a day's work was, except the Dutchmen, Poles, and some dozen others. For all the reft were poor gentlemen, tradefmen, ferving men, libertines, and fuch like, ten times more fit to fpoil a common-wealth, than either begin one or help to maintain one. For when neither the fear of God, or law, fhame, nor the difpleafure of their friends could rule them at bome, there was fmall hope ever to bring one in twenty to be good when thofe reftrictions were removed. Notwithftanding, I confefs that divers amongft them had better minds, and grew much more induftrious than was expected; yet ten good workmen would have done more fubftantial work in a day than ten of them in a week.

And now let us fee how they fared after my departure, and to that end I will read you what hath faid the worthy Doctor *Sims :* "The company from *James Town,* under the command of Captaine *Jobn Sickelmore,* alias *Ratliffe,* went to inhabit *Point Comfort.* Captaine *Martin* and Captaine *Weft,* having loft their boats and neere halfe their men among the Salvages, were returned to *James Town ;* for the Salvages no fooner underftood *Smith* was gone, but they all revolted, and did fpoile and murther all they incountered. Now, wee were all conftrained to live onely on that *Smith* had left for his owne Companie, for the reft had confumed their proportions, and now they had twentie Prefidents with all their appurtenances: Mafter *Piercie*, our new Prefident, was fo ficke, hee could neither goe nor ftand.

" But ere all was confumed, Captaine *Weft* and Captaine *Sickelmore*, each with a fmall fhip and thirtie or fortie men well appointed, fought abroad to trade. *Sickelmore*, upon the confidence of *Powhatan*, with about thirtie others as careleffe as himfelfe, were all flaine, onely *Jeffrey Shortridge* efcaped, and *Pokahontas*, the King's daughter, faved a boy called *Henry Spilman*, that lived many yeeres after, by her meanes, amongft the *Patawomekes. Powhatan* ftill as he found meanes, cut off their Boats, denied them trade, fo that Captaine *Weft* fet faile for *England.*

" Now we all found the loffe of Captaine *Smith*, yea, his greateft maligners could now curfe his loffe ; as for Corne, provifion and contribution from the Salvages, we had nothing but mortall wounds, with clubs and arrowes, as for our Hogs, Hens, Goats, Sheepe, Horfe, or what lived, our commanders, officers and Salvages daily confumed them ; fome fmall proportions fometimes we tafted, till all was devoured ; then fwords, armes, pieces, or anything, wee traded with the Salvages, whofe cruell fingers were fo oft imbrewed in our blouds, that what by their crueltie, our Governours indifcretion, and the loffe of our fhips, of five hundred within fix moneths after Captaine *Smith's* departure, there remained not paft fixtie men, women, and children, moft miferable and poor creatures, and thofe were preferved for the moft part, by roots, herbes, acornes, walnuts, berries, now and then a little fifh : they that had ftarch in thefe extremities made no fmall ufe of it; yea, even the very fkinnes of our horfes.

" Nay, fo great was our famine, that a Salvage we flew, and buried, the poorer fort took him up againe and eat him, and fo did divers one another, boyled and ftewed with roots and herbs; and one among the reft did kill his wife, powdered* her, and had eaten part of her before it was known, for which hee was executed, as hee well deferved; now whether fhee was better roafted, boyled or car-bonado'd, I know not, but of fuch a difh as powdered wife I never heard of. This was that time, which ftill to this day we called the ftarving time; it were too vile to fay, and fcarce to be beleeved, what we endured; but the occafion was our owne, for want of providence, induftrie, and government, and not the barrenneffe and defect of the countrie."

This, methinks, fhould prove a fufficient anfwer

---

* Salted.

to thofe, my maligners, who aver that I ruled them
with a rod of iron, and was the caufe of all their
miferies.

And now, before I quit me of this part of my
life, let me tell you of the juftice of God upon
thofe villain Dutchmen. *Valdo* the *Switzer*, of
whom I have told you before as being an arch
traitor, made a fhift to get to *England*, where,
perfuading the merchants that he had difcovered
rich mines, and how he would do them great fervices, was very well rewarded, and returned with
my Lord *De la Warr*, who arrived at *Virginia* on
the 9th of June, 1610. He was foon found out
to be an impoftor, there being, of courfe, no mines,
fo no one would have aught to do with him, and
he perifhed miferably. His two conforts and bofom
friends, *Adams* and *Francis*, fled again to *Powhatan*,
to whom they promifed what wonders they would
do on the arrival of my Lord *De la Warr*, would
he but fuffer them to go to him. But the King,
feeing they would be gone, replied, " You that
would have betrayed Captain *Smith* to me, will
certainly betray me to this great Lord, in order to
make your peace;" and fo he caufed his men to
beat out their brains.

CHAPTER XXII.

WHAT pains and tortures I fuffered from my wound during the paffage to *England* no man can conceive, and I was very long in recovering my health, even with the aid of the moft experienced chirurgeons and phyficians. I had fore need of reft after my arrival, for befides that my life, all through, had been a bufy and a ftirring one, the hardfhips and anxieties of the laft two years had told upon me more than aught previoufly; fo that I looked for and enjoyed my reft. But I ftill took a keen intereft in all the news I could hear pertaining to *Virginia*, which, however, I will not tell you now, as it belongeth not to mine own perfonal adventures, but I may not fail to tell you of what I heard of that *nonpareil* of *Virginia*, my very good and dear friend, *Pocahontas*. After my departure, faith was not kept with *Powhatan* as I had done, and he was at enmity with the colonifts, and had fome in captivity. *Pocahontas* had now little influence with him, and had never been to *James Town* fince I left, but was living at *Patawomeke* with a friend named *Iapazaws* and his wife, thinking herfelf there unknown.

That rough old fea dog, Captain *Argall*, was then (1612) with his fhip in the Colony, and he

was fent to the river *Patawomeke* to trade for corn,
and he entered into a great acquaintance with
Iapazaws, who was an old friend of mine, and
indeed of all our nation ever fince we had difcovered
the country.   Now Captain *Argall*, finding from
this Chief that *Pocahontas* was there, devifed a
notable fcheme to poffefs himfelf of her, and holding her as hoftage, till that *Powhatan* fhould return
the men he had in captivity, and reftore the guns,
&c., he had ftolen.   In order to effect his defign,
he worked on the avarice of *Iapazaws*, and promifed him a copper kettle, if he could but bring
her on board, affuring him that he would in no
wife hurt her, but only keep her till they could
conclude a peace with her father.

What favage could have withftood fuch a bribe ;
he would have fold his very felf for it, and the
crafty *Iapazaws* played his part right cunningly.
Although his wife had feen and been in many
fhips, yet he caufed her to feign a great defire to
fee one, and by his inftructions fhe did fo importune
him, that he threatened to beat her for her im-
portunity, at which fhe wept bitterly.   But at laft
he told her, if *Pocahontas* would go with her,
he was content ; and thus did they betray my poor
innocent maid on board the big canoe.   *Argall*
feafted them all very kindly in the cabin ; *Iapazaws*
oft-times treading on his foot to remind him that he

had done his part. When the Captain faw his time, he perfuaded *Pocahontas* to go into the gun-room, feigning that he wanted to fpeak alone with *Iapazaws*, which was only that fhe fhould not perceive that he was in any way guilty of her captivity. After a while he fent for her again, and told her before her friends that he muft keep her prifoner for awhile, and that fhe muft go with him, and help to compound peace betwixt her country and the colonifts, and then, and not till then, fhe fhould fee *Powhatan*. *Iapazaws* and his wife played their parts to admiration, beginning to howl and cry as faft as *Pocahontas* did; but, at laft, the Captain's fair perfuafions pacified her; *Iapazaws*, with his wife, copper kettle, and other toys, went merrily on fhore, and my little maid was carried to *James Town*. A meffenger was forthwith fent to her father, telling him how they had got poffeffion of his daughter, *Pocahontas*, whom he loved fo dearly, and that if he wanted her again he muft ranfome her with the men, fwords, pieces, tools, &c., he had fo treacheroufly ftolen.

Now this was but unwelcome news to *Powhatan*, becaufe he loved both his daughter and our commodities well, and it was a hard matter for him to choofe between them; fo that it was not till three months after, that he returned any anfwer, and then, by perfuafion of his Council, he

fent back feven men, but he took great care that
each bare with him an unferviceable mufket; and
by them he fent word that when his daughter was
delivered to him, he would make fatisfaction for
all injuries done, give five hundred bufhels of
corn, and be for ever friends. That which he
fent was received in part payment, but they at
James Town well knew this crafty old fox, and
returned anfwer that his daughter fhould be well
ufed, but that they could not believe that the reft
of the arms were either loft or ftolen from him,
and, therefore, until he fent them, his daughter
would be kept.

This anfwer, it feemed, much difpleafed him,
for no more was heard from him for a long time
after. At length, when the colonifts had fome
leifure to attend to fuch matters, Sir *Thomas Dale*,
with one hundred and fifty men, embarked in
Captain *Argall's* fhip, and fome other veffels
belonging to the colony, and went up his own
river, to his chief habitation, having with them
Pocahontas, his daughter. The favages received
them with many fcornful bravados, proudly
demanding why they were come thither; the
reply was, they had brought *Powhatan's* daughter,
and to receive the ranfom for her that was promifed, or elfe they would have it perforce.
Nothing difmayed at this, the Indians anfwered

that if they came to fight, they were welcome, for they were provided for them, but adviſed them, if they loved their lives, to retire, elſe they ſhould be ſerved as they had done Captain *Ratliffe.* The coloniſts replied they would pre-ſently have a better anſwer, but they were no ſooner within ſhot of the ſhore, than the ſavages welcomed them with a flight of arrows.

Being thus juſtly provoked, they manned the boats, and a party went on ſhore, who burned all their houſes, and took from them everything they could find. The next day they went higher up the river, when the inhabitants aſked why their houſes had been burned; the reply to which was another queſtion, why had they been ſhot at? They anſwered it was ſome ſtraggling ſavages, and made many other excuſes that they intended no hurt, but were friends, on which the Engliſhmen told them they came not to hurt, but to viſit them as friends alſo.

Upon this a peace was concluded, and, forth-with, meſſengers were deſpatched to *Powhatan*, whoſe anſwer, as they ſaid, could not be expected for four and twenty hours, for it would take that time for the meſſengers to go and return. They alſo ſaid that the Engliſhmen they had, were run away, for fear that they ſhould be hanged, but that *Powhatan's* men had run after them; as for the fwords and pieces, they fhould be brought next day, but this was only an excufe to gain time, for the next day they came not.

So they went higher up the river, to a houfe of *Powhatan's*, named *Matchot*, where they faw about four hundred men, well appointed, who dared them to land, a challenge which was at once accepted. The favages fhowed no fign of fear at all, nor offered to refift the landing, but walking boldly up and down, demanded to confer with the Captain, to find out his reafon for coming in that manner, and to have truce till they could but once more fend to their King to know his pleafure; which, if it was not agreeable, they would cheerfully fight, and defend their own as beft they could. But this was only to defer the time, in order that they might carry away their provifions; ftill, it fuited the colonifts to pretend to believe it, and they promifed a truce till the next day at noon, when, if fighting was to be done, due notice of it fhould be given by the noife of drums and trumpets.

Upon this promife, two of *Powhatan's* fons came to vifit their fifter, and at fight of her, finding her well, (for they had heard to the contrary), they much rejoiced, and promifed they would perfuade her father to redeem her, and for ever be friends with the Englifh. And thefe two

brethren came on board, and ſtayed there, whilſt
Maſter *John Rolfe* and Maſter *Sparkes* went to
Powhatan to acquaint him of the buſineſs. Kindly
were they entertained, but not admitted to the
preſence of *Powhatan;* but they ſpake with
Opechancanough, his brother and ſucceſſor. He
promiſed to do all he could with *Powhatan,* and
thought all would be well. So it being April,
and time to prepare the ground and ſet the corn,
the expedition returned to *James Town,* pro-
miſing to wait for the performance of their
arrangement till the next harveſt.

But *Pocahontas* was never thus redeemed, for
ſhe had fallen into a gentler bondage, and yet one
that was harder to break. Long before this,
Maſter *John Rolfe,* of whom I have but juſt ſpoken,
an honeſt gentleman, and of good behaviour, had
been in love with *Pocahontas,* and ſhe with him,
which thing at that inſtant he made known to Sir
Thomas Dale, in a letter, wherein he intreated his
advice, and *Pocahontas* acquainted her brother
with it, which reſolution Sir *Thomas Dale* well
approved. The noiſe of this marriage ſoon came
to the knowledge of, *Powhatan,* and it ſeems to
have been a thing acceptable to him, as appears
by his ſudden conſent, for within ten days he ſent
Opachiſco, an old uncle of hers, and two of his
ſons, to ſee the manner of the marriage, and to do

in that behalf what they were requefted, for the
confirmation thereof, as his deputy.   And married
they were, about the firft of April, 1613, *Pocahontas* having been converted to Chriftianity, and
baptized under the name of the Lady *Rebecca*.

And ever fince that time there hath been
friendly trade and commerce, as well with *Powhatan* himfelf, as all his fubjects.

———

CHAPTER XXIII.

ALTHOUGH I refted, I was not idle, for I
helped Mafter *William Simons* in his work
entitled, " A Map of *Virginia*."   But it was not
for an old rover like me to lie abed when there was
man's work to be done, fo that after a time, and
my wound was whole, which took long, I looked
around me for frefh adventures, which in thofe
days were not long a coming to thofe who looked
out for them.   Now you may remember that in
the Letters Patent granted by his Majefty in 1606
for the limitation of *Virginia*, did extend from 34
to 45 degrees, which was divided into two parts,
namely, the firft colony, and the fecond.   The
firft was to the honourable City of *London*, and
fuch as would adventure with them to difcover and

take their choice where they would, betwixt the degrees of 34 and 41.

The second was appropriated to the cities of *Briftol*, *Exeter*, and *Plymouth*, &c., and the Weft parts of *England*, and all thofe that would adventure and join with them, and they might make their choice anywhere betwixt the degrees of 38 and 45, provided there fhould be at leaft an hundred miles' diftance between thefe two Colonies, each of which had laws, privileges, and authority, for the government and advancing their feveral plantations alike. Now this part of *America* hath formerly been called *Norumbega*, *Virginia*, *Nufkoncus*, *Penaquida*, *Cannada*, and fuch other names as thofe that ranged the coaft pleafed.

But, becaufe it was fo mountainous, rocky, and full of ifles, few have adventured much to trouble it; notwithftanding, that honourable patron of virtue, Sir *John Popham*, Lord Chief Juftice of *England* in the year 1606, procured means and men to poffefs it, and fent Captain *George Popham* as Prefident, Captain *Rawley Gilbert* as Admiral, Captain *Edward Harlow*, Mafter of the Ordnance, Captain *Robert Davis*, Sergeant-Major, Captain *Elis Beft*, Marfhall, Mafter *Seaman*, Secretary, Captain *James Davis* to be Captain of the fort, and Mafter *Gomez Carew*, Chief Searcher. All thefe were of the Council, who, with fome hundred

more, were to ftay in the country; they fet fail
from *Plymouth* the laft day of May, 1606, and
came to *Monahigan* on the 11th of Auguft. At
Sagadahock, nine or ten leagues fouthward, they
planted themfelves at the mouth of a fair navigable
river, but the coaft all thereabouts was moft
extremely ftony and rocky; and that very fevere
frozen winter was fo cold, they could not range,
nor fearch the country. Their provifion was fo
fmall, that they were glad to fend all but 45
of their company back again; their noble Prefident,
Captain *Popham*, died, and not long after arrived
two fhips well provided with all neceffaries to
fupply them, and another came fome fmall time
after, by whom they learned the death of the Lord
Chief Juftice, and alfo of Sir *John Gilbert*, whofe
lands there, the Prefident, *Rawley Gilbert*, was to
poffefs, according to the adventurers' directions;
but the colony regarding their continuance there
as hopelefs, they all returned to *England* in the
year 1608: and thus the plantation was begun, and
ended, in little more than a year.

Captain *Harlow* went out again to difcover an
Ifle, fuppofed to be near unto *Cape Cod*, but he
found it not, fo he returned, bringing fome favages
with him. Sir *Francis Popham* fent one Captain
Williams divers times to *Monahigan* only to trade
and bring home fifh, but of plantations was no

more heard. For all this, as I liked *Virginia* well, though not their proceedings, fo I defired alfo to fee this country, and fpend fome time in trying what I could find out as a reafon for all thefe evil rumours and difafters.

So I made advances to them, which were accepted, and in the month of April, 1614, I made my firft voyage to *New England.* The expedition was undertaken at the charge of Captain *Marmaduke Roydon*, Captain *George Langam*, Mafter *John Buley*, and Mafter *William Skelton*, with two fhips from *London*, and I chanced to arrive at *Monabigan*, an ifle of *America*, in 43' 4" of northerly latitude. Our idea was there to take whales, for which intent we had on board one *Samuel Crampton*, and others expert in that faculty, and alfo to try and find a mine of gold or copper ; if thefe failed, then were we to fall back upon fifh and furs to make our adventure pay. We found this whale-fifhing a coftly conclufion; we faw many of them, and fpent much time in chafing them, but could not kill any; they being a kind of *Jubartes*, and not the whale that yields fins and oil, which we expected.

As for the gold, that was all a device of our Mafter's, fo that he might get a voyage, to which end he projected it, for truly he had no knowledge of fuch matters. So we had to fall back upon fifh and fur, and the prime of both thofe feafons were paft, by reafon of our late arrival, and long lingering after whales. In our ignorance, we thought their feafons ferved at all times, but we found it otherwife, for by the midft of *June* the fifhing failed, yet in *July* and *Auguft* fome were taken, but not fufficient to defray fo great a charge as our ftay required: of dried fifh we made about forty thoufand, and of cured fifh about feven thoufand. Whilft the failors fifhed, I, and eight others who could beft be fpared, ranged the coaft in a fmall boat, and we got for trifles near eleven thoufand beaver fkins, one hundred marten's, and as many otter's; the moft of which we obtained within the diftance of twenty leagues. We ranged the coaft, both eaft and weft, much further, but eaftward, our commodities were not efteemed, they were fo near the French, who knew their wants, and who traded with the favages, at fuch long diftances that they went further than the precinéts of their own diftriéts.

With thefe furs, train oil, and dried fifh, I returned to *England* in the bark, and arrived fafely back, within fix months of our departure from the *Downs*. The beft of the fifh fold for £5 the hundred; the reft, by reafon of ill ufage, from £3 to 50s. The other fhip ftayed to fit herfelf for *Spain* with the dried fifh, which was fold at *Malaga*

at forty rials* the quintal, each hundred weighing
two quintals and a half. But one *Thomas Hunt*,
the master of the ship, (after that I was gone),
thinking to prevent the plan I had of there making
a plantation, and hoping to thereby keep this
abounding country to himself, and still in obscurity,
so that only he, and some few merchants more,
might enjoy wholly the benefit of the trade, and
profit, of this country, did betray four and twenty
of those poor savages aboard his ship, and most
dishonestly and inhumanely, (for they treated me
and all my men with kind usage), carried them with
him to *Malaga*, and there for a little private gain,
he sold those poor unfortunate silly savages for rials
of eight; but this vile act kept him ever after from
any other employment to those parts.

Now I taken a draught of this coast, and called
it *New England*, yet did *Hunt*, his consorts, and so
many others who after my successful return, went
thither next year, persist in drowning that name,
by calling it *Cannaday*, that at last I presented the
map, with a discourse, to his Royal Highness
Prince *Charles*, now His most Gracious Majesty,
humbly intreating him that he would change the

---

* A Rial was worth ten shillings in England. There
seems to have been an error; otherwise the fish fetched a
Rial apiece! Even if it were the *Rial of Eight* (Ruding, v. ii.
p. 60) or Piece of Eight of Robinson Crusoe, which was
worth 4s. 6d., it would still be a high price.

barbarous names of fome of the places, for such
Englifh names, that pofterity might fay Prince
Charles was their godfather, and this he did, as a
few of the names will show.

Cape Cod he changed to *Cape James.*		
Chawum	,,	*Barwick.*
Accomack	,,	*Plymouth.*
Sagoquas	,,	*Oxford,* &c. &c.

Returning in the bark, it was my ill luck, as it
afterwards turned out, to put into *Plymouth*, where
I imparted my opinions of this unregarded country
to divers whom I thought my friends, and who
were interefted in the dead Patent. By them I was
fo encouraged, and affured to have the managing of
their authority during my life, and they made me
fuch large promifes, that I engaged myfelf with
them to undertake it. When I came to *London* I
found others equally eager to avail themfelves of
my fervices, but having pledged myfelf to them at
Plymouth, I could not go from my word.

CHAPTER XXIV.

IT was not, however, till next year (1615), and after many vexations, that I really, and in earneft, did get away. I was employed by many of my friends in *London*, and Sir *Ferdinando Gorges*, a noble knight, who much affected thefe forts of adventures, and he it was who perfuaded the Reverend Dean of *Exeter*, Doctor *Sutliffe*, and divers merchants of the Weft, to entertain the idea of an expedition to this plantation. Much labour indeed had I to bring them and the *Londoners* to join together, becaufe the *Londoners* have moft money, and the Weftern men are moft proper for fifhing; and it is near as much trouble, and much more danger, to fail from *London* to *Plymouth* than from *Plymouth* to *New England*, fo that half the voyage would be thus faved; yet, as I faid before, hard work had I before I could prevail, fo defirous were they both to be Lords of that fifhery.

I was to have only fixteen men, *i.e.*, four gentle-men, eight foldiers, and two men and two boys, who were to learn to be failors, but I expected great help from the favages, to whom I was well, and favourably, known. When I returned firft from *New England* to *Plymouth*, I was promifed four good ſhips ready prepared to my hand by the next Chriſtmas, ſo that in January, with two hundred pounds in caſh for adventure, and ſix gentlemen well furniſhed, I went from *London* to *Plymouth*, where I expected to find my ſhips, but I found no ſuch matter ; and, moreover, many who had pro-miſed me help, were now unwilling to afford it. Notwithſtanding, at laſt, with a labyrinth of trou-ble, though the greateſt of the burden lay on me and a few of my particular friends, I was furniſhed with a ſhip of two hundred tons, and another of fifty, and in the larger one I ſet ſail, having had the dignity conferred on me of Admiral of *New Eng-land.* But ere I had ſailed one hundred and twenty leagues, ſhe brake all her maſts and leaked ſo badly, that each watch, in order to keep her afloat, we had to pump ſome five or ſix thouſand ſtrokes. All we could do was to ſet her ſprit ſail, ſo as to keep her ſpooning before the wind, till we could rig up a jury maſt, when there was nothing elſe to do but to return to *Plymouth,* or founder at ſea.

My Vice-Admiral, not knowing of my miſ-fortunes, proceeded on his voyage, whilſt I managed to get a ſmall bark of ſixty tons, with which I again ſet ſail on the 24th day of June, and this voyage turned out to be a moſt eventful one for me. For we had not been out many days when we were chaſed by one *Fry*, a pirate, to whom my maſter,

mate, and pilot, together with divers others, importuned me to yield.   But I would not, and after
much fwaggering, came to fair terms with him,
fwearing if they were broken I would rather fink
the fhip than yield.   They thought it ftrange that
a bark of threefcore tons, and but four guns, fhould
ftand upon terms with them, they being eighty
expert feamen, in an excellent fhip of one hundred
and forty tons, and thirty-fix caft pieces of ordnance.   Yet when they came to know who I was,
they would have yielded to me and carried us
anywhere, for many among them had been old
foldiers of mine, and they had but lately run from
Tunis, where they had ftolen this veffel, and were
now fhort of victual ; but I rejected their offer,
which afterwards we all repented, confidering them
too unruly.

After we made the *Azores*, we encountered, at
Fayal, two French pirates, one of two hundred
men, the other of thirty. My men would not fight
until that I threatened that I would blow up the
fhip rather than yield before I had fpent all my
powder. So that together by the ears we went,
and at laft we got clear of them, for all their fhot.
But it was only to fall into a greater evil, for at
Flores we were chafed by four French men-of-war,
the Admiral being a veffel of one hundred and
forty tons, and ninety men ; the others good fhips,

and as well provided.   Much parley we had, they vowing they were *Rochellers*, who had a commiffion from their King to let true men pafs, but to take Portugals, Spaniards, and pirates.   They requefted me to fhow my commiffion, which was under the Great Seal, and I went on board for that purpofe; but they refpected it not, nor even their own words, for they kept me prifoner, rifled my fhip, manned her with Frenchmen, and difperfed my crew among their fleet.

Within five or fix days their numbers had increafed to eight or nine fail, and then they gave us back our fhip and moft of our provifion, promifing to remedy the defects the next day, and fo they did. My crew, however, had got mutinous, and were all for returning to *England*, but when, after fome trouble, I perfuaded them they were as near to New *England*, as to the Old, the major part refolved to proceed with me.   The French Admiral fent for me again, and I went on board his veffel, which fcarce had I done, when he efpied a fail and gave chafe, whereby my mutineers finding an opportunity, in the night, ran away, leaving me on board the Admiral's fhip, with fimply the clothes I had on, my cap, breeches, and waiftcoat, for I had no coat, by reafon of the heat.   The mutineers fhared amongft them my clothes, arms, and whatfoever I had, and, feigning that they feared I fhould turn my fhip into a man-of-war, they returned to *Ply-mouth*.

Now the caufe why the French detained me was, that my mafter and mate had told them that I meant to revenge myfelf, when I came to the *Cod Bank*, or in *New found land*, on all the French I could there encounter, and how I would have fired the fhip had they not over perfuaded me; alfo, that for the value of a bifcuit, if I had once again my arms, I would rather fink my veffel than that they fhould have the leaft thing from me. Of courfe this treachery, and thofe lies, were only that they might get rid of me, fo, they having left, perforce I had to go with the Frenchmen.

Being a fleet of eight or nine fail, they watched for the *Weft India* fleet, till ill weather feparated us from the other eight; ftill we fpent our time among the Ifles of the *Azores*, during which cruife I wrote an account of how I had been treated, and of my miferable eftate, hoping to have been able to fend it to his Majefty's Council, by fome fhip or other. At laft we were chafed by one Captain *Barra*, an Englifh pirate, in a fmall fhip, with fome twelve pieces of ordnance, about thirty men, and all of them near ftarved. Very courteoufly did they feek relief of us, and our captain gave them fuch fair promifes, that at laft they betrayed Captain *Wolliftone*, his lieutenant, and four or five of his

men aboard of us, and then muft needs try to take
the reft perforce.   All this time, as indeed ever it
was when we met with Englifhmen, my part was to
be prifoner in the gun-room, and not to fpeak to any
of them upon my life; yet had *Barra* knowledge
what I was.   Then *Barra* perceiving well the
intents of thofe Frenchmen, made ready to fight,
and *Wolliftone* regarded not their threats; fo they
parleyed for fome fixteen hours longer, and then
the Frenchmen returned their prifoners, and alfo
imparted fome victual upon a fmall compofition.
But whilft they were thus bartering, a carvel, before
their faces, got under the Caftle of *Gratiofa*, from
whence they beat us with their ordnance.

They fpared nor large, nor fmall, and I mind me
well they took a fmall Englifh veffel of *Poole*, from
New found land; the great cabin was at that time
my prifon, from whence I could fee them pillage
thefe poor men of all they had, and half their fifh;
and, when they were gone, they fold their poor
clothes by an outcry at the mainmaft, and it was
fuch a paltry booty that it fcarce gave each man
feven pence a piece.

It may, perchance, be fomewhat wearifome, but
I muft tell you of the divers veffels we met, and of
their fate, fo that you may have a good idea of
what a pirate's life was in thofe latitudes.   Not
long after, they took a *Scot*, freighted from St.

Michael's to *Briftol*, but he had better fortune than the others, for, having but taken from him a boat's loading of fugar, marmalade, fuckets, and such like, they defcried four fails, after whom they ftood, and furling their main fails waited for us to fight. But the Frenchman's fpirit was content when he faw the Englifh red croffes. Within a very fhort time after, we chafed four Spanifh fhips that came from the *Indies;* we fought with them four or five hours, tore their fails and fides with many a fhot betwixt wind and water, yet not daring to board them, loft them, for which all the failors, for ever after, hated the Captain as a profeffed coward.

A poor carvel of *Brazil* was the next we chafed; and, after a fmall fight, in which thirteen or fourteen of her crew (which was indeed the better half of them) were wounded, we took her, with three hundred and feventy chefts of fugar, one hundred hides, and thirty thoufand rials of eight.

The next was a fhip of *Holland*, which had loft her conforts in the Straits of *Magellan*. Her, alfo, thefe Frenchmen, with fair promifes, cunningly betrayed to come aboard them to fhow their com- miffion, and fo made prize of all. The moft of the Dutchmen we took aboard the Admiral, and manned her with Frenchmen, who, within two or three nights afterwards, ran away with her to *France*. Within a day or two after, we met a

Weft India man-of-war, of one hundred and fixty tons; before noon we fought with her, and took her. This was a rich prize, for fhe had on board one thoufand one hundred hides, fifty chefts of cochineal, fourteen coffers of wedges of filver, eight thoufand rials of eight, and fix coffers of the King of *Spain's* treafure, befides the good pillage, and rich coffers of many wealthy paffengers.

CHAPTER XXV.

TWO months they kept me in this manner, making me manage their fights againft the Spaniards, and keeping me a clofe prifoner when they fought with any Englifh. Now, though the Captain had oft broke his promife, which was to put me on fhore the *Ifles,* or the next fhip he took; yet at the laft he was contented I fhould go in the carvel, which was loaded with fugar, to *France,* and accordingly I went on board her. He, him-felf, feemed refolved to keep the feas, but the next morning we all fet fail for *France,* and that night we were feparated from the Admiral and the rich prize by a ftorm. Within two days afterwards, we were hailed by two *Weft India* men, but when they faw us hoift the French colours, they gave us their broadfides, fhot through our main maft, and fo left us. With much ado we arrived at the *Aiguillon*, not far from *La Rochelle*, where, inftead of performing the great promifes with which they had always fed me, of double fatisfaction, and full content for all my loffes, befides ten thoufand crowns, which was generally concluded I fhould have, they kept me five or fix days, a prifoner in the carvel, accufing me to be him that burnt their Colony in *New France*, to force me to give them a difcharge before the Judge of the Admiralty, and fubmit myfelf to their courtefy for fatisfaction, or elfe I fhould lie in prifon, or even a worfe mifchief might happen to me. The times then were very lawlefs, when the Prince de Condé was with his army in the field, and every poor lord, or man in authority, was as a little king to himfelf ; for this injury that was done me was by them that propofed this voyage, and not by the failors, for they were cheated of all, as well as I, by a few officers aboard, and the owners afhore.

As good luck would have it, there came fuch a ftorm as beat them all under hatches, and I watched my opportunity to get afhore in their boat, whereinto, in the dark night, I fecretly got, and, with a half pike that lay by me, I put adrift, hoping to land on *Rat Ifland*, but the current was fo ftrong, and the fea ran fo high, that I went drifting to fea, till it pleafed God that the wind fhifted with the turn of the tide. I was the whole of that fearful night—fome twelve hours—in the gufts and rain, on the fea, tired with fculling, and baling out the water, which I expected every minute would fink me, till at laft I was ftranded on an oozy Ifle by *Charron*, where certain fowlers found me near drowned, and half dead with water, cold, and hunger.

One does not always meet with difinterefted friends in this world, and thefe faid fowlers would not help me without reward ; fo I pawned my boat (which was the only thing of value I poffeffed) to them, to find means to take me to *La Rochelle*, where I underftood our man-of-war, and the rich prize, in which was the Captain, and the thirty thoufand rials of eight we took in the carvel, had been driven on the rocks and wrecked, the Captain and half his company drowned, on the very fame night in which I efcaped in a little boat, by the mercy of God, far beyond all men's reafon or my own expectation. When I arrived at *Rochelle*, I made my complaint to the Judge of the Admiralty. He gave me many good words and fair promifes, and ere long, many of them that had efcaped drowning told me how they had heard the news of my own death. Some of thefe I caufed to be arrefted, and as their feveral examinations did confirm my complaint, it was held proof sufficient, and the Judge gave me a certificate under his hand, ftating that he believed my ftory to be true, which I prefented to Sir *Thomas Edmonds*, then our Englifh Ambaffador, at *Bordeaux*, where it was my chance to fee the arrival of the King's great marriage from *Spain*.

Here it was my good fortune to meet my old friend Mafter *Crampton*; grieved at my lofs he willingly, and as far as in his power lay, did fupply my wants, as did alfo Madam *Chanoyes*, of *Rochelle*, whom I moft efpecially thank, for that fhe did fuch kindnefs to me, a ftranger. But I have ever found refcue and protection in my greateft dangers from women. The beauteous Lady *Tragabigzanda*, when I was a flave to the Turks, did all fhe could to fuccour me. When I overcame the Bafhaw of *Nalbrits* in *Tartaria*, the charitable Lady *Callamata* fupplied my neceflities. In the utmoft of many neceflities, that bleffed *Pocahontas*, the daughter of the great King of *Virginia*, oft faved my life. And now, when I efcaped the cruelty of pirates and moft furious ftorms, a long time alone in a fmall boat at fea, and driven afhore in *France*, the good lady Madam *Chanoyes* bountifully afflifted me. Indeed, I may fay that I was more beholden to the Frenchmen that efcaped drowning in the man-of-war, Madam

Chanoyes, and the lawyers of *Bordeaux*, than all the reft of my countrymen I met in *France*.

Of the wreck of the rich prize, fome three thoufand fix hundred crowns' worth of goods came afhore, and were faved in the carvel, and I iffued a procefs of attachment upon them. I could not then ftay for the ending of my fuit, but the Judge promifed I fhould have juftice, and fo it proved, for I fince received my fair fhare of what there was to divide. But under the colour and pretext to take pirates and *Weft India* men (becaufe the Spaniards will not fuffer the French to trade with the *Weft Indies*), any goods from thence, though they take them upon the coaft of *Spain*, are lawful prize, or from any of the Spaniard's territories out of the limits of *Europe;* and as they betrayed me, though my commiffion was under the Great Seal, fo did they rob and pillage twenty fail of Englifhmen more, befides thofe I knew not of, in the fame year.

Leaving thus my bufinefs in *France*, I returned to *Plymouth*, to find thofe treacherous mutineers who had thus buried me among the French ; and not only buried me, but with fo much infamy, as fuch treacherous cowards could fuggeft, to excufe their villanies. Such of the chieftains of this mutiny as I could find, I laid by the heels, and the reft confeffed the truth. I alfo heard how my

Vice-Admiral, who unwittingly parted company with me when I fprung my mafts, had done well on his voyage, and returned; and that from *Plymouth* fome four or five fail had gone there a-fifhing, and from *London* as many. And to my thinking, as I perfuade myfelf, there be fifh fufficient to freight four or five hundred fail, or as many as will go; for this fifhing ftretcheth along the coaft from *Cape Cod* to *New found land,* which is feven or eight hundred miles at the leaft; and hath its courfe in the deeps, and by the fhore, all the year round; the fifh keeping their haunts and feedings as the beafts of the field and the fowls of the air.

On my return, after punifhing my mutineers, I took a little reft, and writ a "Defcription of *New England,*" with my map thereof, and then I fet about another voyage thither, which came to nought.

T

CHAPTER XXVI.

AND now, bethink you what news I heard?
Nought lefs than that Sir *Thomas Dale*,
having, to his thinking, fettled all things in good
order, made choice of one Mafter *George Yearly* to
be the Deputy Governor in his abfence, left
Virginia, accompanied by *Pocahontas*, my moft
dear little maid, and her hufband, and they landed
at *Plymouth* on the 12th day of June, in the year
1616. As I have before faid, fhe had been
converted to Chriftianity, and baptized under the
name of the Lady *Rebecca*. Her real name was
Matoaka, and fhe was only called *Pocahontas*,
becaufe that the favages did think that, did we know
her real name, we fhould have the power of cafting
an evil eye upon her. By the diligent care of
Mafter John *Rolfe*, her hufband, and his friends,
fhe was taught to fpeak fuch Englifh as might well
be underftood, had been well inftructed in Chriftianity, and was become very formal and civil in
her behaviour, after our Englifh manner. She
alfo had by him a child, whom fhe loved very
dearly, and the Treafurer, and Virginia Company
took order for the maintenance both of her and
her baby: befides which, there were divers perfons

MATOAKA ALS REBECCA FILIA POTENTISS PRINC: POWHATANI IMP: VIRGINIÆ. ✤

Ætatis suæ 21. A°. 1616.

Matoaks als Rebecka daughter to the mighty Prince Powhatan Emperour of Attanoughkomouck als virginia converted and baptized in the Christian faith, and wife to the worth Mr. Joh Rolff.

of great rank and quality who were very kind to her; and before fhe arrived in *London*, I, being defirous of in part repaying her former courtefies, made her qualities known to the Queen's moft excellent Majefty, and to her Court, and I writ a little book to this effect to the Queen, of which the following is an abftract :—

> " To the moft high and vertuous Princeffe,
>   " Queen *Anne** of Great Britaine.
> " MOST ADMIRED QUEENE,
>   " The love I beare my God, my King, and Countrie, hath fo oft emboldened mee in the worft of extreme dangers, that now honeftie doth conftraine me to prefume thus farre beyond my felfe, to prefent your Majeftie this fhort difcourfe : if ingratitude be a deadly poyfon to all honeft vertues, I muft bee guiltee of that crime, if I fhould omit any means to be thankfull. So it is,
>
> " That fome ten yeeres agoe being in *Virginia*, and taken prifoner by the power of *Powhatan* their chiefe King, I received from this great Salvage exceeding great courtefie, efpecially from his fonne *Nantaquas*, the moft manlieft, comelieft, boldeft fpirit, I ever faw in a Salvage, and his fifter *Pocahontas*, the King's moft deare and wel-beloved daughter, being but a child of twelve or thirteene

---

* Confort of James I.

yeeres of age, whofe compaffionate pitifull heart, of my defperate eftate, gave me much caufe to refpect her; I being the firft Chriftian this proud King and his grim attendants ever faw: and thus inthralled in their barbarous power, I cannot fay I felt the leaft occafion of want that was in the power of thofe my mortall foes to prevent, notwithftanding al their threats. After fome fix weeks fatting amongft thofe Salvage Courtiers, at the minute of my execution, fhe hazarded the beating out of her own brains to fave mine, and not only that, but fo prevailed with her father, that I was fafely conducted to *James Towne*, where I found about eight and thirtie miferable poore and ficke creatures, to keepe poffeffion of all thofe large territories of *Virginia*, fuch was the weakneffe of this poore Commonwealth, as had the Salvages not fed us, we directly had ftarved.

And this reliefe, moft gracious Queene, was commonly brought us by this Lady *Pocahontas*. Notwithftanding all thofe paffages when inconftant Fortune turned our peace to Warre, this tender Virgin would ftill not fpare to dare to vifit us, and by her our jarres have beene oft appeafed, and our wants ftill fupplyed. Were it the policie of her father thus to imploy her, or the ordinance of God thus to make her His inftrument, or her extraordinary affection to our Nation, I know not; but of

this I am fure; when her father with the utmoft
of his policie and power, fought to furprize mee,
having but eighteene with mee, the darke night
could not affright her from comming through the
irkefome woods, and with watered eies gave me
intelligence, with her beft advice to efcape his furie,
which had hee knowne, hee had furely flaine her.
James Towne with her wild traine fhe as freely
frequented, as her father's habitation; and during
the time of two or three yeeres, the next under
God, was ftill the inftrument to preferve this
Colonie from death, famine, and utter confufion,
which if in thofe times had once been diffolved,
Virginia might have lien as it was at our firft
arrivall to this day. Since then, this bufineffe
having beene turned and varied by many accidents
from that I left it at: it is moft certaine, after a
long and troublefome warre after my departure,
betwixt her father and our Colonie, all which time
fhee was not heard of, about two yeeres after, fhee
herfelfe was taken prifoner, being fo detained neere
two yeeres longer, the Colonie by that meanes was
releived, peace concluded, and at laft, rejecting her
barbarous condition, was married to an *Englifh*
Gentleman, with whom, at this prefent, fhe is in
England; the firft Chriftian ever of that Nation,
the firft *Virginian* ever fpake *Englifh*, or had a
childe in marriage by an *Englifhman*, a matter

furely, if my meaning bee truly confidered and well underftood, worthy a Princes underftanding.

" Thus, moft gracious Lady, I have related to your Majeftie, what at your beft leifure our approved Hiftories will account you at large, and done in the time of your Majefties life, and however this might bee prefented you from a more worthy pen, it cannot be from a more honeft heart, as yet I never begged anything of the State, or any, and it is my want of abilitie, and her exceeding defert, your birth, meanes, and authoritie, hir birth, vertue, want and fimplicitie, doth make me fo bold, humbly to befeech your Majeftie to take this knowledge of her, though it be from one fo unworthy to be the reporter, as myfelfe, her hufbands eftate not being able to make her fit to attend your Majeftie: the moft and leaft 1 can doe, is to tell you this, becaufe none fo oft hath tried it as my felfe, and the rather being of fo great a fpirit, how ever her ftature; if fhe fhould not be well received, feeing this Kingdome may rightly have a Kingdome by her meanes ; her prefent love to us and Chriftianitie, might turne to fuch fcorne and furie, as to divert all this good to the worft of evill, where finding fo great a Queene fhould doe her fome honour more than fhe can imagine, for being fo kinde to your fervantes and fubjects, would fo ravifh her with content, as endeare her deareft bloud to effect that, your Majeftie and all the Kings honeft fubjects moft earneftly defire: And fo I humbly kiffe your gracious hands."

This fcripture of mine had good effect, for the Queen moft gracioufly received her, and all the ladies of the Court vied with each other as to who could do her fervice.

I was about this time preparing to fet fail a third time for *New England*, and, although my expedition came to nought, I could not ftay to do her that fervice I defired, and fhe well deferved; but, hearing fhe was at *Brentford*, with divers of my friends, I went to fee her. The fight of me called up a flood of recollections, and fomewhat overcame her, for, after a modeft falutation, without faying a word, fhe turned about, and obfcured her face, as not feeming well contented; and in that humour, we all, her hufband and myfelf, left her for two or three hours, and I, thinking her fomewhat fulky, repented myfelf having written that fhe could fpeak *Englifh*.

But not long after, fhe began to talk, and reminded me well what courtefies fhe had done; saying, "You did promife *Powhatan*, what was yours fhould be his, and he the like to you; you called him father, being in his land a ftranger, and by the fame reafon fo muft I do you:" which, though I would have excufed, I durft not have allowed her to ufe that title, becaufe fhe was a King's daughter. With a bright look fhe turned her face full towards me, and faid, " Were you afraid to come into my father's country, and caufe fear in him and all his people (but me), and fear you here that I fhould call you father? I tell you then I will, and you fhall call me child, and fo I will be for ever and ever your countrywoman. They did tell us always you were dead, and I knew no other, till I came to *Plymouth;* yet *Powhatan* did command *Uttamatomakkin* to feek you, and know the truth, becaufe your countrymen will lie much."

This favage, of whom fhe fpake, was one of *Powhatan's* Council, and was, amongft them, held to be an underftanding fellow. The King fent him, as they fay, purpofely to number the people here, and to inform him well what we were and what was our ftate. Arriving at *Plymouth,* according to his directions he got a long ftick, whereon by notches he did think to have kept the number of all the men he could fee, but he quickly wearied of that tafk. Coming to *London,* where many were defirous to hear him and fee his behaviour, he met me by chance, and we renewed our acquaintance. Then he told me *Powhatan* had bidden him to find me out, fo that I might fhow him our God, the King, Queen, and Prince, of all of whom I fo

much had told them. Concerning God, I told him
the beft I could; the King I had heard he had
feen, and the reft he fhould fee whenever he liked.
He denied ever having feen the King, till by
circumftances he was fatisfied that he had.   Then
faid he very fadly, " You gave *Powhatan* a white
dog, which *Powhatan* fed as himfelf, but your
King gave me nothing, and I am better than your
white dog."

During the fhort time I was in *London*, divers
courtiers and others, my acquaintances, went with
me to fee *Pocahontas*, and they generally concluded,
that they did think God had a great hand in her
converfion, and that they had feen many *Englifh*
ladies worfe favoured, proportioned and behavioured,
and, as fince I have heard, it pleafed both the King
and the Queen's Majeftie honourably to efteem her.
And fhe went about, accompanied by that honourable Lady, the Lady De la Warr, and that
honourable Lord her hufband, and divers other
perfons of good quality, both publicly at the
Mafks, and otherwife, to her great fatisfaction and
content, which doubtlefs fhe would have told her
people, had fhe lived to arrive at *Virginia*.

But that, alas! fhe was fated not to do.   The
Treafurer, Council, and *Virginia* Company, having
well furnifhed Captain *Samuel Argall* for his outward voyage, the Lady *Pocahontas*, or *Rebecca*,

with her hufband and others, embarked in the good
fhip called the *George*, but fhe was taken ill, and,
when the fhip lay at *Gravefend*, it pleafed God to
take this young lady to His mercy. She made not
more forrow for her unexpected death, than joy to
the beholders to hear and fee her make fo religious
and godly an end. She was buried in the chancel
of the church at *Gravefend* on 21ft day of March,
$\frac{1616}{1617}$ * being then in the twenty-fecond year of her
age. Her hufband grieved forely for her, but he
returned with *Argall*, leaving his little child, *Thomas*,
at *Plymouth*, with Sir *Lewis Stukly*, who earneftly
defired the keeping of him. Poor little maid! I
forrowed much for her thus early death, and even
now cannot think of it without grief, for I felt
towards her as if fhe were mine own daughter. Her
father, *Powhatan*, lived not long after her, for he
died in April, 1618.

---

* The church of St. George at Gravefend, where fhe was
buried, was burnt down in 1727, but the regifters were
preferved, and in that of her burial there is a curious error
as to the date, May being written inftead of March : " 1616,
May 2j. Rebeca Wrothe, wyff of Thomas [*fhould be John*]
Wroth, gent., a Virginia Lady borne, was buried in the
Chauuncle." Here, then, we have two errors, one in Rolfe's
Chriftian name, and the other in the date, which muft
neceffarily be March, for in an account of how " The
Government devolved to Captaine Samuel Argall, 1617," it
fays, " In March they fet faile, 1617, and in May he arrived
at *James* Town ; " and in the Calendar of State Papers
(Domeftic Series) it fays, " Mar. 29, 1617. The Virginian
Woman died at Gravefend on her return."

I went not to *New England,* nor could I get any
suitable employment. New men have arisen, and
no place can now be found for me, who have been
wont to be a leader among men. But when the
most sad and terrible news came of the massacre of
nigh upon 400 of the settlers, by the savages, on
the 22nd day of March, 1622, then I wrote to
the Right Worshipful the Company of *Virginia,*
offering to go with 100 soldiers and 30 sailors, if
they would provide such, with victual, munition,
and such necessary provision, and, by God's
assistance, we would endeavour to enforce the
savages to leave their country, or bring them into
that fear and subjection that every man should
follow his business securely.

How think you that my offer was treated?
Their answer to me was that the charge would be
too great; their stock was decayed, and they did
think the planters should do that work themselves,
if I could find means to effect it. They did think
I might have leave of the Company, to do it at
mine own cost, provided they might have half the
pillage; but I think there are not many that would
strive much for that employment, for, except it be
a little corn which at some time of the year may be
had, I would not give twenty pounds for all the
pillage to be got among the savages in twenty
years. So I went not, nor have I had aught to do

with *Virginia* since, save that in the year 1623 His Majesty's Commissioners for the re-formation of *Virginia* desired me to give them my experience to guide them, and to that end propounded to me seven questions, which I answered at length to the best of my ability.

L'ENVOY.

I HAVE thus writ the adventures of my dear old friend, as he fpake them, and have no more to add to them. From that time forth, he led a peaceful, harmlefs life, beloved of all that knew him.   As he himfelf hath writ, " I thanke God I never undertook any thing yet, any could tax me of careleffneffe or diſhonefty, and who is hee to whom I am indebted or troublefome ?   Ah ! were my accufers but to change cafes and places with me but 2 yeres, or till they had done but fo much as I, it may be they would judge more charitably of my imperfeĉtions. But here I muft leave all to the triall of time, both my-felfe, *Virginia's* preparations, proceedings, and good events, praying to that great God, the Proteĉtor of all goodneffe, to fend them as good fucceffe as the goodneffe of the aĉtion and country deferveth and my heart defireth."

In his lifetime he wrote many books, and I have fet them down in the order as they were written, as followeth :—

" A true relation of fuch occurrences and accidents of noate as hath hapned in Virginia fince the firſt planting of that Collony, which is now refident in the South part thereof, till the laſt returne from thence."   1608.

" A Map of Virginia ; with a defcription of the Coun-trey, the commodities, people, government and reli-gion."   1612.

" A Defcription of New England."   1616.

" New Englands Trials."   1620.

" An Accidence, or the Pathway to Experience neceffary for all Young Seamen, &c." 1620.

" The Generall Hiftorie of Virginia, New England
and the Summer Ifles, &c.   1624.

" The True Travels, Adventures, and Obfervations
of Captain John Smith in Europe, Afia, Affrica, and
America, from Anno Domini 1593 to 1629," &c.

" Advertifements for the Unexperienced Planters of
New England or any where," &c.   1631.

And " The Seaman's Grammar."

At the time of his death he was at work on, and left
unfinifhed, " A Hiftory of the Sea."

After his death, a loving friend, I may not fay who,
but I know full well, put up a tablet to his memory, on
the fouth fide of the Quire of St. Sepulchre's Church,
where he was interred, and thus it runs :—

" To the living Memory of his deceafed Friend Captain
JOHN SMITH, fometime Governour of *Virginia*, and
Admiral of *New England.* Who departed this Life the
21ft of June 1631.

Accordiamus, Vincere eft Vivere.

Here lyes one conquered that hath conquered Kings,
Subdu'd large Territories, and done Things
Which to the World impoffible would feem,
But that the Truth is held in more efteem.
Shall I report his former Service done
In honour of his God and Chriftendom ?
How that he did divide from Pagans three
Their Heads and Lives, Types of his Chivalry.
For which great Service, in that Climate done,
Brave *Sigifmundus*, King of *Hungarion*,
Did give him as a Coat of Armes to wear,

Thefe Conquered Heads got by his Sword and Spear.
Or fhall I tell of his Adventures fince
Done in *Virginia*, that large Continent?
How that he fubdu'd Kings unto his Yoke,
And made thofe Heathen flee, as Wind doth Smoke:
And made their land, being of fo large a Station,
An Habitation for our Chriftian Nation,
Where God is glorify'd, their Wants fupply'd;
Which elfe, for Neceffaries muft have dy'd.
But what avails his Conquefts, now he lyes
Interr'd in Earth, a Prey to Worms and Flyes?
O! May his Soul in fweet *Elyfium* fleep,
Until the Keeper that all Souls doth keep,
Return to Judgment; and that after thence,
With Angels he may have his Recompence."

And as fome of you haply would fain read his laft Will and Teftament, which was written on the day of his death, I have tranfcribed it as under:—

"IN THE NAME OF GOD. AMEN. The one and twentieth daie of June in the feaventh yeare of the reigne of our Soveraigne Lord Charles by the grace of God King of England, Scotland, France and Ireland, defender of the faith, &c. I, *Captain John Smith*, of the parifh of St Sepulchers, London, Efqui^r, being ficke in bodye, but of perfect mind and memory, thanckes be given unto Almightie God therefore, Revoking all former wills by me heretofore made, doe make and ordaine this my laft will and teftament in manner following-inge. Firft, I comend my foule into the handes of Almightie God my maker, hoping through the merittes of Chrift Jefus my Redeemer to receive full remiffion of all my finnes and to inherit a place in the everlafting kingdome, my body I comitt to the earth from whence it came, to be interred according to the difcrec'on of myne executors hereunder named, and of fuch worldlie goodes wherof it hath pleafed God in his mercie to make me an unworthie Receaver, I give and bequeath them as hereafter followeth. Firft, I give and bequeath unto Thomas Packer, Esq*, one of the Clerkes of His Ma^tes Privy Seale and to his heires for ever, all my houfes, landes, tenementes and hereditamentes whatfoever fcituate lyinge and beinge in the parifhes of Lowthe and Greate Carleton in the Countie of Lincolne, togeather with my coate of armes. Item, my will and meaninge is that in confiderac'on therof the faid Thomas Packer fhall difburfe and paye all fuch fomes of money and legacies as hereafter in this my will are given bequeathed and referved not exceeding the fome of fowerfcore poundes of lawfull money of England, that is to faie : Firft, I referve unto my felfe to be difpofed of as I fhall thinck good in my life tyme the fome of twentie poundes. Item, he fhall difburfe about my funerall the fome of twentie poundes. Item, I give and bequeath out of the refidue of the faid fourfcore poundes as followeth, vizt, I give and bequeath unto my much honored and moft worthie freind Sr Samuel Saltonftall, Knight, the fome of fyve poundes. Itm, to M^ris Tredway the fome of fyve poundes. Itm, to my fifter Smith the widowe of my brother, the fome of tenn poundes. Itm, to my cofen Steven Smith and his fifter the fome of fixe poundes thirteene fhillinges and fower pence betweene them. Itm, to the faid Thomas Packer, Joane his wife, and Eleano^r his daughter, the fome of tenn poundes among them.

Item, to Mr Reynoldes the fay M^r * of the goldfmiths
Hall, the fome of fortie fhillinges, all wch legacies my
meaning and will is fhall be paid by the faid Thomas
Packer his heires executors or adminiftrators w^thin one
yeare after my deceafe. Item, I give unto Thomas
Packer fonne of the above fayd Thomas Packer my
trunck ftanding in my chamber at Sr Samuell Saltonftalls
houfe in St Sepulchres Parish, togeather with my beft
fuite of apparell of a tawney color, vizt hofe doublet
jerkin and cloake. Item, I give unto him my trunke
bound wth iron barres ftanding in the houfe of Richard
Hinde in Lambeth, togeather wth halfe the bookes therein,
to be chofen by the faid Thomas Packer and allowed by
myne executors, and the other halfe parte of the bookes
I give unto Mr John Tredefkin † and the faid Richard
Hind to be divided betweene them. Item, I nominate
apointe and ordaine my faid much honored friend S^r
Samuell Saltonftall and the faid Thomas Packer the
elder, joynt executors of this my laft will and teftament;
the marke of the faid John Smith. Read acknowledged
sealed and delivered by the faid Captaine John Smith to
be his laft will and teftament in the p^rfence of us who
have fubfcribed our names; per me Willmu' Keble Sn^r,
civitatis London, Willm Packer, Elizabeth Sewfter,
Marmaduke Walker his marke, witnes."

---

* The Aſſay Maſter.
† John Tradeſcant, whoſe collection is merged in the
Aſhmolean Muſeum, Oxford.

APPENDIX.

King James Ist's Letters Patent to Sir Thomas Gates, Sir George Somers, and others, for two several Colonies and Plantations, to be made in Virginia, and other Parts and Territories of America. Dated April 10, 1606.

I. JAMES by the Grace of GOD, King of England, Scotland, France, and Ireland, Defender of the Faith, &c.

WHEREAS our loving and well difpofed fubjects, Sir Thomas Gates, and Sir George Somers, Knights, Richard Hackluit, Clerk, Prebendary of Weftminfter, and Edward Maria Wingfield, Thomas Hanham, and Ralegh Gilbert, Efqrs., William Parker and George Pophani, Gentlemen, and divers others of our loving Subjects, have been humble Suitors unto us, that We would vouchfafe unto them our Licence, to make Habitation, Plantation, and to deduce a Colony of fundry of our People into that Part of America, commonly called VIRGINIA, and other Parts and Territories in America, either appertaining unto us, or which are not now actually poffeffed by any Chriftian Prince or People, fituate, lying, and being all along the Sea Coafts, between four and thirty Degrees of Northerly Latitude from the Equinoctial Line, and five and forty Degrees of the fame Latitude, and in the main Land between the fame four and thirty, and five and forty Degrees, and the Iflands thereunto adjacent, or within one hundred Miles of the Coaft thereof.

II. AND to that End, and for the more fpeedy Accomplifhment of their faid intended Plantation and Habitation there, are defirous to divide themfelves into two feveral Colonies and Companies; The one confift-ing of certain Knights, Gentlemen, Merchants, and other Adventurers, of our City of London and elfewhere, which are, and from time to time fhall be, joined unto them, which do defire to begin their Plantation and Habitation in fome fit and Convenient Place, between four and thirty and one and forty Degrees of the faid Latitude, alongft the Coafts of Virginia, and Coafts of America aforefaid; And the other confifting of fundry Knights, Gentlemen, Merchants, and other Adventurers of our Cities of Briftol and Exeter, and of our Town of Plimouth, and of other Places, which do join themfelves unto that Colony, which do defire to begin their Planta-tion and Habitation in fome fit and convenient Place, between eight and thirty Degrees and five and forty Degrees of the faid Latitude, all alongft the faid Coaft of Virginia and America as that Coaft lyeth.

III. WE, greatly commending, and gracioufly accept-ing of, their Defires for the Furtherance of fo noble a Work, which may, by the Providence of Almighty God, hereafter tend to the Glory of his Divine Majefty, in propagating of Chriftian Religion to fuch People, as yet live in Darknefs and miferable Ignorance of the true Knowledge and Worfhip of God, and may in time bring the Infidels and Savages living in thofe parts, to human Civility, and to a fettled and quiet Government; DO, by thefe our Letters Patents, gracioufly accept of, and agree to, their humble and well intended Defires.

IV. AND do therefore, for Us, our Heirs, and

Succeffors, GRANT and agree, that the faid Sir Thomas
Gates, Sir George Somers, Richard Hackluit, and
Edward Maria Wingfield, Adventurers of and for our
City of London, and all fuch others, as are, or fhall be,
joined unto them of that Colony, fhall be called the *firft
Colony;* And they fhall and may begin their faid firft Plantation and Habitation, at any Place upon the faid Coaft of
Virginia or America, where they fhall think fit and convenient between the faid four and thirty, and one and
forty Degrees of the faid Latitude ; And that they fhall
have all the Lands, Woods, Soil, Grounds, Havens,
Ports, Rivers, Mines, Minerals, Marfhes, Waters, Fifhings, Commodities, and Hereditaments, whatfoever, from
the faid firft Seat of their Plantation and Habitation by the
Space of fifty Miles of Englifh Statute Meafure, all along
the faid Coaft of Virginia and America, towards the Weft
and South weft, as the Coaft lyeth, with all the Iflands
within one hundred Miles directly over againft the fame
Sea Coaft; And alfo all the Lands, Soil, Grounds, Havens,
Ports, Rivers, Mines, Minerals, Woods, Waters, Marfhes,
Fifhings, Commodities, and Hereditaments, whatfoever,
from the faid Place of their firft Plantation and Habitation
for the Space of fifty like Englifh Miles all alongft
the faid Coafts of Virginia and America, towards the Eaft
and North Eaft, or towards the North, as the Coaft
lyeth together with all the Iflands within one hundred
Miles, directly over againft the faid Sea Coaft ; And
alfo all the Lands, Woods, Soil, Grounds, Havens,
Ports, Rivers, Mines, Minerals, Marfhes, Waters, Fifhings, Commodities, and Hereditaments, whatfoever, from
the fame fifty Miles every way on the Sea Coaft, directly
into the main Land by the Space of one hundred like

Englifh Miles ; and fhall and may inhabit and remain
there ; fhall and may alfo build and fortify within any the
fame, for their better Safeguard and Defence, according
to their beft Difcretion, and the Difcretion of the
Council of that Colony ; And that no other of our
Subjects fhall be permitted, or fuffered, to plant or
inhabit behind, or on the Back fide of them, towards the
main Land, without the Exprefs Licence or Confent of
the Council of that Colony, thereunto in Writing firft
had and obtained.

V. AND We do likewife, for Us, our Heirs, and Succeffors, by thefe Prefents, GRANT and agree, that the faid
Thomas Hanham, and Ralegh Gilbert, William Parker,
and George Popham, and all others of the Town of Plimouth in the County of Devon, or elfewhere, which are, or
fhall be joined unto them of that Colony, fhall be called the
Second Colony; And that they fhall and may begin their faid
Plantation and Seat of their firft Abode and Habitation, at
any Place upon the faid Coaft of Virginia, and America,
where they fhall think fit and Convenient, between eight
and thirty Degrees of the faid Latitude, and five and forty
Degrees of the fame Latitude ; and that they fhall have
all the Lands, Soils, Grounds, Havens, Ports, Rivers,
Mines, Minerals, Woods, Marfhes, Waters, Fifhings,
Commodities, and Hereditaments, whatfoever, from the
firft Seat of their Plantation and Habitation by the Space
of fifty like Englifh Miles, as is aforefaid, all alongft the
faid Coafts of Virginia and America, towards the Weft
and South weft, or towards the South, as the Coaft
lyeth, and all the Iflands within one hundred Miles,
directly over againft the faid Sea Coaft : And alfo all the
Lands, Soils, Grounds, Havens, Ports, Rivers, Mines,

Minerals, Woods, Marfhes, Waters, Fifhings, Commodities, and Hereditaments whatfoever, from the faid Place
of their firft Plantation and Habitation for the Space of
fifty like Miles, all alongft the faid Coaft of Virginia and
America, towards the Eaft and North eaft, or towards
the North, as the Coaft lyeth, and all the Iflands alfo
within one hundred Miles directly over againft the fame
Sea Coaft; And alfo all the Lands, Soils, Grounds, Havens,
Ports, Rivers, Woods, Mines, Minerals, Marfhes,
Waters, Fifhings, Commodities, and Hereditaments,
whatfoever, from the fame fifty Miles every way on the
Sea Coaft, directly into the main Land, by the Space of
one hundred like Englifh Miles ; And fhall and may inhabit and remain there ; and fhall and may alfo build and
fortify within any the fame for their better Safeguard,
according to their beft Difcretion, and the Difcretion of
the Council of that Colony ; And that none of our
Subjects fhall be permitted, or fuffered, to plant, or
inhabit behind, or on the Back of them, towards the
main Land, without the exprefs Licence of the Council of
that Colony, in Writing thereunto firft had and obtained.

VI. PROVIDED always, and our Will and Pleafure
herein is, that the Plantation and Habitation of fuch of
the faid Colonies, as fhall plant themfelves, as aforefaid,
fhall not be made within one hundred like Englifh Miles
of the other of them, that firft began to make their Plantation, as aforefaid.

VII. AND We do alfo ordain, eftablifh, and agree,
for Us, our Heirs and Succeffors, that each of the faid
Colonies fhall have a Council, which fhall govern and
order all Matters and Causes, which fhall arife, grow, or
happen, to or within the fame feveral Colonies, according

to fuch Laws, Ordinances, and Inftructions, as fhall be, in that behalf, given or figned with Our Hand or Sign Manual, and pafs under the Privy Seal of our Realm of England ; Each of which Councils fhall confift of thirteen Perfons, to be ordained, made, and removed, from time to time, according as fhall be directed and comprifed in the fame Inftructions ; And fhall have a feveral Seal, for all Matters that fhall pafs or concern the fame feveral Councils ; Each of which Seals fhall have the King's Arms engraven on the one Side thereof, and his Portraiture on the other ; and that the Seal for the faid firft Colony fhall have engraven round about, on the one Side, thefe words : *Sigillum Regis Magnæ Britanniæ, Franciæ & Hiberniæ* ; on the other fide this Infcription round about : *Pro Concilio primæ Coloniæ Virginiæ.* And the Seal for the Council of the faid fecond Colony fhall alfo have engraven, round about the one Side thereof, the aforefaid words : *Sigillum Regis Magnæ Britanniæ, Franciæ & Hiberniæ* ; and on the other Side, *Pro Concilio fecundæ Coloniæ Virginiæ.*

VIII. AND that alfo there fhall be a Council eftablifhed here in England, which fhall, in like manner, confift of thirteen Perfons, to be, for that purpofe, appointed by Us, our Heirs, and Succeffors, which fhall be called our *Council of Virginia* ; And fhall, from time to time, have the fuperior Managing and Direction, only of and for all Matters, that fhall or may concern the Government, as well of the faid feveral Colonies, as of and for any other Part or Place, within the aforefaid Precincts of four and thirty and one and forty Degrees, above mentioned ; Which Council fhall, in like manner, have a Seal, for Matters concerning the Council or Colonies, with the like Arms and Portraiture, as aforefaid, with this Infcription, engraven round about on the one Side; *Sigillum Regis Magnæ Britanniæ, Franciæ & Hiberniæ;* and round about the other Side, *Pro Concilio fuo Virginiæ.*

IX. AND, moreover, We do GRANT and agree, for Us, our Heirs and Succeffors, that the faid feveral Councils, of and for the faid feveral Colonies, fhall and lawfully may, by Virtue hereof, from time to time, without any Interruption of Us, our Heirs, or Succeffors, give and take Order, to dig, mine, and fearch for all Manner of Mines of Gold, Silver, and Copper, as well within any Part of their faid feveral Colonies, as of the faid main Lands on the Back fide of the fame Colonies; And to HAVE and enjoy the Gold, Silver, and Copper, to be gotten thereof, to the Ufe and Behoof of the fame Colonies, and the Plantations thereof; YIELDING therefore, to Us, our Heirs and Succeffors, the fifth Part only of all the fame Gold and Silver, and the fifteenth Part of all the fame Copper, fo to be gotten or had, as is aforefaid, without any other Manner of Profit or Account, to be given or yielded to Us, our Heirs, or Succeffors, for or in Refpect of the fame.

X. AND that they fhall, or lawfully may, eftablifh and Caufe to be made a Coin, to pafs current there between the People of thofe feveral Colonies, for the more Eafe of Traffick and Bargaining between and amongft them and the Natives there, of fuch Metal, and in fuch Manner and Form, as the faid feveral Councils there fhall limit and appoint.

XI. AND We do likewife, for Us, our Heirs and Succeffors, by thefe Prefents, give full Power and Authority, to the faid Sir Thomas Gates, Sir George Somers,

Richard Hackluit, Edward Maria Wingfield, Thomas Hanham, Ralegh Gilbert, William Parker, and George Popham, and to every of them, and to the faid feveral Companies, Plantations, and Colonies, that they, and every of them, fhall and may, at all and every time and times hereafter, have, take, and lead in the faid Voyage, and for and towards the faid feveral Plantations and Colonies, and to travel thitherward, and to abide and inhabit there, in every the faid Colonies and Plantations, fuch and fo many of our Subjects, as fhall willingly accompany them, or any of them, in the faid Voyages and Plantations ; With fufficient Shipping and Furniture of Armour, Weapons, Ordinance, Powder, Victual, and all other things neceffary for the faid Plantations, and for their Ufe and Defence there : PROVIDED always, that none of the faid Perfons be fuch, as fhall hereafter be fpecially reftrained by Us, our Heirs, or Succeffors.

XII. MOREOVER, We do, by thefe Prefents, for Us, our Heirs and Succeffors, GIVE AND GRANT Licence unto the faid Sir Thomas Gates, Sir George Somers, Richard Hackluit, Edward Maria Wing- field, Thomas Hanham, Ralegh Gilbert, William Parker, and George Popham, and to every of the faid Colonies, that they, and every of them, shall and may, from time to time, and at all times for ever here- after, for their feveral Defences, encounter, expulfe, repel, and refift, as well by Sea, as by Land, by all Ways and Means whatfoever, all and every fuch Perfon and Perfons, as without the fpecial Licence of the faid feveral Colonies and Plantations, fhall attempt to inhabit within the faid feveral Colonies and Plantations, or any of them, or that fhall enterprife or attempt, at any time hereafter, the Hurt, Detriment, or Annoyance, of the faid feveral Colonies or Plantations.

XIII. GIVING AND GRANTING, by thefe Prefents, unto the faid Sir Thomas Gates, Sir George Somers, Richard Hackluit, Edward Maria Wingfield, and their Affociates of the faid firft Colony, and unto the faid Thomas Hanham, Ralegh Gilbert, William Parker, and George Popham, and their Affociates of the faid fecond Colony, and to every of them, from time to time, and at all times for ever hereafter, Power and Authority to take and furprife, by all Ways and Means whatfoever, all and every Perfon and Perfons, with their Ships, Veffels, Goods, and other Furniture, which fhall be found trafficking, into any Harbour or Harbours, Creek or Creeks, or Place, within the Limits or Precinéts of the faid feveral Colonies and Plantations, not being of the fame Colony, until fuch time, as they, being of any Realms or Dominions under our Obedience, fhall pay, or agree to pay, to the Hands of the Treafurer of that Colony, within whofe Limits and Precinéts they fhall fo traffick, two and a half upon every Hundred, of any thing, fo by them trafficked, bought, or fold; And being Strangers, and not Subjeéts under our Obeyfance, until they fhall pay five upon every Hundred, of fuch Wares and Merchandifes, as they fhall traffick, buy or fell, within the precinéts of the faid feveral Colonies, wherein they fhall fo traffick, buy, or fell, as aforefaid; WHICH Sums of Money or Benefit, as aforefaid, for and during the Space of one and twenty Years, next enfuing the Date hereof, fhall be wholly employed to the Ufe, Benefit, and Behoof of the faid feveral Plantations, where fuch Traffick fhall be made; And after the faid one and twenty Years

ended, the fame fhall be taken to the Ufe of Us, our
Heirs, and Succeffors, by fuch Officers and Minifters, as
by Us, our Heirs and Succeffors, fhall be thereunto
affigned or appointed.

XIV. AND We do further, by thefe Prefents, for
Us, our Heirs, and Succeffors, GIVE AND GRANT
unto the faid Sir Thomas Gates, Sir George Somers,
Richard Hackluit, and Edward Maria Wingfield, and to
their Affociates of the faid firft Colony and Plantation,
and to the faid Thomas Hanham, Ralegh Gilbert,
William Parker, and George Popham, and their Affociates of the faid fecond Colony and Plantation, that they,
and every of them, by their Deputies, Minifters, and
Factors, may tranfport the Goods, Chattles, Armour,
Munition and Furniture, needful to be ufed by them, for
their faid Apparel, Food, Defence, or otherwife in Refpect of the faid Plantations, out of our Realms of England
and Ireland, and all other our Dominions, from time to
time, for and during the Time of Seven Years, next
enfuing the Date hereof, for the better Relief of the faid
feveral Colonies and Plantations, without any Cuftom,
Subfidy, or other Duty, unto Us, our Heirs, or Succeffors,
to be yielded or payed for the fame.

XV. ALSO We do, for Us, our Heirs, and Succeffors, DECLARE, by thefe Prefents, that all and
every the Perfons, being our Subjects, which fhall dwell
and inhabit within every or any of the faid feveral
Colonies and Plantations, and every of their Children,
which fhall happen to be born within any of the Limits
and Precincts of the faid feveral Colonies and Plantations, fhall HAVE and enjoy all Liberties, Franchifes,
and Immunities, within any of our other Dominions, to

all Intents and Purpofes, as if they had been abiding and born, within this our Realm of England, or any other of our faid Dominions.

XVI. MOREOVER, our gracious Will and Pleafure is, and we do, by thefe Prefents, for Us, our Heirs, and Succeffors, declare and fet forth, that if any Perfon or Perfons, which fhall be of any of the faid Colonies and Plantations, or any other, which fhall traffick to the faid Colonies and Plantations, or any of them, fhall, at any time or times hereafter, tranfport any Wares, Merchandifes, or Commodities, out of any of our Dominions, with a Pretence to land, fell, or otherwife difpofe of the fame, within any the Limits and Precincts of any the faid Colonies and Plantations, and yet neverthelefs, being at Sea, or after he hath landed the fame within any of the faid Colonies and Plantations, fhall carry the fame into any other foreign Country, with a Purpofe there to fell or difpofe of the fame, without the Licence of Us, our Heirs, and Succeffors, in that Behalf firft had and obtained; That then, all the Goods and Chattles of fuch Perfon or Perfons, fo offending and tranfporting, together with the faid Ship or Veffel, wherein fuch Tranfportation was made, fhall be forfeited to Us, our Heirs, and Succeffors.

XVII. PROVIDED always, and our Will and Pleafure is, and we do hereby declare to all Chriftian Kings, Princes, and States, that if any Perfon or Perfons, which fhall hereafter be of any of the faid feveral Colonies and Plantations, or any other, by his, their, or any of their Licence and Appointment, fhall, at any time or times hereafter, rob or fpoil, by Sea or by Land, or do any Act of unjuft and unlawful Hoftility, to any Subjects of Us, our Heirs, or Succeffors, or any the Subjects of any

King, Prince, Ruler, Governor, or State, being then in
League or Amity with Us, our Heirs, or Succeffors, and
that upon fuch Injury, or upon juft Complaint of fuch
Prince, Ruler, Governor, or State, or their Subjects, We,
our Heirs, or Succeffors fhall make open Proclamation,
within any of the Ports of our Realm of England, com-
modious for that Purpofe, That the faid Perfon or Perfons, having committed any fuch Robbery or Spoil, fhall
within the term to be limited by fuch Proclamations,
make full Reftitution or Satisfaction of all fuch Injuries
done, fo as the faid Princes, or others fo complaining,
may hold themfelves fully fatisfied and contented ; And,
that, if the faid Perfon or Perfons, having committed fuch
Robbery, or Spoil, fhall not make, or caufe to be made,
Satisfaction accordingly, within fuch Time fo to be limited,
That then it fhall be lawful to Us, our Heirs, and Succeffors, to put the faid Perfon or Perfons, having committed
fuch Robbery or Spoil, and their Procurers, Abettors
or Comforters, out of our Allegiance and Protection ;
And that it fhall be lawful and free for all Princes and
others, to purfue with Hoftility the faid Offenders, and
every of them, and their and every of their Procurers,
Aiders, Abettors, and Comforters, in that Behalf.

XVIII. AND finally, We do for Us, our Heirs,
and Succeffors, GRANT and agree, to and with the faid
Sir Thomas Gates, Sir George Somers, Richard Hackluit, and Edward Maria Wingfield, and all others of the
firft Colony, that We, our Heirs and Succeffors, upon
Petition in that Behalf to be made, fhall, by Letters
Patent under the Great Seal of England, GIVE and
GRANT, unto fuch Perfons, their Heirs and Affigns,
as the Council of that Colony, or the moft Part of them,

shall, for that purpose, nominate and affign, all the Lands, Tenements, and Hereditaments, which shall be within the Precincts limited for that Colony, as is aforesaid, TO BE HOLDEN OF US, our Heirs, and Successors, as of our Manor of East Greenwich, in the County of Kent, in *free and common Soccage* only, and not *in Capite.*

XIX. AND do, in like manner, GRANT, and agree, for Us, our Heirs, and Successors, to and with the said Thomas Hanham, Ralegh Gilbert, William Parker, and George Popham, and all others of the said second Colony, that We, our Heirs, and Successors, upon Petition in that Behalf to be made, shall, by Letters Patent, under the Great Seal of England, GIVE and GRANT unto such Persons, their Heirs and Assigns, as the Council of that Colony, or the most part of them, shall, for that purpose, nominate and affign, all the Lands, Tenements, and Hereditaments which shall be within the Precincts limited for that Colony, as is aforesaid, TO BE HOLDEN OF US, our Heirs, and Successors, as of our Manor of East Greenwich in the County of Kent, *in free and common Soccage* only, and not *in Capite.*

XX. ALL which Lands, Tenements, and Hereditaments, so to be passed by the said several Letters patent, shall be sufficient Assurance from the said Patentees, so distributed and divided amongst the Undertakers for the Plantation of the said several Colonies, and such as shall make their Plantations in either of the said several Colonies, in such Manner and Form, and for such Estates, as shall be ordered and set down by the Council of the said Colony, or the most Part of them, respectively, within which the same Lands, Tenements, and Hereditaments shall lye or be; Although exprefs Mention of the true Yearly Value or Certainty of the Premifes, or any of them, or of any other Gifts or Grants by Us or any of our Progenitors or Predeceffors, to the aforefaid Sir Thomas Gates, Knt., Sir George Somers, Knt., Richard Hackluit, Edward Maria Wingfield, Thomas Hanham, Ralegh Gilbert, William Parker, and George Popham, or any of them, heretofore made, in thefe prefents, is not made, Or any ftatute, Act, Ordinance, or Provifion, Proclamation, or Reftraint, to the contrary hereof had, made, ordained, or any other Thing, Caufe, or Matter whatfoever, in any wife notwithftanding. IN WITNESS whereof, we have caufed thefe our Letters to be made Patents ; Witnefs Ourfelf, at Weftminfter, the tenth Day of April, in the fourth Year of our Reign of England, France, and Ireland, and of Scotland the nine and thirtieth.

Lukin

Per breve de privato Sigillo.

Copy of the Seal of Virginia.

The Copy of a Letter fent to the Treafurer and Council of Virginia from Captain Smith, then Prefident in Virginia.

RIGHT HONORABLE, &c.,

I received your Letter, wherein you write, that our minds are fo fet upon faction, and idle conceits in dividing the Country without your confents, and that we feed *You* but with ifs and ands, hopes and fome few proofes; as if we would keepe the myftery of the bufineffe to ourfelues: and that we muft expreffly follow your inftructions fent by Captain *Newport:* the charge of whofe voyage amounts to neare two thoufand pounds, the which if we cannot defray by the Ships returne, we are like to remain as banifhed men. To thefe particulars I humbly intreat your Pardons if I offend you with my rude Anfwer.

For our factions, unleffe you would haue me run away and leaue the Country, I cannot prevent them: becaufe I do make many ftay that would els fly any whether. For the idle Letter fent to my Lord of *Salifbury*, by the Prefident and his confederats, for diuiding the Country, &c. What it was I know not, for you faw no hand of mine to it; nor euer dream't I of any fuch matter. That we feed you with hopes, &c. Though I be no fcholer, I am paft a fchool boy; and I defire but to know, what either you, and thefe here doe know, but that I have learned to tell you by the continuall hazard of my life, I have not concealed from you any thing I know; but I feare fome caufe you to beleeue much more then is true.

Exprefly to follow your directions by Captain *Newport*, though they be performed, I was directly againft it; but, according to our Commiffion, I was content to be overruled by the maior part of the Councell, I feare to the hazard of us all; which is now generally confeffed when it is too late. Onely Captaine *Winne* and Captaine *Waldo* I have fworne of the Councell, and Crowned *Powhatan* according to your inftructions.

For the charge of this Voyage of two or three thoufand pounds, we have not received the value of an hundred pounds. And for the quartred boat to be borne by the fouldiers over the Falles, *Newport* had 120 of the beft men he could chufe. If he had burnt her to afhes, one might have carried her in a bag, but as fhe is, fiue hundred cannot, to a navigable place aboue the Falles. And for him at that time to find in the South Sea, a Mine of Gold, or any of them fent by Sir *Walter Raleigh*: at our Confultation I told them was as likely as the reft. But during this great difcovery of thirtie myles,* (which might as well have been done by one man, and much more, for the value of a pound of Copper at a feafonable tyme), they had the Pinnace and all the Boats with them, but one that remained with me to ferue the Fort. In their abfence I followed the new begun workes of Pitch and Tarre, Glaffe, Sope afhes, and Clapboord, whereof fome fmall quantities we have fent you. But if you rightly confider, what an infinite toyle it is in *Ruffia* and *Swethland*, where the woods are proper for naught els, and though there be the helpe

---

* *Newport's* expedition to the *Monacans.*

both of man and beaſt in thoſe ancient Common-wealths, which many a hundred years have vſed it, yet thouſands of thoſe poore people can ſcarce get neceſſaries to liue, but from hand to mouth. And though your Factors there can buy as much in a week as will fraught you a ſhip, or as much as you pleaſe; you muſt not expect from us any ſuch matter, which are but a many of ignorant miſerable ſoules, that are ſcarce able to get where-with to liue, and defend ourſelues againſt the inconſtant *Salvages:* finding but here and there a tree fit for the purpoſe, and want all things els the Ruſſians haue. For the Coronation of *Powhatan,* by whoſe advice you ſent him ſuch preſents, I know not; but this give me leaue to tell you, I feare they will be the concluſion of vs all ere we heare from you againe. At your Ships arrivall, the *Salvages* harveſt was newly gathered, and we going to buy it, our owne not being halfe ſufficient for ſo great a number. As for the two ſhips loading of Corne *Newport* promiſed to provide vs from *Powhatan,* he brought us but fourteene Buſhels; and from the *Monacans* nothing, but the moſt of the men ſicke and neare famiſhed. From your Ship we had not proviſion in victuals worth twenty pound, and we are more than two hundred to live vpon this; the one half ſicke, the other little better. For the Saylers (I confeſſe) they daily make good cheare, but our dyet is a little meale and water, and not ſufficient of that. Though there be fiſh in the Sea, foules in the ayre, and Beaſts in the woods, their bounds are ſo large, they ſo wilde, and we ſo weake and ignorant, we cannot much trouble them. Captain *Newport* we much ſuſpect to be the Authour of thoſe inventions. Now that you ſhould know, I haue made

you as great a difcovery as he, for leffe charge than he
fpendeth you every meale; I haue fent you this Mappe
of the Bay and Rivers, with an annexed Relation of the
Countries and Nations that inhabit them, as you may
fee at large. Alfo two barrels of ftones, and fuch as I
take to be good Iron ore at the leaft; fo divided, as by
their notes you may fee in what places I found them.
The Souldiers fay many of your officers maintaine their
families out of that you fend vs; and that *Newport* hath
an hundred pounds a yeare for carrying newes. For
every mafter you haue yet fent can find the way as well
as he, fo that an hundred pounds might be fpared, which
is more than we haue all, that helpe to pay him wages.
Cap. *Ratliffe* is now called *Sicklemore*, a poore counterfeited Impofture. I haue fent you him home, leaft the
company fhould cut his throat. What he is, now every
one can tell you: if he and *Archer* returne againe, they
are fufficient to keepe vs alwayes in factions. When
you fend againe I intreat you rather fend but thirty
Carpenters, hufbandmen, gardiners, fifher men, blackfmiths, mafons, and diggers vp of trees, roots, well
provided; then a thoufand of fuch as we haue: for
except wee be able both to lodge them, and feed them,
the moft will confume with want of neceffaries before
they can be made good for anything. Thus, if you
pleafe to confider this account, and of the vnneceffary
wages to Captaine *Newport*, or his fhips fo long lingering
and ftaying here (for notwithftanding his boafting to leave
vs victuals for 12 moneths, though we had 89 by this difcovery lame and ficke, and but a pinte of Corne a day for
a man, we were conftrained to giue him three hogfheads
of that to victuall him homeward), or yet to fend into

Germany or *Poleland* for glaffe-men and the reft, till we be able to fuftaine our felues, and relieue them when they come. It were better to giue fiue hundred pound a tun for thofe groffe Commodities in *Denmarke*, then fend for them hither, till more neceffary things be provided. For in over-toyling our weake and vnfkilfull bodies, to fatisfie this defire of prefent profit, we can fcarce ever recover our felves from one Supply to another. And I humbly intreat you hereafter, let us know what we fhould receiue, and not ftand to the Saylers courtefie to leaue us what they pleafe, els you may charge vs with what you will, but we not you with anything. Thefe are the Caufes that haue kept us in *Virginia*, from laying fuch a foundation, that ere this might haue given much better content and fatisfaction; but as yet you muft not looke for any profitable returnes; fo I humbly reft.

www.ingramcontent.com/pod-product-compliance
Lightning Source LLC
Chambersburg PA
CBHW020946030726
47496CB00005B/1381